Things I LeaRNeD While I was DeaD

KATHRYN CLARK

faber

First published in 2025
by Faber and Faber Limited
The Bindery, 51 Hatton Garden
London, EC1N 8HN
faber.co.uk

Typeset in Plantin by M Rules
Printed and bound by CPI Group (UK) Ltd, Croydon, CR0 4YY

A CIP record for this book
is available from the British Library

ISBN 978-0-571-38586-7

Printed and bound in the UK on FSC® certified paper in line with our continuing
commitment to ethical business practices, sustainability and the environment.
For further information see faber.co.uk/environmental-policy

Our authorised representative in the EU for product safety is
Easy Access System Europe, Mustamäe tee 50, 10621 Tallinn, Estonia
gpsr.requests@easproject.com

1 3 5 7 9 10 8 6 4 2

'**Sucked me in from the start.**'
Kenechi Udogu, author of *Augmented*

'**A life-affirming message,** one that makes
you think about family and ethics and loss.'
Tracy Darnton, author of *Ready Or Not*

'An emotional pull that **refuses to let you go.**'
Melissa Welliver, author of *Soulmates
and Other Ways to Die*

'I could not put it down . . . **I loved
every second of it!**'
S. A Gales, author of *iNSiDE*

'Compelling and poignant, this is a breathtaking
debut from an **exciting new voice.**'
Steve Voake, author of *Blood Hunters*

'**A must read for all teenagers.**'
Mel Darbon, author of *What The World Doesn't See*

'**Unforgettable!** Pulls you into Calico's fierce,
heartbreaking, and hopeful fight for her sister.'
Finbar Hawkins, author of *Witch*

'**Haunting yet heartfelt,** this story packed
an emotional sucker punch.'
Gina Blaxill, author of *Love You to Death*

About the Author

Kathryn Clark is a graduate of the Bath Spa MA Writing for Young People. Her work has been long/shortlisted in awards including Times/Chicken House, Mslexia Children's Novel, Bath Children's Novel and Searchlight Novel Opening. She was runner-up in the Book Pipeline Novel Contest and winner of the Arvon Novel Opening Competition. *Things I Learned While I Was Dead* was a winner of Faber's inaugural Imagined Futures Prize for eco YA sci-fi. Kathryn works as a freelance writing mentor. She lives in Gloucestershire with her family and two dogs.

For my sister, Ali

A Note from the Author

This book deals with issues that include physical and mental illness, violence, death, references to suicide, consent and climate change. If these are difficult subjects for you, please take the best care of yourself and know that you are not alone.

These are difficult subjects for me too. Calico's story grew out of my own anxiety about death, the loss of a friend as a teenager, and caring for someone I love while they were seriously ill. It was also influenced by the inequality we see all around us. How some voices are suppressed, ignored or shouted down.

Writing about the things that scare and anger me is a way of trying to make sense of the world, of life, of death. And so, although this story goes to some dark places, it is also full of resilience, love and the hope that humans can, and will, do better.

Resources can be found at the back of the book.

Day Zero

Calico

Cold. Dark. Sharp.

Pins, needles. In my toes. Fierce. Furious.

'Here we go.' An American man. Gnarly voice.

Pins, needles swarm through my body.

My body. Me. Calico Brown.

A mallet hits my heart, full force.

Silence.

'Come on,' says the voice.

Thud. Thud. Thud. A drum in my chest.

'Yes!'

'Stats, please.' Another voice. Soft, Spanish.

Numbers over numbers.

Warmth. Thud. Thud. Thud.

'We have some eye movement.'

'So soon? Prep for optical test.'

'Removing tape.'

BRIGHT.

TOO BRIGHT.

'Pupils reactive and responsive.' There's a blur by my side. 'Calico, if you can hear me, blink twice.'

Blink? How do I . . . ?

Oh. Yeah. Blink. Blink.

'Prep to extubate.' The soft Spanish voice is right beside me. 'Calico, you have a tube in your throat. You don't need it any more. I'm going to take it out.'

Whaaaaaaaaaaaaaaaaaaaaaaaat?

My blinks go into overdrive.

'It's okay. You're ready.' Warmth on my shoulder. A hand. 'I want you to breathe out of your mouth for as long as you can, okay?'

Blink. Blink.

'Good. Now, Calico …'

Breathe out. Haaaaaaaaaaaaaaaaaaaaah. Icicles rip at my chest, my throat. My body fights against the jagged tearing, silent screaming.

'It's out. Breathe, Calico.'

But I can't, I can't breathe, I'm suffocating. My throat's in shreds.

A cough rattles me, shaking my bones, my heart, my lungs …

And I breathe.

'Welcome back.' There's a smile in the voice.

Tiny lights flicker through the darkness inside me.

My heart. Thud. Thud. Thud.

Rivers of blood pulse round my body.

Is it my blood?

Lucas said they'd drain it all away when I died.

Fill my body with chemicals instead.

Replace it when they brought me back.

Is someone else's blood in my veins now?

Blood.

Blood from a stone.

That means impossible.

Blood.

Thicker than water.

That means family.

Family.

Mum. And Asha.

Asha. Ohmygod. Asha. Open, mouth. Speak.

My voice doesn't work.

'All right. That's enough for today,' the blur says. 'We're going to sedate you, Calico, for the next part of the procedure.' She moves away. 'Commence anaesthesia.'

No! Wait.

Numbness creeps over me. I lose the warm rush of blood, the flickers of light.

Where is she?

Where's my sister?

Where is Asha?

1.

asha

it starts at the end

it starts at the end,
what should have been the end,
would have been the end,
of any other story.

you should be
ashes
in an urn now,
asha
in an urn.
you should be
on your way now –
a soul soaring up to heaven,
a spirit seeking home –
not tethered to this body
that only ever gave you pain.

but perhaps
Death
is not the end
of every story
any more

2.

Calico

I dream of Asha.

Asha. Asha. Her name is like breathing.

I am breathing. The taste of the air – stagnant – is in my mouth and nose. The world is hazy, like I'm inside a cloud.

I push up to sitting. My muscles and joints work smooth and sure, like they did before. I blink away the haze.

Where am I?

There's no one else here. The room is stark and cold, bare concrete walls, two brown doors, no windows.

Is this the facility in America?

It's nothing like the website pictures – all high-shine white and metal. Unease squirms inside me, but I push it away. Doesn't matter what it's like, I'm here now. And so is Asha. That recruiter, that doctor – Lucas – said we'd be transported to the US. *Impossible to get anyone into the country alive*, he'd said. *But dead, you're not a person any more, you're research materials.* And he'd told me again how I'd saved Asha. How the two years of research I'd signed up for would help them cure her. How the scientists at the facility would bring us both back to life.

An icy shiver runs down my neck. They did it. I'm

awake. Alive. I can feel air moving in my windpipe. My lungs expand, contract. I can feel the rhythm of my heart, the music of being, my body singing. I never took much notice of it before. Asha's body, falling apart, got all the attention. Mine just did what it was supposed to.

Asha.

Where is she?

I have to find her.

I push away the grey sheet and blanket, swing my legs over the edge of the bed. The cement floor is rough beneath my feet. There's a scuffed wooden desk and chair to my left. Above, a shelf holds piles of folded clothes. I pick out a black cotton vest top and shorts. Loose trousers, faded to grey. Old, worn soft, they smell of faded rosemary and eucalyptus. I put them on and pull a baggy jumper over the top. Chunky hand-knitted socks. There aren't any shoes.

The first door I try slides open at the touch of my hand. The bathroom. There are mouldy spatters on the once-white walls. No mirror. I splash tepid water over my face. The towel is coarse against my newborn skin.

The other door must be my way out of here. I stand in front of it and take a deep breath, fill my lungs with air and hope. Asha is on the other side. She has to be.

I press my palm against the door. It doesn't move.

The website didn't say anything about being locked in.

I need to get out of here. I have to find Asha. To explain.

I bang and shout till my hands sting and my voice gives out. But no one comes.

It's so quiet. I can't hear another living thing.

I slump on to the floor. The concrete's chill seeps into my bones. Or perhaps it was already there, left over from the freezing.

The door suddenly slides open, startles me to standing. A bear of a man, wearing hospital scrubs, looms. Thick neck, shaved head, grey stubble on a craggy face. His massive tattooed arms are folded across a barrel chest. Tattoos of clocks without hands and a crucifix that trails into a dagger dripping blood.

I back away towards the bed, my heart hammering.

But he smiles kindly as he steps inside the room. 'Well, look at you, kid.' The gnarly American voice from when I first woke up. 'Got yourself out of bed and dressed, so soon after reanimation. That's quite something. Take a seat.' He gestures to the bed and I sit. 'I'm Earl, head nurse here at the Fates Family Facility.'

'Where's Asha?' My voice creaks. 'We came in together. She's my sister. I need to know she's all right.'

'Sorry, kid. I don't know anything about her.'

It's like he's punched me. I'm winded. The air disappears.

'Hey, don't stress,' he says. 'I don't know nothing about you, or anyone else here either. It ain't allowed.'

'But she's my sister—'

'Look, kid. Folk end up here for a lot of different reasons. Best we don't know how they lived. Or how they died. Got to be sure we treat everyone the same. No judgement. No discrimination.' He rubs a hand over his tattooed forearm.

I take a gulp of air.

This doesn't mean something bad has happened to Asha. Plus, if Earl doesn't know anything about us, he doesn't know how we ended up here. What happened that night I left Asha alone.

'Sorry, kid. I get it's tough,' Earl says. 'But you're doing amazing. How 'bout I get you something to eat and drink.'

The door closes behind him.

I rest my head on the pillow.

Inside, I'm hollow. Empty.

Did they take something from me while I was asleep?

Not asleep.

Dead.

I was dead.

And so was Asha.

All those years of sickness, of fighting to get Asha help, and then I didn't have a chance to tell her I'd found a way to save her, that everything would be okay.

Little seeds of sadness and doubt drip into the hollow.

What if I haven't done enough?

What if it hasn't worked?

Earl bustles back in. 'Cry it out, kid.'

Sniff away the tears. I'm not a girl who cries.

I sit up with my back against the wall, push away the sadness, push away the doubts.

Earl puts a tray of food and a cardboard folder on the desk. He sits facing me, too big for the chair. I can't take my eyes off the dagger tattoo.

'Losing it's kind of normal after what you been through,' he says. 'Enough to bake anyone's noodle.' He's so calm, solid. Like an ancient rock letting the sea wash over him. Like he's been here before, seen a thousand, thousand people rise from the dead, and it's no big deal. 'Okay?' he asks.

I nod. But the hollow inside is still there.

'You want a drink?' He passes me a glass of water.

I take a sip. It runs cold through my body.

'Here.' He hands me a bowl of murky-pond-looking stuff. It smells of mushrooms and something sour.

I feel sick. 'Err, no thanks.'

'You got to eat, kid.'

'Not this though.'

'Yes, this.' He shakes his head. 'Okay. I'll leave it here. Have some later. We'll take a look at the paperwork instead.'

He removes a tatty sheet of paper from the folder and hands it to me.

The Fates Family Foundation – HEALE Programme

Human Enhancement and Life Extension – Cryogenics, Nano and Bio Research

Mission statement:

To enhance and extend life through the development of cryogenic suspension, reanimation, and nano-biotechnologies.
'Do no harm'

Study subjects will:

- be monitored physically and mentally.
- participate in nano-biomedical trials as required.
- contribute to research modules: Rehabilitation, Resocialisation, Remembering.

Facility rules

1. Respectful behaviour is expected at all times.
2. Intimate contact between participants is forbidden.
3. Interaction with anyone outside the facility is not permitted.

'I can't even talk to my mum?'

Earl shakes his head.

My heart patters too fast. What exactly have I signed up for? That Lucas – he didn't tell me about any of this. But then there wasn't time. We had to move so quickly.

'Any more questions?' Earl asks.

'No.' I push away the doubt. None of it matters to me. Only one reason I signed up. To save Asha. I'll do whatever I have to, like I promised I would.

'You sure, kid?'

'Okay, I have one question. When do I start?'

Earl laughs, a great rumble. 'I like your attitude. How 'bout right now?' He takes a notebook and pencil from the folder. 'This is your Remembering Book. Writing helps with your manual dexterity and cognitive function. So that's something you can be getting on with.'

'What should I write about?'

'Memories, how you're feeling, anything you want, really. It's yours.' He shifts out of the chair. 'I'll let you get some rest, kid.'

'Wait, Earl. What day is it?'

He smiles. 'Day one, kid. Day one.'

3.

Day one. Not really an answer. I wrap the blanket round me, sit at the desk and open the dusty blue notebook. My Remembering Book. The pages are thin and yellowed, cheap recycled paper. It smells damp, like it's been stored in some garage or attic.

I've only ever written what I had to, for school or whatever. Answering questions. Or making lists. I'm not good at creating something out of nothing like Asha does. But Earl said to write my memories down and I've got a lot of those. All with Asha. And this is *for* Asha. What I have to do. I pick up the thick wooden pencil.

Day 1

My fingers find it hard to bend, and the writing comes out like a little kid's.

Everything happened so fast. I don't even know the last words Asha said to me.

I chew the end of the pencil. How do I remember?

I close my eyes, block out where I am. The dull walls. The cold.

Asha. Late summer. At home.

Sunset has painted the walls of Asha's room pink. We sit on her bed and I run the brush through her hair. It's fine and brittle, like everything about her.

'You hate me,' Asha says.

Her words slide into me, sharp.

'No, I don't.'

She turns to face me. 'You do. You can't go to the party, and it's all my fault.'

'No.' But there's a splinter of truth in what she says.

'You shouldn't have to give up your life because of me.' She coughs.

'It's a stupid party, not my whole life.'

'But you never get invited anywhere.'

'Thanks a lot.' I prod her with the hairbrush, even though it's usually true. This party is a pre-year thirteen thing so everyone's included, even me.

'Mum should've stayed in tonight,' Asha says.

'Yeah, well, she had a gig. Money! She couldn't say no.'

'I really want you to go to the party.' Asha's eyes are bird bright. 'Please. Take photos. Tell me about it tomorrow. It'll be like I was there.'

There's a glimmer inside. A bit of me wants to go. To be normal, not the big sister of the dying girl. And if it's for Asha, what she wants … 'Maybe I could go,' I say. 'For a little while.'

She smiles, moves up the bed to her pillows.

Her eyes close. Dark lashes rest like feathers on her cheeks.

I plug her phone into the charger, drip lavender oil on the duvet. Her journal's open on the bedside table, the page edged with intricate purple spirals around her poem:

> truth
> is not
> a solid thing.
> time wears rock
> paper thin.
> the tiny breeze
> from a
> butterfly wing
> melts mountains
> into sand.

I stay till Asha's breathing softens into sleep. I pause at her bedroom door.

Am I really doing this?

I force myself downstairs.

Mum's gin bottle is on the kitchen table. I take a swig. It warms my throat, my chest.

Yes. I am really doing this. Leaving Asha.

For her. And a little bit for me.

I step out into the fading light.

The party's in a field a mile away. I cut across the common. The tired, end-of-summer grass catches at my legs, and that splinter scratches at my heart.

What Asha said.

That I hate her.

I could never hate her. But maybe, for a minute, I didn't love her? Or didn't love her enough. Maybe, for a moment, I wished she was already dead.

Shame washes over me. I stop writing, open my eyes, get up and pace the small, dull room. This is so hard.

But I've done harder things for Asha. I make myself sit at the desk again, go back in my mind.

I'm walking to the party. I pass the old oak. Last time we were here, it was Easter. Asha sat leaning against the tree, timing me as I ran circuits, training for a race I never got to compete in. The diagnosis came the day before the meet.

The music from the party calls to me, louder and louder. It's nearly dark now. There are tiny white lights like stars in the trees. I go through a gate in the dry-stone wall. Woodsmoke. I say hello to a few people from school, but they're all in groups or couples. So I lose myself in the blur of bodies and music. There's a hum of happiness over the thumping bassline, like the earth's heartbeat in time with mine. I meld with the moment, let everything else go.

The music slows and people come together, silhouettes in the smoke.

18

I move to the wall, take out my phone and attempt a photo for Asha. Not sure it will come out. It won't capture the way everything feels and sounds and smells anyway.

She's not a part of this.

I'm not a part of this.

But I'm on the edge of it. The edge of life. The life I'll have when Asha's gone.

Why did I come? To see who I'll be? A different me? What was I thinking?

The stars, the lights, turn to streaks.

Without Asha, there is no me.

There is no me.

4.

Asha

in between

you and Death
played games for years.
catch-me-if-you-can,
hide-and-seek.

you had tricks
that kept him at bay.
the pen spiralling
on the page.
the purple poems
mesmerised him.
and singing slowed him too.
he'd pause to listen.
but always
he lurked there
in the corner
of your room,
the corner
of you.

and where is Death now?
is he the hider
or the seeker?
and what about you, asha?
are you dead?
are you living?
or are you somewhere
in between?

5.

Calico

'Hey, kid.' Earl arrives with another tray of food.

'Is it the morning?' I ask. So strange having no windows. It ranges from dark to dusk in here, never gets any brighter, and I haven't found a light switch.

'Sure.' He puts my breakfast on the desk. 'You didn't eat much yesterday.' His craggy face is creased with concern.

'Not hungry,' I say. Today's offerings don't look much more tempting. A bowl of cement-type stuff with black bits in it. A steaming cup of grey liquid that smells like a damp dog. 'I don't like being locked in here. When can I get out of this room?'

'You drink your tea, you eat your porridge –'

'Yes.' I pick up the bowl and force in a mouthful. It's both gritty and oily somehow.

'– you urinate, you defecate –'

'Euww.' I gag.

Earl sighs. 'You're in here till you got your bodily functions under control, is what I'm saying, kid. Okay?'

'Okay.'

'So you going to eat some more?'

I force down another mouthful. I have to if I want to get out of here and find Asha. My intestines groan and rumble, but I finish it.

After Earl leaves, I lie still for a bit and try not to puke.

Maybe a shower will help. The water is a lukewarm drizzle. The soap is a hard block that smells like tar. After a few minutes the water stops, and I can't get it to come back on. But I feel a bit better.

Earl comes back at lunchtime, bringing lentil soup and dry crackers.

He smiles at my clean breakfast tray. 'Good on yer, kid.'

The last thing I want is to eat again, but I think of Asha. The chemo killed her appetite. I would chat about nothing to distract her while popping tiny bites of Marmite toast into her mouth. Mum would grind up tablets and hide them in chocolate ice cream.

This is nothing compared to what Asha went through.

I make myself swallow soup and chew crackers. There's a lot of gurgling in my guts but I don't feel sick any more. I take out the Remembering Book and read through what I wrote yesterday. It's so vivid. *I was coming back from the party.*

Day 2

When I get home, the house reeks of lavender. I run up to Asha's room. The bottle's smashed on the floor. Her pink bed is empty.

There's a note from Mum.

They're at the hospital.

My heart plunges.

I shouldn't have left Asha. Whatever's
happened, it's all my fault.

Asha's not on the children's ward this time. She's in
the ITU. A nurse buzzes me in.

Mum's voice fills the room. 'The Lord's my
shepherd …'

Shit. If she's singing hymns, it's bad. Panic
patters inside me.

Asha's chest barely moves with each little
bird breath. Mum's lost in a trance. Her fingers
trace the shape of Asha's face; a heart, a heart, a
heart …

How … what … I was only gone two hours.

'What happened?' I ask, my voice cracking.

Mum doesn't answer. She doesn't look at
me. Doesn't move her gaze from Asha's face. She
keeps singing.

'Why isn't anyone doing anything? Where's the
doctor?'

'… My soul He doth restore again …'

An alarm slices the room, jolts me. Mum's
fingers falter, her voice drops away. The machine
Asha's attached to flashes red.

A nurse appears at Mum's side. She mutes the
alarm, lifts Asha's fragile wrist, feels for a pulse.

'It won't be long now, Ruth,' the nurse says softly.

'What do you mean?'

23

'I'm sorry. We've done all we can.'

'No. No.' This can't be right. 'What happened?'

Mum looks at me at last. Her eyes are shadows. 'I – I don't know. I found her unconscious.'

No. No. Months, she still had months. And hope. The drug trials. Immunotherapy. There's always another way. Only a few hours ago, she was so alive, so Asha. Yes, she was ill, but not like this.

Guilt swamps me. I should've been there with her. Whatever it is, whatever went wrong, I could've stopped it.

'I shouldn't have left her,' I say.

Mum shakes her head, turns back to Asha.

A chill threads through my body. Mum blames me too.

She starts to sing again: 'The Lord's my shepherd, I'll not want …'

But I do want.

I want my little sister alive. I want her well. I didn't mean it when I half wished her dead. I want her to live a real life. To write her poems. To go to parties.

And I want to never go through that moment – the one where her next breath doesn't come.

'Sing with me, Calico,' Mum says in a pause between verses.

But I can't. I'm done with God. I sang all the

hymns first time around. I prayed and prayed. It didn't help Asha. Didn't stop the illness seeping back into her. What kind of god lets a fourteen-year-old die?

And I can't be here, with Mum singing words she doesn't believe in either, while Asha fades away. I need to do something. There must be something I can do. There's always another way. Another transfusion. More bone marrow. New medication. A different doctor. I have to get out of here. I have to do something.

A flood of adrenalin. My heart beats too fast, like it did back then.

The need to do something, it's so strong, the need to save Asha.

I throw the Remembering Book across the room.

I want to get out of here. To go outside.

I want to run across the common past the old oak. There's no space in here.

I stride instead. Three paces, hit the wall, turn and pace again, over and over until I'm dripping in sweat. A twinge in my belly makes me run for the bathroom.

Earl will have to let me out now.

6.

asha

hourglass

mum sang spiders' webs
of sticky silk and words,
and melody and love,
to catch you, trap you,
stop your flight.

but Death was stronger
even than her love.
and Death had
stalked you, shrunk you,
hollowed out
the bones of you.

his knuckles cracked,
his breath smelled
of deep damp earth.

as
the
last
grit
drifted
through
his hourglass,
you hovered
in half-light,
not quite
being.

7.

Calico

'Hey,' a not-Earl voice says. A boy stands in the doorway.
He's golden brown, smooth-skinned, sun streaks in a
mess of hair. Eyes like the sea. About my age, my height,
wearing a scrub top and baggy board shorts. He's a lot
prettier than Earl.

'Who are you?' I ask.

'Um.' He looks round the room like he's searching
for an answer. 'Gabe,' he says at last.

'You work here?' I ask.

'Kind of helpin' out.'

'Are you part of the study?'

He shakes his head. 'So, you ready for the tour?'

'I'm getting out of this room?'

He smiles, nods.

Asha. I'm up and across towards him so fast, Gabe
has to step out of my way. He smells of outside, of
cigarettes and sun on skin. He drops something as he
moves. It's smooth and black, shaped like a plectrum. I
hand it back to him.

'Thanks.' He presses it and the door opens.

I follow him out into a dimly lit, narrow corridor, so
long I can't see either end of it. This is nothing like the
photographs on the website. A breath of cool air caresses
the back of my neck and I shiver. The door slides closed

behind us. The hallway is lined with more doors, all the same dark brown, all with numbers burned into the wood. Mine is 225.

'Okay?' Gabe says softly. 'It's this way.'

The rough concrete floor catches at my socks as we walk. Paint peels from the walls in places, like pale skin shedding. The lamps morph between weak light and shadow. I feel like I'm underground or in a submarine, claustrophobic, closed in, desperate for air, for light, for life. For Asha. She could be on the other side of any of these doors. I stop beside one, press my hand to it. Nothing happens.

'This is the East Wing—' Gabe's voice echoes off the walls ahead. 'Hey, what you doin'?' he asks.

'I'm trying to find someone. A girl—'

Gabe runs his fingers through his hair. 'They told me not to talk about the patients.'

Patients? Not study participants. Perhaps Asha's a patient, still getting treatment. That makes sense. She was so ill.

'Come on,' Gabe says.

I catch him up. Get the cigarette and sun scent again.

'Like I was sayin', we're in the East Wing.'

'What are all these rooms?'

'The cells.'

'What?'

'Joke. Well, sort of. This place was a prison back in the day.'

The walls close in around me. Prison. Maybe it's what I deserve.

We reach a corner. The light is brighter here. There's a lobby with several swing doors off it. The floor is smoother, polished.

Gabe points left. 'Through there's the labs and offices. And staff quarters.'

'You all live here too?'

'Yeah. We're in the middle of goddam nowhere, so not much choice.' He shakes his head. 'The hospital wing's through there too.'

Hope lifts me. Maybe that's where Asha is. I rush forwards.

'Hey.' Gabe catches my arm gently. His skin is warm. 'You can't go wanderin' off by yourself. There's rules, y'know.'

'Yeah, I noticed.' The hollow inside echoes with emptiness.

'We're goin' this way.' Gabe turns and heads down another corridor.

'Where is everyone?' I ask.

'You sure ask a lot of questions,' he says.

We walk along. There are fewer doors here, but they're the same dark brown. Some have words burned into them instead of numbers. A strong, acrid smell permeates the air.

'That's the laundry.' Gabe points to a room on the left. 'You'll be spendin' some time there as part of your rehab.'

'Rehab? I'm not an addict.'

'Rehabilitation – just means chores really.'

'Right,' I say. Lucas kept that quiet. The website had beautiful people brought back to life hanging about somewhere that looked like a spa. They certainly weren't doing the laundry in an old prison.

'The kitchen's down there.' Gabe gestures. 'And here's the—'

'Day room,' I say. That's what's burned into the door. Makes me think of an old people's home.

Gabe unlocks it and we go in.

It's laid out a bit like the school canteen with a shuttered hatch between this room and the kitchen. Mismatched, worn tables and chairs. Scuffed walls. The smell of old onions.

A voice crackles from Gabe's pocket. He pulls out a walkie-talkie, turning away from me. I look around trying to find a phone or a laptop, but most of the tables are bare. In the far corner there's a space cleared. A few sets of dumbbells are on the floor. And there's a punch bag.

'Um, I got to go deal with the supplies delivery.' Gabe fiddles with the walkie-talkie. 'I'll have to take you back to your room now.'

'Oh no – can't I stay here?'

'I ain't s'posed to leave you.' He pulls at his hair. 'But guess if I lock you in, it's okay.'

'Thanks.'

'Don't – um – do anything.'

'Like what? Nothing *to* do in here.'

'All right. I'll be back in a while.' He heads out the way we just came in.

But there's another door in the opposite wall. And it's ajar, not locked. Maybe I can get to the hospital wing through there.

No. On the other side is a small room with a dull painting on the wall and some dust-coloured sofas.

My heart heaves. Someone is sprawled across one of them. But it's not Asha. It's a boy. White, tall, angular. He's got on the same baggy clothes as me, plus a black beanie, pulled so low it covers half his face. His mouth moves like he's talking, but no sound comes out.

'What did you say?' I ask.

He doesn't answer but lifts his head and looks at me. Dark brown eyes and sallow skin. A jagged scar inches out from under the hat, like red fingers cradling his cheek.

He gets up, takes hold of a broom leant against the wall, and starts half-heartedly sweeping.

This is no use. He's no help.

I head back to the day room. Try and open the main door.

'Only the staff can do that.' The boy has followed me.

'Hey, you're English too,' I say.

'Well spotted.'

'Where from?'

'Nottingham.'

'I'm Calico.'

'Jem.' His head twitches.

31

I gesture at the door. 'There must be a way to open this. What if there's a fire or something?'

'We're fucked.' He puts the broom in a corner. 'Or not, depending on your point of view.'

'What?'

'Depending how you ended up in here.'

'How?'

'Or why.' He picks up a Remembering Book and slouches over to me.

I nod like I know what he's on about. 'So we're trapped in here till someone lets us out?'

He slumps into a chair. 'Yeah. Like the fucking cryopod all over again.'

The world goes still. He was frozen too.

'Are there more of us – I don't know the word – frozen, defrosted?'

'Reanimates. That's what they call us. More like inmates if you ask me. Can't take a piss in here without it being logged down.'

'But there are others?'

'Yeah.'

'Have you met a girl called Asha?'

'No.'

The hollow inside me deepens.

'You sure? She looks a bit like me, but younger, thinner.'

He stares at me. Dark, dark eyes. 'No one like you.' His head jerks. 'Sod off, Stan,' he whispers to his shoulder.

I turn away from him. How am I going to find her?

I walk round the room searching for anything that might help me. I spot something phone-like but when I get closer it's a tatty pack of playing cards. There's a draughts board on another table, pieces missing. It's a depressing space.

I reach the gym corner. The punch bag looks well battered. I put on some padded gloves and give it a whack. The force judders up my arm. It feels good.

Two years I'm going to be here. Apparently locked in one room or another. By myself or with some muttering stranger.

Asha. That's why I'm here. That's why I signed up.

I keep punching, until tiredness takes me over and I go back to the main entrance.

Jem's totally still, cheek on the table, eyes closed. Panic prickles at me. Is he even breathing?

'Hey.' I touch his back lightly. 'Are you okay?'

Just then, Earl barges in.

'What the . . .' he says.

I drop my hand. I don't think he saw.

Jem raises his head.

'What are you two doing in here together unsupervised?' Earl frowns.

'Don't ask me,' Jem says.

'Gabe, was it?' Earl snorts. 'That boy! Never thinks.'

'You gonna grass him up to Doctor Fates?'

Earl glares at Jem.

33

'Who's Doctor Fates?' I ask.

'The creep who runs this place.'

'Show a little respect, Jem.' Earl sighs. 'Right. Let's get you two back to your rooms.'

'Aren't we getting a trip to the hospital wing?' Jem says. 'To be on the safe side.'

Hope flickers as Earl pauses. That's exactly where I want to go.

Earl rubs at his tattooed forearm. 'You didn't touch each other, did you?'

'What?' I say. 'No.'

Jem's head jerks. 'Two people can be locked in a room together without hooking up, you know, Earl.'

'If you say so, kid.'

Jem grimaces at me. Or maybe it's a smile.

I smile back.

We follow Earl down the corridor.

Jem's back to his muttering. 'Sod off, Stan,' he says. 'Don't bring him into it.'

Earl stops. Room 226. 'Here you are, kid.' He lets Jem in and I get a glimpse of a huge drawing stuck to his wall made from notebook pages joined together. A picture of a boy's face. So real, so detailed, it's like a photograph.

'And here *you* are.' Earl opens my door. 'Guess you met your neighbour.' He stands there rubbing his stubbled cheek. 'Didn't think you'd run into anyone else today. I should've gone over the rules.'

'I read the rules, Earl.'

34

'I have to report what happened.'

'Nothing happened.' Report it to who – this Doctor Fates?

'You were standing real close to Jem.'

'I was just making sure he was okay.' There's edginess in my chest. Earl was so calm before, now he seems stressed. 'What's it matter anyway?'

'Your recovery's been fast, but your immune system's still adapting.'

'I feel fine.'

'Have to assume your body might not be able to fight off infection yet. And there are new viruses all the time.' He looks at me. 'The treatments don't always work, you know.'

The treatments don't always work?

What does that mean?

What about Asha and her cure?

8.

I feel so trapped by this place. The ex-prison. Maybe it's the lack of windows, daylight. It's vast but empty. Where is everyone? All the workers and the study participants? It doesn't feel like a place people come back to life. More like somewhere they go to rot. Unease slithers inside me, slimy and foul. I signed us up for this. What if I did the wrong thing? Tears glaze my vision but I scrub them away.

It's no good thinking like that. I'm here. Have to get on with it. For Asha. And for Mum. All I can do right now is the Remembering Book. I flick back to what I last wrote.

City Hospital. I'd just left Mum and Asha.

<u>Day 4</u>

The corridor is bright after the ITU. Beside me a vending machine rattles and hisses. Coffee smell slaps my face.

'Calico?' A smooth American voice.

I turn. He's wholesome-looking, twenties maybe. How does he know my name?

He holds out his hand. 'I'm Lucas,' he says. 'I'm here to help you save your sister.'

Hope lurches inside me.

He flashes his security pass. The photograph doesn't capture the intensity of his eyes when he says: 'Death is not the end.'

Oh right, I get who he is. Scrubbed too clean. Smug vibe. Seen enough of that at church. Golden. Shiny on the outside, dirty on the in.

'I don't have time for whatever religious shit you're selling.'

'Calico—'

'I don't need God. I need a doctor.'

He holds up his hands. 'I am a doctor.'

'They said there's nothing else they can do.' My voice is a whimper.

'I know,' he says.

'I can't believe that's true.' It leaks out of me.

He nods. 'I understand, I do. Anyone who faces losing someone hopes for a miracle.'

He still sounds like a religious freak to me.

'I can't stop Asha dying,' he says. 'But I can bring her back to life. I can give you that miracle.'

He thinks he is God? Did I walk out of the ITU into some parallel world?

'Look at this.' He pulls out an iPad. Taps the screen. Sticks it in front of me.

I scroll down. Videos of scientists in sparkling labs. People oozing health. There's a lot of science. Diagrams and graphs and stats, and long strange words.

'What is it?' I ask.

'Our foundation runs a programme,' Lucas says, 'where the viability of a body can be maintained until a cure is found.'

'What does that even mean?'

'The process is called cryogenic preservation. The body is cooled to an extremely low temperature and stored—'

'You want to freeze Asha?'

He gives me the saddest smile. 'Think of it more as putting her on pause.'

'This can't be real.'

'Cryogenic science has been around a long time,' Lucas says. 'It's used in industry and sports. You've heard of it, I'm sure?'

'Yeah.' Sort of.

'And some people choose to be cryogenically preserved.'

He means rich people.

I get it. Hope costs. 'We don't have any money,' I say.

'Don't worry about that right now,' he rushes on. 'You understand this won't make Asha better? There's no cure for her illness — yet. But we're working on treatments all the time. Once we have one, we'll be able to deliver it to her using nanomedicine. That's the other branch of our research. Until then, she remains suspended and perfectly safe.'

Asha suspended. I see her floating in the night

38

sky among the stars. She'd like that. Suspended.
And safe.

'We don't have much time.' Lucas pulls out a
clipboard. 'The sooner after death we can process
Asha, the better chance she has.'

I shiver. Asha's details – diagnosis, treatment,
are all there on the top sheet of paper.

'How do you know so much about her?'

'You've applied on her behalf to many
experimental programmes, I believe.'

'Yes.'

'All such trials are registered and the details
are recorded by the UK authorities. The Foundation
has a special agreement with them.' He smiles;
perfect white teeth. 'That's why there's no fee,
Calico.'

'Asha can be in the programme for free?'

'Not exactly. What we ask, in lieu of payment,
is that a close relative of the patient participates
in our research. A sibling is ideal.' He looks at me.
'The choice is yours, Calico.'

Guilt jabs at me. It's my fault Asha's here. I
shouldn't have left her. It's not a difficult decision
to make.

'Okay,' I say. 'Research, I can do that. Where do
I sign?'

He blinks. 'I should explain what the research
programme entails first.'

'Whatever it is, I'll do it.'

'Legally, I'm bound to run through this.'
He talks fast. 'If you elect to be cryogenically
processed at the same time as Asha, there's no fee
for your sister's preservation and treatment.'

All the air disappears.

'You mean, I have to be frozen, too?'

'Yes.'

Frozen. Suspended. My life on pause. But then,
Asha being ill has put life on pause anyway.

'How long would I be frozen for?'

'Not long. We've recently perfected the
reanimation process. After you're brought back to
life, you'll be required to participate in our research
for two years.'

Two years. To make up for one night. Two years
of my life.

It's nothing to save Asha.

And precious seconds are passing.

'I'll do it,' I say.

He hands me the clipboard, flips to the next
page. There I am in black and white. Everything
about me. And at the bottom there's a consent
slip. For cryogenic suspension upon death.

'We need parental consent for Asha,' Lucas
says. 'But as you're over sixteen you get to decide
for yourself.'

I hold out my hand for a pen.

'You do understand, Calico,' he says, 'this
process can only be performed on the legally dead.'

A lightning bolt of pure terror strikes me. But I push it away. I gave Asha my blood. I gave her my bone marrow.

'Will it hurt?' My mouth is dry.

'No,' he says. 'You won't feel a thing.'

Asha's going to die. I can save her. But only if I die too.

Quiet settles over me like unexpected snow.

Lucas passes me the pen.

I sign my name.

'And here.' He flips the page.

Consent for voluntary euthanasia.

If I sign this, I'm going to die. My heart bashes against my ribs, like it's fighting me all the way. 'You'll wake me up?' I ask.

'The scientists at the facility will, yes. I promise.' Lucas nods.

Think of it as sleep. I'll be asleep, not dead. I'll wake up again. Asha will be well. Mum will be happy. Maybe she'll forgive me for leaving Asha alone.

I don't read any more of the document. I've made my decision and there's no time anyway. I sign my name again.

Lucas guides me back to the ITU. 'Your mother needs to give consent for Asha.' He taps the clipboard in my hand. 'I'm not allowed in there till she's signed it.'

9.

Earl hustles into my room. 'Doc Perez wants to see you, kid. Maybe bring your Remembering Book, you might have to wait.'

We walk along the run-down hallway, past all the doors. My brain whirs with what happened yesterday. That strange boy, Jem. What Earl said about the treatments not always working. What that means for Asha.

Gabe comes round the corner, smooth skin, baggy shorts. He's with another boy who is all sinew, big eyes, and freckles under a buzz cut. Slightly behind them is a girl. Black hair, pixie cut; dark brown skin. She swing-walks using crutches. Her left leg stops at the knee.

And then we've moved on. Earl unlocks the door to a room that smells like the school science labs, only there's no equipment or specimens anywhere.

Jem lurks in the far corner behind a workbench. He dips his head when he sees me, does his twitch and mutter thing. A shy half-smile. The beanie's pulled so low only the fingertips of his scar show.

'Wait here,' Earl says. 'I'll be back to collect you when Perez is done.'

Jem scuffs over to me once Earl's gone. 'You just missed Veda and Taylor.'

'Oh, I think I saw them. Are they—'

'Yeah, they're inmates too. Taylor's all right. Veda's a bit of an arse-licker.'

'Nice language, Jem.' The soft Spanish voice, from when I woke up.

'Nice timing,' he murmurs.

'Calico? Hi, I'm Sophia Perez.'

She's smaller than me, wearing grey scrubs. Black hair, kind eyes smudged with tiredness. A gold cross hangs from a chain at her neck.

Great. God squad.

'Welcome to the facility,' she says. 'I have a starter pack for you.' She hands me a cardboard folder. 'There's a baseline questionnaire for you to complete.'

I take it over to a bench.

'I'll be with you in a moment, Jem,' she says, going into a side room marked Office.

'Whatever,' he mutters.

I turn to the questionnaire.

Jem hovers beside me. 'You don't have to fill that in. You don't have to give them any information about yourself.'

'But that's what we're doing here, right? Research. They need information.'

Jem taps the facility logo at the top of the questionnaire. 'The HEALE Programme?' he says. 'More like the HELL Programme if you ask me. And *Do no harm*. That's a fucking lie.'

He carries on talking to himself and someone called Stan. But I block it out. I have to. I answer questions about digestion and menstruation, headaches and allergies. It's a normal medical form. Not exactly my deepest secrets.

'In you come, Jem,' Doctor Perez says from her office.

'Nah. I'm good.'

'Jem, come on.' Doctor Perez is in the doorway now. 'Must I call Earl again?' She taps at her wrist.

'You're asking the question, but you've already called him.' Jem's head jerks, his voice getting louder. 'You don't *have* to get Earl. You could choose *not* to get Earl instead of forcing me to do something I don't consent to.'

'You signed up for this, Jem.'

His whole body convulses. 'I did NOT sign up for this and you fucking know it.'

That's why he's so anti everything? But why? If he didn't sign up himself he must've been dying – or already dead – so they saved his life.

Earl marches in, huge tattooed arms swinging, and heads straight for Jem. He's at least twice his size. 'Why you got to make things so hard on yourself, kid?'

Jem darts to the back of the lab. Earl lunges after him. Jem grabs a stool, holds it over his head.

'Cool it, kid.'

Jem roars, chucks the chair full force. It somersaults over benches. Crashes into the wall. My heartbeat ratchets up. I crouch behind the workbench. What the hell?

44

'That's enough.' Earl's voice is like steel.

Jem leaps on to a bench. Earl grabs his leg.

'Don't touch me!' Jem yells.

Earl pulls him down, holds Jem tight. The tattoos bulge: clocks without hands, the dagger dripping blood.

'This. Is. Abuse,' Jem wheezes.

Earl half carries him through the lab. The beanie slips off. Jem's scar is like a bloody handprint on his cheek. Earl wrangles him into the office and Doctor Perez shuts the door behind the three of them.

I'm shaking. 'What – what—'

My mouth's dry. What the hell was that? Earl's a nurse, not a bouncer. He's been so kind to me. Did he really need to force Jem into the other room like that? What about *'do no harm'*? This is a research facility, not a prison any more, so why *are* we locked in our rooms and escorted everywhere? Jem looked so scared.

I need to distract myself. The Remembering Book. *I'd just left Lucas outside the ITU.*

Mum has Asha in her lap. Their eyes are closed. My heart stutters. Is Asha already gone? Did I take too long to decide?

I go over to them, hear Asha's tiny bird breath. Relief washes over me. I stroke her face. 'I'm here,' I whisper.

Mum starts singing again, soft and low. She's moved on from the hymns to an old folk song.

Blood and breath and bone,
threaded through with love and light.
Always in my heart and mind.
I'll carry you through deepest night.

The song goes on and on.

I touch Mum's arm. 'There's a place on a treatment programme,' I tell her.

She opens her eyes, stares at me like I'm someone far away.

'You've got to sign this.' I hold out the clipboard. 'Mum. Please. One last chance.'

All the breaths in the world are waiting.

The song stops.

'One last chance?' Mum whispers. And she's here with me in the real world, not somewhere between life and death with Asha. 'What is this?'

'An experimental treatment, nanomedicine,' I say. 'There's not much time.'

Mum takes the pen. I show her where to sign.

'Is this the right thing to do?' She looks so like Asha when she says it.

I don't know if it's the right thing, but I do know it's something. The only thing. And Mum's always told us to give ourselves the best chance possible, keep our options open.

'Yes.' I bend Mum's fingers round the pen. Her hand trembles but she scrawls her name.

One last chance.

I drop into the chair next to Mum. It hits me, what I'm going to do …

'Calico,' Mum says. 'I need to tell you something—'

But Asha sighs in her arms. And this time, the next breath doesn't come.

Everything's silent. The moment stretches on and on.

My Asha is gone.

Mum sobs.

I wrap my arms around them both. I kiss Asha's forehead. It's warm and smooth beneath my lips. I kiss Mum's cheek, taste her tears.

'We need to move quickly,' the ITU nurse says. She picks up the phone: 'Page Doctor Rahman. Code silver.'

10.

asha

New Game

seems like Death
ran out on you
mid game of hide-and-seek.
left you hiding
in some corner
of the lonely universe.

perhaps Death's
found a new game
and you
don't know
the rules.

11.

Calico

Jem comes back into the lab with Earl. He snatches his beanie off the floor. His face is tear-streaked.

Doctor Perez calls for me from her office. My hands quiver as I gather the papers.

'Come in, Calico.' Doctor Perez sits at a desk. Her dark hair has drifted loose. She looks exhausted. 'Take a seat,' she says.

It's a small space – the wooden desk, two chairs, some cupboards. On the wall, there's the facility logo, and that motto again: *do no harm.* Beneath it are diagrams of enormous terrifying spiders. My skin crawls. Nanomites, it says. Magnified. Lucas mentioned nanomedicine back at City Hospital. That was how they'd fix Asha. I didn't know it meant spiders. But then, I didn't know anything much except I had to save her.

'I'm trying to find my sister,' I say to Doctor Perez.

She looks at me a moment. 'Yes, Earl mentioned you'd asked about her. We're not allowed to discuss any other study participants for reasons of confidentiality. I'm sorry, I know you must be worried about her, but my advice is to wait and see.' She smiles.

There's a flutter of hope inside me. Is she saying she can't tell me, but I'll see Asha soon? I hold on to that.

'I also wondered what the date is.'

'There'll be time to answer all your questions when we get to the debrief. But today is about setting everything up for the research programme. Okay?' Her voice softens. 'First I'd like to apologise for what you had to witness in the lab.'

Jem.

She's sorry it happened? Or she's sorry I *saw* it happen?

'Well, it did shake me up a bit. Is Jem – all right?' I ask.

'As I said, I can't discuss anyone else, but it's a big thing to come to terms with – what you've both been through – emotionally, as well as physically. It takes some longer than others to recover.'

'But he'll be okay?'

She nods vaguely. 'We must get on. Let me review your questionnaire, Calico.'

I pass it over the desk and go to look at the weird nanomite poster on the wall while she reads. They're not spiders at all. They're tiny robots made out of biological material. They repair damage inside human bodies. It gives me a lift imagining how they'll have been used to cure Asha, and I'm smiling as I turn.

But then the world warps.

There, standing in the doorway, is a ghost.

A ghost.

Must be a ghost.

White coat, white hair.

Skin so pale, it's like snow.

A slow, sad smile.

Death-is-not-the-end eyes.

'Lucas?' I whisper.

He nods.

'But you're old,' I say.

How long was I dead?

The air shrinks.

How do I ... breathe?

The room fades.

The floor falls away.

Darkness bats at my face, swirls around me.

I am lost.

12.

'Calico?' An underwater voice.

My heartbeat is so loud it drowns out the rest of the words.

A warm hand on my forehead. Kind eyes smile over me. *Mum?*

No. It's Doctor Perez. Her crucifix dangles above my face. 'Calico, you're safe. Breathe, nice and slow.'

Ohmygod. How long was I dead? How long was I frozen? What about Asha? Oh. God. What about Mum? If Lucas is ancient, how old is she? Is she even still alive?

I scramble to sit. I'm on the floor in the lab. My mind races, trying to catch hold of anything that makes sense. No sign of Lucas. *Old* Lucas. *Was* it a ghost?

'Where is he?'

'Who?' Doctor Perez helps me stand.

'Lucas.'

She frowns. 'You mean Doctor Fates?'

Doctor Fates?

What?

Lucas is Doctor Fates?

Jem's voice is in my head. *The creep who runs this place.*

'I need to see him.' He knows where Asha is, he must do.

'You will,' Doctor Perez says.

52

'Now,' I say. 'He was right here.'

'Let's check you over first.' She sits me on a stool. 'Did you hit your head?'

'Please, I need to see him,' I say. He has all the answers.

She rests her hands on the bench. 'How do you know his first name is Lucas?'

'We met before.'

She shakes her head. 'That's not possible.' Her wrist vibrates.

'What the hell is that?'

'It's my nanocom,' she says. 'A mini computer.'

'Under your skin? Inside your body?'

'Yes.'

So freaky. I want to puke. But it makes this real. I am in the future.

'Come with me,' Doctor Perez says.

I follow her into the hall. She takes me to a lobby with four doors off it. Hospital Wing. Staff Quarters. Administration. Doctor Fates. That's the one she knocks on.

'Come.'

Inside, shelves line the walls. Not much on them – a few stacks of paper. Worn beige carpet. A big polished mahogany desk. No computer. And there he is again. Lucas. Definitely Lucas. Not a ghost, but old. Really old. Hair faded, skin creased, back stooped.

'Take a seat, Calico.' His voice slices the air.

But I don't sit down. I can't be still. My brain chases

questions, too many things I need to know. Asha. Mum. 'What year is it?' I blurt.

Lucas rests against his desk, looks at me through gold-rimmed glasses. Those death-is-not-the-end eyes. 'It's 2070,' he says.

2070.

No no no.

Forty-five years. Forty-five years since we died, me and Asha.

All that time. Gone. I thought I was giving us more time together. I thought I was giving us more options, more choices, more life.

What did I do? What did I do?

No. *Him*. What did *he* do? I snarl, lurch for Lucas.

Doctor Perez grabs hold of me. 'Calm down, Calico.'

'Surely I don't need to sedate you,' Lucas says, ice cold.

The memory slides through me like a needle. Asha's hospital room, the ambulance, the morgue.

'No,' I say. 'Just – why did it take so long?'

'There were a number of complications.'

'Why didn't anyone tell me?' I ask.

'Reanimates are typically informed of the date when they're debriefed,' Lucas says.

He's so sodding calm I want to take the water jug off his desk, smash him with it.

Perez pulls on her damn crucifix. 'Sorry, Calico. I should have told you.'

But none of this is her fault. I never met her before today. She can't even have been born when this happened. I'm older than her. And younger.

I go limp and Doctor Perez leads me to a chair.

'With the AA crisis, and the staff shortage,' she says to Lucas, 'I haven't gotten to her debrief yet.'

'It's quite all right, Sophia,' he says.

But it's not all right. None of this is all right.

'What about Asha? Where is she? And my mum?' The words drop out of me like tiny stones. Forty-five years. 'Is Mum even still alive?'

'We have no way of knowing, Calico,' Doctor Perez says gently. 'We don't have access to any information about your life pre-suspension, or your family. It's all sealed until your two years is up.'

'*He* knows. He knows all about my family. About me. And Asha.'

Lucas walks round behind the desk.

Yeah, you better put some distance between us.

He clears his throat. 'There have been over five hundred subjects stored by the Foundation at one time or another—'

'And you brought them all in yourself, personally, did you? On two-for-one deals?'

'Doctor Fates?'

'A very short-lived recruitment system in the UK, Sophia. Representatives of the Foundation met with subjects to explain the procedure and the study.'

'That level of interaction with participants

55

pre-suspension?' Doctor Perez frowns. 'Surely it's at odds with protocol.'

'Times change,' Lucas says. 'Ethical boundaries move.' His mouth is a pencil-grey line.

Doctor Perez stares at him. Her wrist buzzes.

'You'd better see to that, Sophia,' Lucas says. 'I'll escort Calico back to her room.'

Her fingers flutter to the gold crucifix, but then she nods, and leaves.

Lucas walks beside me through the corridor.

'You promised her,' I say quietly.

'What's that?'

'You promised Mum she'd see us again.'

He looks straight ahead. 'What's a promise but the best of intentions? The world can change in a heartbeat. No one knows what's going to happen the second after a promise is made.'

'Why has it taken so long though? You told me when I signed up that you'd perfected the reanimation technique.'

'I was optimistic. In the early days of reanimation, people didn't survive for long. We had to refine our processes.'

I shudder. I could've been one of those people.

He's silent until we get to my room. He opens the door and gestures for me to go in. I'm desperate to keep him here, to get more information.

'Tell me about Asha, at least,' I say. 'How is she?'

'Sit down, Calico.' He points to the bed. 'I can't discuss another study subject with you.'

'But she's my sister.'

'It doesn't matter.' He drags the chair over from the desk and sits, leaning into my space. The wrinkles on his face are deep. 'You signed up for this, Calico. It was all there in the contract, including a confidentiality clause you just broke by telling Doctor Perez about the way you were recruited—'

'What? But I didn't know.'

'Listen carefully. You cannot discuss the circumstances of your recruitment with anyone. Including the fact that you were healthy and uninjured before you were processed. No one else knows about that.'

'So I have to lie?'

'I'm sure you don't want to be removed from the programme. That would be no good for you. Or your sister.'

He's threatening me. I swallow down bitter rage.

'Please just tell me Asha's okay.'

'You're not stupid, Calico. You know how unlikely it is that Asha would have been reanimated before you, given her condition at the time of death.'

That empty space inside me. The hollow.

Deep down, I knew it. Deep down.

'She's still frozen, isn't she?' I whisper.

'Yes.'

Exhaustion crashes over me.

A moment of Asha, tiny bird. Tiny dead bird.

I wish it was me. Frozen. Still asleep. Unaware.

I close my eyes, get a glimpse of Mum's face the day of the third diagnosis. This was how she felt. The overwhelming tiredness, the I-don't-think-I-can-do-this-again, all I want is to sleep. And I saw her tuck it away, open her eyes, smile and say, *Well, we've beaten it before, we'll do it again.*

It's a moment, only a moment. Tuck it away, Calico. Hide it in the hollow.

'So there's no cure yet?' I ask, my voice heavy. 'Even after all this time?'

'No.'

'But you're still working on it?' I whisper.

'Of course.'

'I want to see her.'

Lucas shakes his head. 'That's not possible. The protocols—'

'Thought you were in charge around here.'

'I am,' he says. 'And we can't have study subjects wandering around the Cryostore. It's for your own good.'

But I won't let this go. I can't.

'The only thing that's good for me is to know Asha's all right. I need to see her even if she is still frozen.'

'You'll have to take my word for it,' he says.

Take his word for it? Trust him? How can I?

But I trusted him before.

It didn't hurt when I died, like he promised. And he

58

did wake me up, like he promised, even if it took longer than I thought it would. A lot longer.

And he did save Asha. I saw him put her in the transportation pod before I died.

'The best way to help Asha now is to focus on the study. It is everything,' he says.

'Lucas—'

'You must follow the rules of the facility – and you can start by showing me some respect – no more Lucas. You will refer to me as Doctor Fates.'

'Okay, but—'

'No more discussion, Calico. You obey the rules, follow the study protocols – otherwise the research will be worthless.' His voice hardens. 'And if that happens, there's no hope for Asha at all.'

I am sinking under the weight of his words.

'Do you understand?' he says.

'Yes,' I whisper.

What else can I do?

He knows I won't risk Asha.

13.

No sleep. It hits me, over and over, like a drummer's inside my head. Asha's still dead. Asha's still dead.

I didn't save her.

I can blame Lucas, old Lucas – Doctor Fates – but it's my fault.

All I can do for Asha right now is follow his rules and protocols, focus on the study.

I take out the Remembering Book again.

Code Silver.

<u>Day 5</u>

In the ITU, Doctor Rahman checks for Asha's pulse. 'Time of death 03:32,' she says. 'Prep for cardiopulmonary support, please.'

'Ruth, I need to take her.' The nurse lifts Asha from Mum's lap and on to the bed. She attaches pads with wires to her chest.

'I don't understand,' Mum says. 'She's gone. It's too late.'

The nurse crouches by her side.

Doctor Rahman's on the phone: 'Page the cryogenic team to ITU.' She comes over to Mum. 'I'm so sorry, Ruth. Once the team arrives, you'll need to leave.'

'No! I have to stay with her.'

'They need to prepare the girls for transit, Ruth. I don't think you want to be here for that.'

'The girls?' Mum says.

Doctor Rahman nods at me.

'I had to sign up, too, Mum,' I say.

'I don't understand,' she says. 'Sign up for what?'

'Some research. That's all.'

'For both Asha and Calico,' Doctor Rahman says slowly, 'the process is post-mortem.'

'Post-mortem?' Mum asks.

'It means after death.'

Mum is silent, still.

The door smashes open. Lucas bursts in with a team of paramedics.

'All set?' he asks.

Doctor Rahman nods and passes him the paperwork.

The cryogenics team swarm over Asha. They put bags of ice around her head, attach a machine to the wires on her chest. They lift her on to a trolley, pull a sheet over her, cover her face.

'Let's go,' Lucas says.

'Wait! I need to say goodbye to her.'

'It's not goodbye, Calico. You're coming with us.'

'No. Not yet.'

'Calico, get in the wheelchair, please,'
Lucas says.

'Mum!' I try to reach her, but someone's got
hold of me. There's a sting in my arm.

'That's the tranquilliser in.' A wheelchair
bumps the back of my knees. 'Take a seat, please.'

I fold into it. 'Mum!'

The nurse is at her side, talking quietly.

Mum lets out a low groan, like the earth
splitting open.

'Mum?'

She stands and turns to Lucas. 'There's been
a mistake,' she says. 'Calico didn't know what she
was doing. I didn't know what she was doing.'

He shakes his head. 'Don't you want to save
Asha?'

'Not like this.'

'I'm sorry,' he says. 'It's too late.'

'No.' Mum grabs at him. 'No. It can't be.'

Lucas takes her hands in his. 'I know what it's
like to lose someone you love, Ruth. And I promise, I
promise, I'll bring them back to you.'

Mum stumbles to me. Her eyes are huge with
terror. Her fingers trace my face.

'What have you done?' she says. 'Oh, Calico,
what have you done?'

What have I done? What have I done?

I lie back on the bed. It's so quiet here in the facility.

No noise, no rhythm of home. I turn on to my side and wish Asha would come like she did when she was small. After I started school, she didn't like it, me being away from her all day. She said I smelled different when I came home, like I wasn't me. At night she'd sneak into my bed in her bright pink pyjamas. Her hot little body clinging to my back, she'd sing softly in my ear until she fell asleep mid-word. Mum would pull her off me sometime in the night. *Come on, little limpet.* That was years and years ago. Before the first diagnosis. Then it was Asha who smelled different. No amount of Mum's essential oils could hide it. That hospital smell.

14.

asha

bone

the first time,
hospital smells, hospital spells.
magic medicine took away pain,
made you float.

when it came back at eleven.
calico said she'd had enough
of god,
and all the talk of heaven.

the holy grandparents muttered
about the sins of the mother,
and how the three of you
would go to hell together.

third time, calico said:
there's always another way.
she wrote to judges and MPs
doctors and drug companies
treatment trials and
millionaires and billionaires
and research centres
and charitable foundations.

she was a dog
and you, asha,
were the bone

15.

Calico

All last night Asha darted across my dreams and I woke up to a memory of her. Small and naked, flitting around the garden, her body slick and raspberry-coloured.

Grandma opened the back door and screamed.

Mum and her singing student ran out from the house.

'What on earth's happened?' Mum asked.

Grandma caught Asha, like a tiny tiddler in a towel.

'I thought it was blood,' Grandma said. 'I thought it was blood.'

'Calico painted me!' Asha clapped her crimson palms together.

Mum laughed; the student smiled. Grandma frowned.

Asha had asked me to paint her. Wanted to be a robin. She'd shivered and giggled when I brushed the watery paint on her sun-warm skin.

Oh, Asha. She was so tiny, and the disease got so big. It filled up our lives, the searching for any chance we could to save her, keeping all the options open. That's what Mum said. Preparing for choices we didn't know we'd need to make, hoping for the future. And here I am now, really *in* the future. And I'm on my own. But I'm still looking to Asha. Still looking *for* her. Still trying to save her.

I'm no good at being by myself. I don't do alone. I do taking care of Asha. Helping Mum. Holding it all together.

Or do I?

First, I put my trust in God. Then medicine. Put my trust in Lucas sodding Fates. That was stupid.

This is all my fault. If I hadn't left Asha, gone to that party, none of this would've happened. I wouldn't have even met Lucas – Doctor Fates. Wouldn't be here, trapped in this building.

But Asha's here too.

In the Cryostore. Fates let that slip.

I don't need him to take me to her. I can find her myself.

There is always another way.

16.

'Time for rehab, kid. You're on kitchen duty today.'

I'm jittery, jogging along the corridors trying to keep up with Earl's bustling strides. I check for any signs to the Cryostore, but there aren't any.

'Here we are,' Earl says.

The kitchen is a long room with under-counter drawers and cupboards on both sides. Ceramic pots of wooden utensils on the work surface. It smells musty, mushroomy.

Someone is washing dishes.

'Calico, this is Taylor.'

'Hi.' It's the boy I saw in the hallway. He's about my age, slight and lean under old clothes like mine. A freckled face and buzz-cut hair.

'Right, kid.' Earl rubs a hand over the dagger tattoo. 'Remember the rules.'

I nod.

'I'll leave you to it, then.'

'Hey.' Taylor smiles. 'How y'doing?'

'I'm—' I was going to ask if he'd seen Asha. Like I've asked everyone else here. But now I know she's still frozen and no one's seen her.

'That good, eh?' Taylor says, drying his hands.

I nod.

'You want some tea?' He pulls out a tall stool

and gestures for me to sit.

He lights the stove and puts a blackened kettle on to boil. I feel like I've woken up back in the past, not the future.

'It's all right to feel weird and confused,' Taylor says softly. 'You did die, you know. And now you've come back. It's a helluva shock.'

'Yeah.' Treacherous tears prick at my eyes, but I will not let them fall. 'I just found out I – died a lot longer ago than I thought.'

Taylor looks at me. 'That must mess with your head.'

'It really does. I – I – don't know if my mum's still alive.'

'Oh shit. That's tough.'

Taylor gets out two chunky mugs. 'Did you get a letter from your mom or anything?'

I shake my head but inside there's a flicker of hope. 'Did you?'

'Yeah. I died seven years ago, and when I was reanimated they gave me letters from my folks. So I know they're okay. Or at least they were eighteen months back.'

'I thought we weren't allowed contact with anyone outside the facility.'

'Think it depends how you ended up in here. I was knocked down by a drunk driver – didn't know anything about it. My mom and pop explained in their letters so I didn't freak out. Too much, anyways.' He smiles and rummages in some stone pots, pulling out dried leaves and flowers. When he pours water over them, sage and chamomile scent the air. I get a vision of Mum amongst her pots of herbs.

Mum.

I won't have a letter from her. I know that. It sits heavy like a stone in my chest. How she looked at me that last time in the ITU. Her eyes full of blame.

'Here you go,' Taylor says.

I blink away more threatening tears. 'Thanks.' I breathe in the steam.

There's something about this, sitting in a kitchen with a hot mug – a familiar ritual maybe, or the kindness of a stranger – that comforts me.

'I need to get on with the lunches, but you take it easy.' Taylor opens a cupboard full of glass jars. Flour, lentils, dried beans, dehydrated mushrooms. From another cupboard he brings a huge bowl over to the counter. He shows me the sludgy contents. 'Lentils soaked overnight. Looks delicious, eh?'

'Um—'

He laughs. 'No need to be polite with me. I know it's disgusting. Most of the food here is.' He tips the sludge into a pan and adds salt, dried mushrooms and herbs. 'I try my best when I'm on cooking duty, but there's not much you can do to make this stuff look or taste any better.'

'Why *is* it so bad?'

'I guess they don't have access to much fresh food.

We're in an arid zone so they can't grow their own. We only get supplies every few months so it's mostly dried or dehydrated. Not that it matters – you'd need a knife or two to prepare fresh meat and veg.'

'There aren't any knives?'

'Nope. Not for us anyways. No sharp objects or anything that could be made into one. That's why there's no mirrors. Guess they don't want folk hurting themselves.'

'Oh.' I think about what Earl said, how it was better not to know how reanimates had lived or died. I think about muttering Jem.

'Is it like this everywhere? Outside the facility, I mean?'

'Oh no. My folk have plenty of fresh food at home. We grow our own crops and raise animals, feed ourselves and the community.'

'Must've been a disappointment when you woke up here.'

He grins. 'Yeah. But I'm so, so glad to be alive, and in this body, you know, it's worth eating this crap for two years.'

I guess two years isn't so bad when you know what's waiting for you on the outside. My mind turns to Mum again.

'You want to help make the crackers?' Taylor asks.

'Sure.' I welcome the distraction. I'd rather be doing than thinking.

We mix flour, salt and water into a paste. Taylor

heats a flat pan on the stove and smears dough over it. After a minute he flips it and after another minute it goes on a rack to cool. We repeat this over and over while the soup bubbles on the stove, and Taylor talks in his gentle voice about his mom and pop, his three older brothers, the horses on his family ranch. It soothes me, and I jump when Gabe comes in with a trolley.

'Hey, guys.'

'Hi.' Taylor grins. 'You're on slop duty today then?'

'Yeah.' Gabe messes with his sun-streaked hair.

'Lucky you.'

We load up trays with soup and crackers. Gabe takes most of them away on the trolley. Taylor rolls up the hatch between the kitchen and the day room and we scoot over the counter.

'Hey, Veda.'

The girl I saw yesterday sits facing us. Her crutches lean against the table.

'Hello, Tee,' she says. 'And you must be Calico.'

'Yeah. Hi.'

Taylor brings our food over to the table.

'Delicious,' Veda says.

'You being rude about my cooking again?'

They both laugh. Their ease makes me feel on the outside. It's like being back in the school canteen. The hollow inside me gapes. I miss Asha so much. I miss being known by someone.

I force down a few crumbs of cracker and stir my soup while the others eat.

'I got you something,' Taylor says to Veda, reaching into his pocket. 'Happy re-birthday!'

'An apple!' Veda holds it to her nose and inhales. 'Thank you.'

'I swiped it the other day when the supplies came in.'

'Re-birthday?' I ask.

'Taylor loves any excuse to celebrate,' Veda says. 'Today is the anniversary of when I was reanimated.'

'A year?'

'Yes.'

'And you, Taylor?'

'Longer. I've only got five months left and then I'm out of here.'

'So you know what the date is?'

'Not exactly.'

'I mark the days in my Remembering Book.' Veda taps the journal next to her.

She keeps it with her then, like Jem does. I wonder why they do that.

'Do you know Jem?' I ask.

'Yeah,' Taylor says. 'You met him?'

I nod.

'He was the last person reanimated before you, only about six months ago.'

'And still very much adjusting to being alive,' Veda says.

'Yeah,' I say. 'He doesn't seem to want to be here.'

'Well, it's tough,' Taylor says. 'Think he went through a lot of trauma – before he died. And he can't

72

seem to get his head round his mom signing him up for the programme.'

'I suppose everyone's different.' Veda traces a pattern on the table with her fingertip. 'Even though I didn't know this would happen to me, perhaps I'm more open to the idea of being brought back to life. My parents aren't religious, but my nani believes in reincarnation. I spent a lot of time with her when I was little.' She brushes the table. 'You seem to be coping well, though, Calico – in rehabilitation and resocialisation already.'

'What's resocialisation?'

'This is.' She laughs. 'Interacting with your peers. You must have a lot of questions. I know I did when I woke up.'

'Yeah. I do. Have either of you got a phone?'

Taylor smiles, shakes his head. 'No, sorry.'

'But there's one somewhere in this place, right?'

'I've never seen one,' Veda says.

'What? How about a laptop?'

'No,' she says.

'No computers or phones or anything?'

'That's right.'

'Do you mind me asking, Calico, when did you die?' Veda says.

I take a deep breath. '2025.'

She nods. 'So back then, in your first life, you were used to having a lot of personal tech – cell phones, computers?'

'Yeah.'

'Those devices are history now.'

'There are no phones or laptops at all?'

'Not like you're thinking,' Taylor says.

'Mostly biologically integrated tech. You may have seen the staff here using nanocoms implanted in their wrists. They can communicate with them.'

'Oh. Is that what those are?'

Veda nods.

'How do the staff talk to the outside world though?'

'Radio, most likely,' Taylor says. 'That's what we use on the ranch.'

No way of getting in touch with Mum, then. No way of finding out if she's even still alive. The hollow inside me expands. What else has happened in the world out there? So much I want to know. But that's not going to help me or Asha. I need to focus on the here and now.

'Do you know where the Cryostore is?' I ask.

Veda and Taylor exchange a glance.

'Yes,' Veda says.

A little ember of hope glows. 'Where?'

She clears her throat. 'Did you know this building was a prison in the past?'

'Yes.'

'Well, the Cryostore used to be death row.'

No.

The cruelty of it is like a punch to the head.

I'm spinning, inside and out. Everything blurs and the world disappears.

17.

asha

loop

they say life
flashes
before your eyes
when you die,
but this is more
a
s l o w – m o t i o n
replay:
memories,
on repeat
on repeat.

like you missed
something important
first time around,
and now you're
stuck in a loop
in a loop,
looking for
the truth.

18.

Calico

I am empty and weighed down at the same time. Doctor Perez says it's grief. But it's not. I will not grieve while there's still hope. She says I need to eat and rest more. Think about happy memories of Asha, before she was ill. She has me shut in my room again with nothing to do but write in the Remembering Book.

<u>Day 9</u>

Happy memories. I guess there must be some. It's hard thinking back to before she was ill, like peeling back the layers of a pass the parcel.

Actually, Asha was obsessed with that game for a while. She'd played it at someone's party and after that she'd wrap up random objects — a pebble, a cauliflower, a jelly baby. She loved watching me and Mum opening the parcel. She liked making us laugh—

This is no good. I need to write a list. It makes me calmer, having a list. That's what I did when I was trying to help Asha before. A list of solicitors. I'd talk to each one for the free half hour they offered. That's how I managed to get round the law and give Asha my bone marrow when I was underage. And I had a list of experimental treatments, and research trials. And kindly rich people.

To do:

1. Find a way to contact Mum. Or at least find out if she's okay.
2. Find out how far along they are with Asha's cure.
3. Find out where exactly the Cryostore is and how I can get into it.
4. Find—

Gabe comes in with breakfast, some kind of beans.

'How you feelin'?' he asks.

'Fine.'

'Well, you got to stay in your room today.' He messes with his hair. 'To get over your faintin' fit.'

'I'm totally okay.'

'Not up to me. Doc's orders.' He turns to go.

No. I'm not sitting in here for another whole day. I've wasted enough time. Forty-five years. Now I know where Asha is, I have to find the Cryostore.

'Gabe, wait.' I leap up and reach out to stop the door closing. It whacks right on to my hand. There's a crack like a whip. Pain sears. My screams ricochet around me.

'Oh man.' Gabe wedges the door open with his foot. Takes my hand gingerly.

There's hammering from the room next to mine. Jem's voice. 'Hey. What the fuck are you doing to her? Hey!' Jem shouts, banging on his door. 'Calico!'

'I'm okay, Jem,' I say. Even though I'm in so much pain I want to puke.

There's a muttered, 'Shut up, Stan,' and then Jem falls silent.

'I should go get Earl,' Gabe says.

'Where is he?'

'Hospital wing.'

'Maybe you should take me to him.'

Gabe pulls at his hair. 'Um, not sure about that.'

I lift my hand towards him. There's deep purple bruising already and a massive lump. 'Is that the bone?' I say.

'Oh man.' His face has gone pale. 'Um. Okay, let's go.'

Every step jars my hand, but I push the hurt aside. Every step takes me closer to finding Asha.

There's the sign: Hospital Wing. Gabe takes me through one lobby, into another with doors marked Ward and Treatment Room. We go in.

'Stay here,' he says. 'I'll go get Earl.'

I sit on a rickety chair. There's another nanomite poster on the wall in here. Those giant freaky spiders stare down at me. I can't stay here.

I edge out towards the ward. My fingertips touch the wooden door, but there are fast footsteps coming. I run back into the treatment room.

'Christ, kid.' Earl douses his hands in some foul-smelling stuff, takes hold of my arm with his massive paw.

'Shit.' I pull away.

'Yeah, kid, you've broken some bones, but we can fix 'em up.'

Doctor Perez appears. 'What happened?'

'Had a fight with a door,' I say.

Earl shakes his head, takes a massive syringe from a box and puts it on a tray next to me, along with some bottles.

Doctor Perez scrubs her hands and picks up the syringe.

'What's in that?' I ask.

'Relax.' She smiles. 'It's a simple bone repair serum.'

'What?'

'A solution containing nanomites.' She points at the poster. 'Miniature bio-bots. They perform microscopic repairs to the bone.'

She's putting those freaky spiders inside me. 'Why don't you put it in plaster?'

'We don't do that any more.' She takes hold of my wrist. 'Brace yourself, Calico. It's going to hurt. I have to inject directly into the bone.'

She positions the syringe over one of the lumps, pushes the end. It's like a frozen shard shattering into me, an ice cream headache, magnified a million.

I turn my head and puke.

Earl is already there with a bowl. 'Normal reaction, kid.' He wipes my face.

Doctor Perez repeats the bone injection twice more. Third time, I don't puke.

Both their wrists start to vibrate at once. Creepy.

'Stay here,' Earl says to me on his way out.

As if.

I go straight to the ward. Fates said Asha's still frozen, but hope can't help itself. I have to look. She might be in here.

A long room, no windows. It's old-fashioned, not like City Hospital. Beds on either side, each with someone in. It's too quiet and still for a ward. There's no bustle of nurses, no whir or beep of machines. They fix you up silent here. Little tiny bio-bots working beneath the surface.

I shake myself. Asha. I'm here to find Asha. I go to the first bed on the left, a spike of hope inside me. The person in it's asleep. Her eyes are closed; her breathing's so shallow, like Asha at the end. But it isn't Asha. This woman is ancient, her skin shrivelled like the last apple in a fruit bowl.

I go to the next bed. An old man, fine grey hair, fluffy like a baby duck; a slug trail of drool from his mouth. His eyes flick open. It makes me jump. But he doesn't see me. He's unaware, barely even here.

And the next one. Hairless; face creased like paper that's been folded over and over. Not Asha.

And the next. Not Asha.

My heart lurches every time I step towards a bed.

On and on – twenty of them on this side of the ward; eighteen on the other. All of them are ancient, hardly alive. And none of them is Asha.

A scuttle, like spiders under my skin, makes me shudder. The nanomites?

I leave the ward and those barely breathing bodies behind.

I stop in the lobby. No sign to the Cryostore. I'll have to get out of here, search the rest of the facility—

'I thought as much ...' An ice-cold voice. Old Lucas – Doctor Fates – sweeps into the lobby.

Shit.

'As soon as I got the nanocom from Earl, I knew you were up to something.'

I hold up my arm. 'I hurt my hand. They fixed me up. I was trying to find the loo.'

'Do I look like I was born yesterday?'

'No. You really don't.'

He grabs my injured hand.

'Ow.'

'Let's get you back to your room.'

'My cell, more like.'

'You agreed to it, Calico.'

'I didn't have the full picture.'

'Well, you do now.'

Rage rips through me. 'Do I?'

He steers me down the corridor, his grip surprisingly strong for someone so old and frail. We walk in angry silence to my room.

He opens the door and we go in.

'You do want Asha to be cured, don't you?' Fates says.

'Yes, you know I do. That's why I'm here.'

'And you want her to be reanimated?'

'Yes. Like you promised.'

'Well then, you need to do as you're told, Calico. No more breaking out of your room.'

Shit.

'And I'll reiterate our last conversation, just so we're clear. No telling people you and I met before you were frozen. You don't want to compromise the integrity of the research data. No telling people about your sister. No more questions. I'll know if you do anything out of line.' He taps his head. 'I have eyes and ears everywhere. I'll know.'

My mouth opens, but there's nothing to say.

'Do you understand?' he asks.

I nod.

'Good.'

The door slides silently shut behind him.

Tiny ice spiders climb my spine. He'll know if I tell anyone about Asha? If I do anything I shouldn't? How? Is there a camera somewhere? I scan the room. There's hardly anything in here. Are there bugs hidden in the ceiling lights or something?

Bugs.

Shit.

There are bugs inside me. The nanomites. Bio-bots. Right now, they're scurrying along my bones, my veins.

The swelling's already gone from my hand, the bruises too. The bones look smooth like they did before.

What happens to these mites once they've done their job? Do they just disappear? What if they have another job to do?

Can they get into my heart? My brain?

Can they tell what I'm thinking?

19.

My eyes are itchy with tiredness. I dreamed nanomites danced inside my eyeballs. It jerked me awake. Spent the rest of the night drinking water and peeing, trying to get rid of them. Like a detox. Not sure if it worked.

I scan the ceilings, the walls, the lights, as Earl and I walk down the corridor. Can't see any cameras or microphones, but I don't even know what to look for. And they could be microscopic, like the nanomites.

What Fates said is on repeat in my head: *No more questions. I'll know if you do anything out of line.*

I need to be good, follow the rules.

Eyes and ears everywhere.

I can't control a shudder.

'No need to be nervous,' Earl says. 'You met most of them already.'

I follow him into the day room. In one corner there's a group of maybe ten people dressed in hospital gowns and robes. The smell of urine and antibacterial spray hits me. Gabe's reading a picture book to them. They're all grey-haired, saggy-skinned. One of them turns as we pass. I smile, but she looks at me like the old ladies at church used to. Silent judgement in her eyes.

'Your group's in there.' Earl points to the small room where I first saw Jem. 'Go on.'

Veda sits writing on her lap. Jem's in the corner nodding and chatting to himself. Taylor's on the sofa. But the three of them are at the edges. The space is filled by the girl coming towards me. She has this sort of gleam. Her hair floats like a fine, coppery halo.

'Well, here she is.' Her laugh is a cascade of coins.

She has on the same loose trousers as everyone else, but her top is tied tight in a knot under her breasts, showing her pale flat stomach.

'Hey, sugar,' she says.

'Hello.'

'I'm Shimmer.'

'Your name's Shimmer?'

She frowns. 'You don't know who I am?'

'I keep telling you, Shimmy,' Veda says. 'You are not so famous. Not everywhere in the world. I had never heard of you, either.'

Shimmer pouts.

'Let it go, girl,' Taylor says.

'I'm Calico.'

'I love your accent,' Shimmy says. 'You're from England?'

I nod.

'So, you know these two then?' She indicates Veda and Jem.

Veda rolls her eyes. 'How would she know us?'

'She's from England.'

'And I keep telling you I'm from India. Your grasp of geography is astoundingly lacking.'

85

'It's all the same to me, sugar. Far away from here.'

'Wish I was far away from here,' Jem says.

'Well, we all wish that too, sugar.'

'Fuck off, Shimmy.'

'Hey, guys,' Taylor says. 'Play nice. It's Calico's first time with us all.'

Veda and Jem go back to their notebooks.

'Should I have brought my Remembering Book?' I ask. 'Earl didn't say to.'

'Oh, no. I just like to keep mine with me,' Veda says.

'And I don't want anyone else getting hold of mine,' Jem says. 'They've got no right to look at it.'

'Trust me, sugar, no one's interested in anything you've got to say.'

'They don't read the Remembering Books though, do they?' Panic picks at me. I don't want anyone looking at my memories. 'I mean, I thought they're not supposed to know anything about our past lives.'

Veda and Taylor share a look.

'What?' I say. 'What is it?'

'Honestly, sugar. I think it's just something to keep us occupied.' Shimmy smiles.

'No. It's important,' Veda says. 'Remembering is how they assess the effects of cryogenics and reanimation on the brain.'

'Who told you that, your lab geek?'

Veda scowls at Shimmy and turns back to me. 'No one's ever read mine. And I actually found it really useful early on. Helped orientate myself, reminded me who I was. But then, I do like to keep my brain active, unlike some people.'

Shimmy laughs. 'Oh, who can be bothered with all that stuff from way back when?'

'I also record everything I learn here,' Veda says. 'This is such an amazing opportunity we've been given. I want to be able to use the knowledge when I leave.'

'You want to be a scientist?' I ask.

'No, I want to work for the Global Eco Government, like my father,' Veda says.

I'm suddenly surrounded by a peachy vanilla scent. Shimmy is really close to me. She touches my arm.

I leap back.

'What's wrong, sugar?'

'We're not supposed to have any physical contact.' I glance about the room, on high alert for cameras again.

'Oh, sugar, no one can see us in here.'

'Can't be sure,' Jem says.

'Oh, don't start, crazy boy.'

'One of us could be a plant.' He stares right at me.

My heart's going too fast. What Fates said pounds in my head. *Eyes and ears.*

'Are *you* a plant, Calico?' Jem says. 'Been brought in to watch us and report back?'

'What are you talking about?' Shimmy says.

Am I a plant? I don't know, with these nano things scuttling through my bones, my body, my brain.

'Only you seem to have made a really quick

recovery. Like, were you even frozen?' Jem says. 'And that girl you asked me about – who is she?'

Asha. I'm not supposed to talk about her. Or how we came to be frozen. This is too hard. The urge to run away overwhelms me. I turn to go.

'Wait!' Shimmy touches my arm again. 'Pay no attention to Jem. He's all smoke.'

Taylor joins us. 'You're shaking, Calico. Why don't you sit down?' He guides me to the sofa. I perch on the arm nearest the exit, suck in deep breaths of air.

'What's going on with you?' Shimmy kneels in front of me.

'I – I'm okay.'

'You can tell us, sugar. We're your friends.'

'She hardly knows us, Shimmy,' Veda says. 'Give her some space.'

'Oh, everyone likes to act like they're the boss of me.'

'Don't you remember what it was like, Shimmy?' Taylor says softly. 'When you first found out?'

'Found out what?'

'What had happened to you. That you'd ... died. When and how you'd died. It was a big shock.'

Jem mutters.

'Is that what it is, sugar? You just found out what happened to you.'

I nod.

There's so much I want to ask them all but I daren't disobey Fates. Maybe the nanomites are transmitting

88

everything back to him. Or maybe someone else in here is a spy. Asha's life is at stake. I'm not risking that.

They're all staring at me.

'I – I found out I'd been frozen for forty-five years.' Is that safe enough to say?

'What!'

'Wow, you're really old, sugar.'

'I am?'

Veda nods. 'That's way further back than the rest of us. And also explains why you wouldn't have heard of Shimmy.'

'What year were you born?' Taylor asks.

'2008.'

'That's crazy,' he says. 'You're older than my parents!'

'And mine.' Veda smiles.

'Ten years before me,' Jem says. 'I'm not the oldest any more.' He does the grimace-smile thing. Does that mean I passed his test, or does he still suspect me?

To be fair, I still suspect myself. Plus my head is trying to get round what Taylor just said.

'So you died when you were seventeen,' Veda says. 'Same as Taylor and Jem. I was sixteen.'

'Can we talk about something else, sugar?'

'Fine,' Jem says. 'What happened to you the other day, Calico? When you were screaming.'

'What? Oh. I hurt my hand.' I hold it up. 'All fixed. By the bone-mending bots or whatever.'

Veda smiles. 'That's great.'

'*That's great,*' Jem mimics. 'It's not great. It's non-consensual, invasive, experimental—'

'Not this again.' Shimmy pouts.

'Nanomites are a well-established treatment,' Veda says.

'I'm not saying they don't fix bones,' Jem mutters, 'but you don't know what else they're doing while they're in there.'

Exactly what I was worried about.

But Veda rolls her eyes. 'There's no evidence to support anything like that.'

'Yeah, you're a conspiracy theorist, Jem,' Shimmy says. 'And I think we've heard about enough from you on that subject, and many others. Why don't you hush now so I can get properly acquainted with Calico.'

Jem does his double head jerk, whispers into his shoulder.

'So, what's your story, sugar?' Shimmy squeezes next to me on the sofa.

Shit. Is *she* the spy? Is Fates testing me?

'Come on, don't be shy.'

Taylor leans across her. 'Calico, you don't have to tell her anything.'

'Oh, *Tay-lor*. I wanna know.'

No telling people you and I met before you were frozen. No talking about your sister.

'It's your story, Calico.' Taylor's big eyes are so earnest. 'Tell it when you're ready. Or not at all. It's up to you.'

'About the only thing you've got any control over in this fucked-up place.'

Can't tell if Jem's on my side or not.

'Let it go, Shimmy,' Taylor says.

'I'm just being friendly.'

'Calico should be asking the questions, anyhow.' Veda smiles at me. 'Ask away.'

So much I want to know, but Fates and his threat hang in my head. I need to get away from anything to do with me and Asha. I go for something harmless instead.

'Um, where actually are we?' I say. 'In the world, I mean.'

'USA,' Veda says.

'Think she's worked that much out for herself,' Jem mutters.

'What's that now, sugar? You joining in the conversation, or talking to yourself?'

Jem gives Shimmy the finger.

'Arizona,' Veda says. 'Go on, what else?'

'I know I asked you this already, but there's definitely no phone in this place?'

Shimmy laughs, like copper coins falling.

'No phones, no computers, TV, anything,' Jem says. 'Why d'you think they give us these?' He taps his Remembering Book. 'Not a lot else to do.'

'So, there's no technology here at all?'

'There's some equipment in the labs,' Veda says, 'but the research is all geared towards nanomedicine and technology using bio.

It's much better for the environment.'

'Plus anything else costs a whole lot of money.' Taylor gestures at the peeling walls. 'And there's not much of that in this place any more.'

'At least until they come up with another crazy project and some idiot who wants to invest in it,' Jem says.

'I wouldn't call the limb-growth project crazy.' Veda points at her left leg.

'Right.' Jem nods. 'I mean, Fates changes the research based on who's giving him the money.'

'Can he do that? Change what we signed up for?' I ask.

'It's in the small print,' Taylor says.

Jem's staring at me. 'You signed up for this?'

Shit. I've said something wrong. 'Er—'

'Oh, now, sugar, you really don't want to go there. You'll get Jem all agitated.'

Jem is twitching more than before. 'You signed up for *this*?'

'What's the big deal?' Taylor shrugs. 'Calico died before any of us did. Maybe things were different back then. Maybe that was the norm.'

'I can't believe someone would agree to this – hell – for themselves.'

A moan cuts him off. It sends goosebumps up my neck. One of the old people I passed earlier hovers in the doorway, hospital gown quivering around his frail body.

'Pay no attention to him,' Shimmy says.

'Who is he?'

'One of the Herd. Old folks. They all are waiting for re-death.'

'What?' Re-death?

Veda shakes her head. 'They're not old. Not as old as they look anyway. There was a problem with their reanimation process.'

Like Fates said. What about Asha? What if it happens to her when she's reanimated?

'What do you mean?'

'Something to do with the synthetic blood products the facility used. It triggered accelerated ageing in some subjects.'

'Your lab geek tell you that?' says Shimmer. 'Lame gossip.'

'No. Scientific fact,' Veda says. 'And they're not called the Herd. They're Agers.'

All those ancient people I saw sleeping in the hospital wing – do they have this accelerated ageing? There were so many of them. And that group in the other room just now. There are a lot more old people here than young.

Gabe appears and leads the old man gently away.

'You don't need to worry,' Shimmy says to me. 'It's not going to happen to any of us. We're the elite.'

Jem gives a brittle laugh. 'Oh, yeah, the elite. The maimed, the broken, the mentally unstable, and the terminally fucking stupid.'

Shimmy flushes. Taylor squeezes her hand.

'We're not elite,' Veda says. 'Teenagers respond best to the reanimation process, that's all. Our brains work differently.' She stands and grabs her crutches, swings herself smooth and quick across to the sofa opposite me. 'Don't worry about all this,' she says. 'Takes a while to get your head straight.'

'Thanks.'

Veda turns to her Remembering Book. Shimmy and Taylor start talking about something else. I let their chat wash over me. My mind is too full. Full of what the world's become. What I've lost. And terror about the nanomites, the accelerated ageing, the treatments not always working. How will I get in touch with Mum if there aren't any phones or computers? How can I get to the Cryostore and find Asha? How do I know who to trust?

'Well, that was my favourite, anyway,' Taylor says to Shimmy.

'Thank you, sugar. It was a big hit.'

'Don't s'pose you'd sing it for me?' Taylor smiles.

'Oh, I don't sing for other people any more. You know that.'

'Shimmer was a big star in her day,' Taylor says to me.

'A singer?'

Shimmy nods.

I have an Asha flash. She's singing in the garden, sitting on the step, shelling peas.

'Calico, Jem.' Earl's bulk blocks the doorway. 'Time's up.'

'I wish,' Jem mutters. He gathers his pencils and Remembering Book.

Think Earl just saved me from talking about things I shouldn't.

I stand up.

Shimmy paws at my arm with her perfect peachy nails. 'Wait,' she says. 'Don't go. We've hardly got acquainted.'

Behind her copper gleam, the pearl skin, the bright blue eyes, there's something else. Shadows, bruises.

'Calico ain't going anywhere, Shimmy,' Earl says. 'She'll be back. You can get to know her then. Wait here with Veda and Taylor, okay?'

'Great,' Veda mumbles.

Earl leads the way with his usual bustling stride. Jem walks next to me. We get to the room with the old people – the not-old people, the Agers. They shuffle around. Sadness hangs over them like mist. I scan them, can't help it, checking for Asha. An old version of Asha.

No. Fates said she was still frozen.

But he said a lot of things.

And not all of them are true.

20.

There's a loud crash, a table falling over. It sends the Agers into a panic. They wander about the corridor behind us, moaning and crying, louder and louder. Gabe stands helplessly by, playing with his hair.

'Dammit,' Earl bristles. 'That boy is useless.'

He strides back the way we've come, moving his huge arms up and down slowly like he's herding cows.

Jem's beside me. 'You shouldn't let them inject you with any of that stuff, you know. It's all experimental. Look at the state of this lot.' He gestures to the Agers.

'I thought Veda said the blood caused the accelerated ageing.'

He shrugs. 'Who knows?'

How does Veda know about this stuff? Why is she so certain? The others act like Jem's paranoid, but I'm not so sure he is.

'What you were saying before,' I say quietly, 'about the nanomites – this is stupid – but, do you think they could use them to, like, read your mind or something?'

'Sure. Anything could happen in this place.' He pushes back his beanie. The scar is stark on his cheek. *'Leave it, Stan,'* he whispers.

'Who *is* Stan?'

'What?' Jem takes hold of my wrist. His fingers are soft on my skin. 'How do you know about him?' he asks.

'You mention him sometimes.'

'Out loud?'

I nod.

'Can you hear him too?' Jem whispers.

'No.'

'Hey.' The scent of cigarettes and sun. Gabe is suddenly right next to us. He glances at Jem's hand on my arm.

Jem drops it.

'Um – Earl says I have to take you back.'

We walk behind him. Jem slows down so Gabe's a little way ahead.

'Stan's my brother,' Jem says. 'He – he died. But he keeps talking to me. Can't shut him up. It's like he's still alive.'

I stop walking. There's a whirlwind inside the hollow. Jem has a dead brother. And they talk to each other?

He must be ill. He's hearing voices.

But what if he's not ill?

What if this is something that happens now? Like the nanomites. I have to ask him how—

'You comin'?' Gabe asks. He's leaning against the wall outside our rooms. *Eyes and ears everywhere.*

'Yeah.'

We get to Jem's open door. The big portrait made of torn-out notebook pages contemplates me. Is that Stan?

Jem goes in, turns back and looks at me in this sad way. Makes me want to tell him that Asha's dead too.

I open my mouth. But I say nothing. Can't risk it. Gabe's right here. And can I trust Jem anyway?

His door slides shut.

'What's goin' on with you two?' Gabe says.

He's closer than I thought.

'Nothing.' I go into my room. I have to be a good girl, follow the rules. Have to be careful if I want to find Asha.

Does Jem really hear his dead brother?

Is that something that happens now?

I can't believe it.

But if he does, why can't I hear Asha?

Shit.

I never tried.

I never thought to try.

Asha? Asha! Are you there?

21.

asha

limbo

perhaps this is it.
this is where you'll stay –
this limbo,
this purgatory.

perhaps this is hell.

perhaps you're not
meant for heaven.

perhaps you just
weren't good enough.

perhaps a life of pain
is not a golden ticket.

perhaps half hoping
is not the same
as faith.

or maybe
it was that thing
you did.

22.

Calico

A night of half-sleep and weird dreams. Mum and Asha singing in low light, unable to see or hear me. My throat is raw from calling them. My heart is sore. And then they're not Mum and Asha any more. They're Veda and Jem, holding my hands, pulling me in different directions, pulling me apart.

I wake with a start.

Asha?

Asha, are you there?

No answer.

The hollow groans inside me.

I push it away. I will not grieve while there's still hope.

I've got two leads on Asha. I need to find out where the Cryostore is. And I need to talk to Jem about Stan. Does he really hear him? And how does that happen? And can Stan hear him back?

On the way to the lab, I stumble along the hallway next to Gabe and his cigarette scent. I'm fractured by tiredness.

'Here you go,' he says.

I make straight for Jem. 'So, about Stan—'

But Doctor Perez calls out from her office. 'Ah great, Calico. Come on through.'

I press down the urge to tell her to piss off. I have to be a good girl, follow the rules. On the surface anyway. I go into her office.

'How's your hand?' she asks.

'Fine. Erm.' I glance at the nanomite poster with the giant spiders. 'I wanted to ask you, about the nanomites, bio-bots whatever – what happens to them after they've fixed the bone?'

'They're absorbed into your tissues.'

Great. Very reassuring.

'Any more fainting?' she asks.

'No.'

'Do you have a tendency to pass out?'

'Nope. Never happened before I was in this place.'

'Hmm.'

'I'm fine. The first time, it was the shock of seeing Lucas so old.'

'Doctor Fates.' She frowns.

'And the second time I hadn't eaten anything.'

'You do seem to have recovered quickly. But I'd still like to test your blood.'

I roll up my sleeve, but she takes hold of my hand and presses a narrow glass cylinder against one of my fingertips. After a few seconds, she holds the other end to her wrist until the nanocom vibrates.

'Is that it?'

'Yes.'

Nothing like the vials of blood they'd take from Asha.

'I'm measuring your hormone levels because you

checked yes to this question.' Doctor Perez points to my baseline questionnaire. 'That you had menstruated prior to cryogenic suspension,' she says.

'So?'

'It's unusual.'

'How come?'

'Since your first life, toxins and hormones leeched into the drinking water, damaging the human endocrine system. Antibiotics stopped being effective for sexually transmitted infections. Fertile females are rare now.' She touches her crucifix. 'It's unlikely you will menstruate again, Calico. We haven't had any fertile female reanimates to date.'

'Oh.' A strange sadness swirls through the hollow.

'I'm sorry. Do you need to take a moment?' she asks. 'It's supervised resocialisation next. Come through when you're ready. They're waiting for us in the lab.'

I don't take a moment. I push away the sadness. I need to focus on finding Asha.

The others sit on high stools around a workbench. I perch next to Veda.

'Okay,' Doctor Perez says. 'Let's talk about hobbies and interests.'

'Not again ...'

'Jem, respect the group, please. Do you want to show us something you've drawn?'

He twitches, mutters into his shoulder. 'Shut up, Stan.'

Shimmy laughs, coins falling. Shakes her copper hair.

'How about you start us off, then, Taylor? What kind of things would you do outside of high school in your first life?'

Shimmy lets out an exaggerated yawn. 'All the little animals ...'

'Oh, well done, Shimmy, you've actually remembered something about somebody else.' Veda slow claps.

'Taylor?' Doctor Perez persists.

'Um, yeah, I'm into animals.'

Jem snorts and starts to doodle in his Remembering Book.

We sit in silence. I glance around the lab, still hopeful, despite everything, that I'll spot a phone or computer, but there's nothing on the workbenches or shelves.

'It's me then, is it?' Veda says at last. 'Again. I think you all know that my hobbies are reading and writing. Not much chance to read here as there aren't many books. So I write instead. Shimmy, your turn.'

'Guess I like to spend time on my appearance, working out, looking nice.' She inspects her fingernails.

'Shallow much?' Jem sniffs.

'Be respectful, please, Jem.' Doctor Perez taps her nanocom.

'What about your singing?' Taylor asks Shimmy.

'Oh, that was my job, sugar, not a hobby.'

'You never sang for the fun of it?'

'Sometimes I used to write my own songs. Liked doing that. Never got to record them though.

Daddy wouldn't let me.'

'Your dad was your manager?' I ask.

'Could call him that.'

'Why don't you write some songs while you're in here?' Jem says.

Doctor Perez nods.

'Oh, what'd be the point? No one'll ever hear them.'

'Does it matter?' Jem says. 'You can do it just for you.'

'We'd love to hear 'em.' Taylor grins.

Shimmy smiles. 'Guess I could.'

'My mum writes songs,' I say. 'She's a singer. And my sister.'

Why am I talking about Asha? I'm not supposed to, but it's so hard not to when I'm always thinking about her.

'What's it like having a sister?' Shimmy says. 'Bet it beats having a brother.'

'You can't say things like that.' Jem's face is pale.

'I can say what I like, sugar. You ain't the boss of me.'

'Guess the truce is over.' Taylor smiles.

'We're on hobbies and leisure today, not siblings,' Doctor Perez says. 'Jem, your turn.'

'Photography. Drawing. Watching old movies with my dad.' A tiny half-smile slips across his face.

'I've never seen a movie,' Shimmy says.

'Me neither.' Taylor and Veda speak at the same time.

'What?' I say. 'How come?'

'How would we watch a movie?' Veda says.

'Cinema, TV—'

'Not in our lifetimes.' Veda smiles sadly.

'Oh, yeah. I don't understand how all the technology suddenly disappeared.'

'It wasn't overnight,' Doctor Perez says. 'It happened gradually. When the peak oil crisis hit, plastic was difficult to make and became incredibly expensive. The metals used in tech had been depleted through overmining, and their costs soared too.'

'It's hard to get my head round it. We're so not rich,' I say. 'But I've got a phone and a laptop. Had, I mean.'

'Same,' Jem says. 'I used to make movies and animations on my phone.' He mutters into his shoulder. '*Shut up, Stan.*'

'My mom and pop used to talk about those days,' Taylor says.

It's weird to think his parents were born after me.

'And even before the peak oil crisis there were problems. My mom's identity got hacked and all their money was stolen. No way to get it back. They couldn't afford the anti-hacking insurance, so it was easier to go without the tech.'

'It's like the world went backwards,' I say.

'No,' Veda says. 'People broke the world. Used up all the resources. Didn't respect it. They let it rot right in front of their eyes. It was only the war that stopped it.'

'War?' I ask.

Veda nods. 'Yes. The Green War. It lasted over three years, back in the forties, before any of us were born.'

'My pop fought in it,' Taylor says. 'And so did Earl.'

'Were they on the same side?' Jem asks.

Taylor shakes his head.

'What about AI though?' I say. 'That was going to be the next thing when I – er – was alive.'

'It didn't really live up to its potential,' Veda says. 'Same issues with availability of materials. And then after the war, the world had changed. They called it redefining wealth. The planet, and people, became more valuable than tech.'

'We seem to have gone off topic again,' Doctor Perez says. 'Calico, why don't you tell us about your hobbies and interests.'

'Um—' My head's spinning with what Veda just said. And anyway, my life was looking after Asha. But in between the illnesses— 'Running,' I say. 'Sprinting. Four hundred metres.'

'That's a tough distance,' Taylor says.

'Yeah, I used to do a lot of training. I miss it actually. Miss being outside. Oh. Maybe I could do some training in the grounds here?'

'That'd be a no,' Jem says. 'They won't let you out.'

Doctor Perez frowns. 'It's for your own safety. But perhaps we can arrange for you to run in the hallways.'

Great.

Back in my room. No chance to talk alone with Jem. No sign of the Cryostore on my journeys to and from the lab. My brain's bursting with this new reality I'm in. The world outside the facility. What will it be like when I get out of here? When *we* get out of here, me and Asha. It feels too big a thing to comprehend. Maybe I'll make more sense of it if I write it down.

But my Remembering Book isn't on the desk. When did I last write in it?

I check on the shelves and in the bathroom. Under the bedcovers, under the bed. There's nowhere else it could be.

My Remembering Book is gone.

23.

'Where's my Remembering Book?' I ask Earl.

'Doctor Fates has it.'

My mind spirals. 'Since when?'

'Since you disrespected him.'

Which time? 'Thought I had to write in it regularly?'

'You'll get it back, kid. Don't worry.' He ushers me out of my room.

My most shameful secrets are in that book. What I did. Leaving Asha that night. And my questions about this place. My plans for finding Asha. I feel sick when I think about Fates reading it. I should have kept it with me like some of the others do. I should've known this would happen.

The hollow inside me is vast. I could disappear into its nothingness if I let myself. But I can't. I won't. Not until I've done everything I can to find Asha. To save her.

I have to find out how things work between Jem and his brother. Crazy as it is, talking telepathically to Asha seems more realistic than getting into the Cryostore right now.

We have unsupervised resocialisation today, in the small room. Jem's right by the door as I go in. Hope surges in me. I'll get a chance to talk to him.

He has a bruise on his cheek.

'What happened?' I reach tentatively for his face.

'Had an altercation with a wall called Earl.'

'What?'

'Part of my "anger management" therapy.'

'He hit you?'

'It was a sparring session,' Taylor says. 'I was there too. Jem refused to wear the protective gear. Earl caught him by accident.'

'Are you okay?'

Jem nods. 'Couple of broken ribs.'

'And let me guess.' Veda drags herself across the space on her crutches, so different to the smooth way she usually moves. 'You won't have any treatment to fix them?'

'No. I won't.'

Taylor goes to help Veda. 'You okay?'

She brushes him off. 'Don't fuss. I'm perfectly capable.'

He flushes and sits down.

'Sorry, Tee.' Veda's smile is tight as she lowers herself on to a chair. 'Doctor Perez was harvesting cells this morning. It's literally draining.'

I think about when I had the nanomites injected into me, how painful it was, how I puked. 'Does it hurt?' I ask.

'Yes. She removes bone marrow and other cells using a large needle attached to a suction device. It hurts a lot.'

'It'll be worth it when you're perfect, sugar.'

'I'm not doing it to be perfect,' Veda spits.

'You're not doing it at all,' Jem says. 'They're doing it to you, forcing you—'

'No one is forcing me to do anything, Jem. These people saved my life. The terms of my repayment to them include two years' participation in their research. Which I am quite prepared to do.'

Jem snorts.

'I'm happy with myself either way, one leg or two. But there's so much potential in this research to help other people.'

'Oh right, Saint Veda.'

'Jem insists his parents wouldn't have signed consent for him to be cryogenically processed,' Veda says to me. 'He thinks there's something underhand about how he ended up here.'

'I *can* speak for myself,' Jem says.

'Oh yeah, sugar. We all know that. And *to* yourself.'

'No way my mum would have signed me up for this,' he says.

'Of course your mother would have signed you up. Any mother would jump at a chance to save their kid.'

'It's true, Jem,' Veda says softly. 'It's what a parent would do.'

'Well, if even Veda and Shimmy agree, it must be true.' Taylor smiles.

'I wouldn't be the one she'd save though.' Jem says it so quietly, I'm not sure the others hear, but it sends goosebumps crawling down my spine. I have a momentary urge to wrap him in a hug.

'Why don't you do some drawing?' Veda points at his Remembering Book.

'Crap distraction technique,' Jem says. 'I did not consent to this. *We* did not consent to any of this.'

'To be fair,' Veda says, 'I was in no position to give consent. I was in anaphylactic shock at the time. But my parents agreed to it on my behalf and I'm happy they did.'

'Same here.' Shimmy nods. ''Bout the only decent thing my daddy ever did. It was a car accident, sugar,' she says to me, eyes skittering left.

'Your dad had already signed you up for this without you knowing,' Jem says. 'That's as bad. You didn't have any say in it.'

'He signed up my whole family. It was a standard thing in the music business. We were all in the car. And we all got frozen.'

What! What? 'Are they in the Cryostore?' I go over to Shimmy on the sofa.

'I don't know what that is.' She turns away from me, to Jem. 'I don't really get what your problem is, sugar. Aren't you glad to be alive? I sure am.'

'I'm glad too,' Taylor says. 'They make you into who you want to be here. That's what they did for me anyway.'

'I know they did,' Jem murmurs.

'They gave me the body I wanted, instead of the one I was born in. They made my outside match my inside. You know how much that surgery would have cost in

111

the real world? And my folks, they support me, but we don't have that kind of money. I'd have had to wait till I'd earned enough – maybe a decade. All that time living as someone I'm not.'

'It's different.' Jem's off again, pacing the room. 'You got what you wanted. You were lucky.'

'Lucky? I didn't actually *want* to die, you know,' Taylor says. 'Getting killed by a drunk driver wasn't top of my list of life goals.'

'How—' I don't know how to ask. Or if I should. Fates. *Eyes and ears.*

'How did I end up in here?' Taylor smiles. 'It was a government scheme for victims of accidents.'

'Yeah,' Jem sneers. 'And how the hell did Fates end up with that contract?'

'He bid for it?' Veda says.

'No way it's that straightforward.'

'Here comes the conspiracy theory.'

Jem says, 'I think—'

'You think waaay too much, sugar.'

'Don't you think I fucking know that?' Jem can't keep still; the words rip right out of him. 'They've taken away our rights, our lives. It's like the Stanford Prison Experiment—'

'Jem,' Veda says, 'that study is ancient, and it's not what's happening here.'

Wait, we studied that in psychology. They ended up turning on each other.

'They brutalised those men,' Veda says.

'Dehumanised them. Gave them numbers instead of names. It's not like that here.'

'You don't think forcing people to have surgery is brutal?' Jem asks. 'Ever seen *One Flew Over the Cuckoo's Nest*? They lobotomised the guy, for God's sake.'

'I don't know what that is,' Shimmy whines.

'It's an old movie,' I say. 'Oh, but you haven't seen any films.'

'Taking away our rights dehumanises us.' Jem's voice is loud now.

'But we know each other,' Taylor says. 'We know who we are.'

'Do we?'

'They don't *force* you to have surgery, anyway,' Shimmy says. 'They suggest it. A perk of being here.'

'Some perk.'

'Well, Nick says I look perfect now.'

Jem pretends to puke.

'Who's Nick?' I ask.

'He's the surgeon. The sweetest guy. Gorgeous too.' Shimmy giggles, leans in to whisper. 'He's gonna be waiting for me when I get out of here. Can't wait for you to meet him when you get your surgeries.'

'I don't need any surgery.'

'Well, yes you do, sugar. Everybody does. He'll fix you up good as new.'

'Fuck's sake, Shimmy,' Jem says.

'I don't need surgery though, do I?'

'No, you don't.' Jem twitches. 'Ignore her, she's on another planet.'

'Oh, come on.' Shimmy pats my belly. 'Everyone has a little imperfection they want taking care of.' She pulls me up to standing. Presses her hands either side of my body and holds my top tight so my waist seems smaller and my breasts look massive. A cartoon version of me.

Jem blushes and looks away.

I free myself from Shimmy. 'I like my body the way it is, thanks.' I've seen Asha sink under anaesthetic too many times. And I had the bone marrow procedure. And, of course, there was the dying. I'm stuck in this place for two years, but I'm never going to let anyone take control of my body like that again. 'I'm with Jem on this.'

He actually smiles. 'Yeah. What's it about – the need to make everyone perfect? Your imperfections are part of who you are.'

'Wouldn't know, sugar.' Shimmy turns to me. 'But Jem doesn't want *any* treatment. Let alone surgery to fix his—'

'Shut the fuck up!' Jem's head jerks violently. 'No, I won't go under the knife of some Perfection Surgeon. My face. My choice.' His fists clench, unclench. 'I get to say no. It's called informed consent.'

'Oh, but sugar, we're the ones who have to look at you.'

Jem leaps up. His skin shines with sweat. 'We are in a fucking experiment,' he shouts at her.

Taylor gets between him and Shimmy.

Jem is shaking. Vibrating. His head veers wildly side to side. A frightened horse, untethered, lost. About to bolt. And the noise he makes. Wild and high, a keening animal. He zigzags across the room.

There's moaning and wailing in the corridor. The Agers are agitated too.

Gabe shouts from out there: 'Cool it, man!'

Jem hurtles towards the doorway. I get to him as blood spurts from his nose and he goes down, a limp tangle of long limbs.

Taylor and I drop beside him at the same time. There's so much blood. I roll Jem into the recovery position. He's much heavier than Asha.

Earl is suddenly here. 'Stand back!' He bends over Jem, checks he's breathing.

'What the hell happened?' Earl glances at me. My jumper's soaked in Jem's blood, clammy against my skin. 'Did he hurt you?'

'No. He had a nosebleed and passed out. He didn't touch me.'

Earl shakes his head.

'Is he going to be okay?' I ask.

'Sure, kid. He's tougher than he looks.' Earl rubs his stubbled chin, scans the room. 'Unlike this one. Shimmy, you okay?' He goes to the sofa. She's curled like a seashell, face hidden. He kneels and talks softly to her.

Jem lurches up to sitting with a sudden scream:

'STAN!' He flails to his feet. Blood and tears stream from his face. 'STAN!' Each time it's like a knife going into me. His pain and loss and fear. I know it so well. It's how I feel about Asha.

'That's enough, kid.' Earl grabs hold of Jem's arm, twists it behind his back.

'Stop it, Earl,' I say, trying to pull him away. 'He's upset. He's not doing anything wrong.'

Earl shakes me off like I'm nothing and brings a brown glass syringe out of his pocket.

'Earl, wait,' I say.

He flips the cork off the end of it.

'NO! NO!' Jem shouts. 'I. DO. NOT. CONS . . .'

'It's this or the straitjacket, kid.' The needle goes into Jem's neck. Earl holds him, a tattooed arm across Jem's chest, till he stops swaying. 'Right. Let's go get you checked over.' Jem's face is blank behind the blood. 'Calico, I'll drop you off on the way,' Earl says. 'You can get cleaned up.'

My heart's in a race. Why did Earl do that? Can't he see how much Jem's suffering? This place – I want to run. Away from all this. But I can't. I can't do anything.

'Come on, Calico.' Earl's already heading out. Jem stumbles along beside him.

His Remembering Book is on the floor.

I scoop it up, lift my bloody top and tuck it into my waistband. It's something I can do. Keep it safe from prying eyes. Keep it safe for Jem.

24.

Back in my room, I'm shaking. I strip off and have a tepid shower. Rinse the blood out of my clothes as best I can in the few minutes of water ration. I'm still frenzied. It's hard to settle. I keep seeing Jem crash to the floor, keep hearing his screams.

Poor Jem. At least I rescued his Remembering Book. Fates won't get his hands on it like he did with mine. I'll keep it with me. Safe.

But what if Jem's really ill? What if he doesn't come back for a while? Or ever? What if there are answers in here about how he and Stan communicate?

Is that selfish, thinking about me and Asha after what Jem's just been through?

I have to wait. He's so paranoid about everything, this way I'll show him he can trust me, and then I can ask him about Stan face to face.

But. It's okay, surely, to take a peek at the last page. The last thing he wrote. The last picture he drew.

I open the Remembering Book and flick from the back to find the most recent entry.

Breath catches in my throat.

It's me. He's drawn me. I look tense, watchful.

Underneath the picture is writing, small and spindly, like a spider's walked through ink. I shouldn't read it. But my eyes skitter over the words.

Told Calico about Stan, she heard me talking to him, i do it out loud apparently. She can't hear him though, that's only me. Yet another way i'm special. Don't know why i told her bout Stan now she's gonna ask me questions bout him & i'm gonna have to lie. Can't tell her i killed him.

Shit.

My heart rattles at my ribcage. All the stuff people have said. Earl and Doctor Perez, why they're not allowed to know how we ended up here, how we died, how we lived. Jem's paranoia. How he lost it in the lab that time. His broken ribs and bruises. And what happened today. Shit. Is he dangerous? And I've stolen his frigging book. Shit.

The Remembering Book slides from my fingers on to the floor, opens randomly. There are more drawings, small and intricate, with sparse words spread across the page.

I should hide this away under my mattress. I pick it up, but can't help it, I turn to the beginning. There's a drawing of a dark-haired boy sat on the floor surrounded by books. Jem. Without his beanie. Without his scar.

Algebraic equations. What the hell am i ever going to need them for? Sat here on my bedroom floor, trying to make sense of them. Again. Retakes suck. Making you do the thing you're worst at over & over. Torture.

Music & laughing come from Stan's room. That doesn't help. He's never had to retake anything in his life. Neither have his mates. All back from uni for some reunion.

One of them comes out of Stan's room, along the landing & into the loo. Clank of seat against cistern. A thundering piss. No flush.

Quiet tap on my door & it eases open.

'Hey, Jem.' It's Zach. 'What you doing?' he asks.

'Revision.'

'On a Friday night?'

'Yeah.' Some of us don't have an eidetic memory.

Zach wanders over to the wardrobe, peruses the photos stuck there. 'Where'd you get these?'

I squirm. 'They're mine. I mean, I took them. For A-level photography.'

'What?' He's looking at the one of Ella's bare back morphing into a cello. 'You made this?'

'Yeah. All of 'em.'

'You got these girls to strip off & pose so you could take photos of them?'

'Yeah.' I'm waiting for a punchline, something dirty, but he's moved on to the one of Ed, bare-chested, merged with the sax, side-on silhouette.

Zach examines it so long i turn back to the algebra.

'Jem?' The toe of his Converse touches my foot.

i look up.

He takes the chewing gum out his mouth, flicks it into the bin.

'It's Friday night,' he says. 'You should come out

119

with us.' He takes my arm, yanks me up. We're so close
i can see the tips of his eyelashes are blond.

Zach doesn't step back. He kisses me, swift &
soft on the lips. He tastes of spearmint & smoke.
His hands rest on my hips. He leans in again. This is …
Zach is … kissing me. Is this a joke?

Stan's door bangs open down the landing. Tomo
calls out: 'Christ, Zach, you taking a dump or what?'

Zach lets go of me. Wipes his mouth with the
back of his hand.

'In here talking to Jem,' he shouts. 'He's coming
out with us.'

i'm pulled along in Zach's slipstream. Everything is
clear & sharp. Stan is flushed, hyper, singing along
with the music from his phone. Is he high?

It's cold out, first glints of frost. We get in Stan's
car. i sit in the front. Put my seat belt on. Stan turns
the heat up. Tomo & Zach are in the back. Music's
pumping. The car lurches backwards off the drive. A
horn blares, short & angry.

'Should you be driving?' i ask.

'Who are you? Mum?' Stan raises a lazy hand at
the neighbour he nearly smashed into & then we're
off. Down the road, out along the high street & on to
the bypass. Lights blur by.

Music.

Acker acker

Boom boom

Zach sits behind me, leaning forward, his hands on the sides of my seat like he's holding my shoulders. The hairs on my neck stand up.

Acker acker

Acker acker

Boom boom

Stan sings, shouts.

We're at the bit where 60 goes to 30 but we're not slowing down

Acker acker

Zach's breath on the back of my neck

We pass the lamp post draped in dead flowers

Acker acker boom

Boom

Boom

Stan brakes hard & sudden on the bend.

Boom!

Not the music. Something else.

Crunch.

Stan flies forward. Glass shatters, spatters. The car is full of diamonds.

Upside down. i am upside down. Chest & belly pinned by the seat belt. Too tight to breathe. Blood runs over my face. Stan's trainer is on the ceiling but the rest of him is gone.

Not Tomo though. He's still here. Strapped in. Can't see his face, head's turned away from me like he's looking out of where the window used to be.

Zach's head's at an angle that's not natural, not right. His eyes are wide open. Unblinking. Staring at me.

There are footsteps.

Someone says, 'Ambulance, please. And police.'

Police? Shit. Stan'll get in trouble now. No seat belt. Loaded. I should have stopped him driving. Why didn't I stop him?

'Stan,' I croak. He needs to get away.

'Hey, one of them's awake in there,' a voice says.

Then close to my ear: 'Can you hear me, son?'

'Yeah,' I say.

'What's your name?'

'Jem.'

'Help's on the way, Jem. We'll get you out. Anyone else ali ... awake in there?'

'No,' I say. 'They're all asleep.' But as I say it I'm not so sure.

Tomo's asleep. But Zach ... pretty sure he winked at me. Is this some kind of joke? Like the kissing? Is this some kind of dream?

Oh God. Poor Jem. What he's been through. I hurt for him.

I flick through the pages. Lots of drawings, not many words. Until:

awake. alive. fuck. alive? you don't want to be. feels the same as when you woke up from the coma after the accident. scar on your face, body bruised, brother dead & buried without you there. all of it your fault. you should have stopped him driving stoned, why didn't you stop him? it's all your fault. following Zach, diamonds in your eyes, making you blind.

perhaps you're not alive after all. perhaps this post-apocalyptic Breakfast Club is hell.

but, your heart. you can feel it beating steady. hear it inside your own head. because it's still your head. still full of all the stuff that made you want to stop. being.

that blissful moment of unconsciousness, slipping into death. that moment was paused, rewound & you are back to all the pain of being. all the pain of being you.

Oh, no, Jem. No.

No.

He didn't want to be alive. That's why he's so angry that he's here.

He feels guilty. He blames himself for Stan dying. Like me with Asha.

I wish I could see him, tell him I understand. That we're the same. And that I'm so glad he is alive.

25.

asha

alone

this space seems edgeless
empty, blank.
worse than life.
worse than death.

you are alone.
no mum.
no calico.
they would help you.
they would know
what to do
or they'd find out for you.

what can you do on your own
in this vast and dark unknown?

26.

Calico

Earl brings me dinner. Some kind of lentil gloop, some kind of rice gloop, and some dried apple. The dagger tattoo is stark on his arm.

'Is Jem okay?' I ask.

'Kid, you know I can't—'

'Talk about anyone else. Yeah. Shit. I know that—'

'Language.' He raises a craggy eyebrow.

'Okay – sorry, but it's pretty scary having someone collapse and bleed all over you. Can't you tell me if he's going to be okay without giving away any confidential stuff?'

Earl rubs his stubbled chin. 'He's fine, all right. Back in his room.'

'What's wrong with him?'

Earl rolls his eyes. 'I can't—'

'Okay, forget it.'

'It's all up here.' He taps his head.

'Can't you help him with that?'

'I'm trying, kid.'

'By breaking his ribs?'

'That what he told you?' Earl shakes his head. 'Eat up.' And he's gone.

I force down the so-called food and read through Jem's Remembering Book again. This time, I scan for any clue about how he and Stan talk to each other. But there's nothing. Maybe Jem doesn't know how it works. Maybe Earl's right and it's all in his head.

I drift into semi-sleep. But panic rattles me awake, time and again. Dream thieves steal Jem's book from under my pillow. I have to keep checking it's there. Tomorrow. I'll give it back to him tomorrow.

27.

I wake with dragging pain low in my belly and back. Familiar but unplaceable. Until I stumble to the loo and see the blood. Period.

Shit. No tampons or sanitary towels in the cupboard. I tear a strip off one of the worn towels. Wodge it into a kind of pad in my shorts. It's soaked through immediately. How am I supposed to deal with this?

I'm standing in my vest and shorts with blood running down my legs when the door slides open. Gabe.

'Um – you okay?' he says, pushing back his hair.

'I'd be better if you could knock before you come in.'

'Should I go get Earl?' he asks.

'No! Doctor Perez.'

'Sure.'

I get some more towels, sit on one and cover myself with the other. Don't know why I didn't think I might be due. Guess being dead for forty-five years makes you lose track of time. I was always regular before. Must remember the day – thirteen.

I get an Asha flash – her asking me why I had a giant plaster in my knickers when I had my first period. She never started hers. They harvested her eggs though. Before the first round of treatment. They're frozen too. It was weird thinking about Asha being a mum; she was a little girl at the time. And I was too. I'd never even thought about having babies. Still haven't. Mum said that was normal and I didn't need to think about it until I was older. Or ever, if I didn't want to. But she was giving Asha that option for when she was grown up. Trying to stop the illness from taking her choices away.

There's a knock. 'Calico. It's Sophia Perez. I'm coming in.'

It's a moment before the door opens.

'What's happened?' She rushes to the bed.

'My period started.'

'Oh.'

'Yeah. Have you got any tampons?'

'No.'

'What am I supposed to do then?'

'I'll figure something out.' She frowns. 'Why are you so sure you're menstruating?'

'What else would it be?'

'There are a number of issues related to cryogenic processing and reanimation.'

'Oh. Right. Should I be worried?'

'Lie down, I'll examine your abdomen.' Her hands are warm and gentle on my skin. 'Everything seems fine.'

'Yeah, it feels like a normal period,' I say.

She goes to the bathroom and washes her hands. Brings me another towel.

'Did you have many ... before?' she asks.

I laugh. 'Yeah. I started when I was twelve.'

'Twelve!' she says.

'What's so weird about that?'

'Young girls don't tend to menstruate now.' She sits me up. 'As I mentioned before, fertile females are rare.'

She touches her crucifix, lost in thought.

'Rare in a good way?' I ask, but I can guess the answer.

Doctor Perez shakes her head. 'This is difficult,' she says.

'Why?'

'There are so many ethical boundaries I need to consider. But my overriding duty is to my patients.' She pauses, stares at the ground. 'I don't like to ask you this, Calico,' she says. 'But please keep the menstruation between the two of us. No need for Earl or Doctor Fates to know.'

Another person asking me to lie. 'Why?' I whisper.

'It's just better this way. Safer for you. Trust me.' Her fingers rest on the crucifix at her throat.

Not sure I can trust her any more than I do Lucas Fates. That gold cross doesn't mean a damn thing. But I'll keep quiet until I find out more. I don't want to end up in a worse situation than I am already. Safer for me means safer for Asha.

'What about Gabe?' I say. 'He saw the blood.'

'I'll speak to him. Let me go do that right now, and find something better than these towels.'

'Wait,' I say. 'Aren't there, like – cameras in here, or bugs?'

'No,' she says. 'Not in the bedrooms or bathrooms. That would be a violation of privacy.' She leaves.

Not in the bedrooms or bathrooms. That's something. But this place is so full of secrets. Lies. Maybe Jem's not wrong to be paranoid. Maybe he's not paranoid at all.

When Doctor Perez returns, she holds out a paper bag. 'Here,' she says. 'Some surgical pads. The best I could do.'

The pad doesn't have any adhesive so I wrap a strip of towel around it to hold it in place. It's bulky and rubs my thighs.

When I go back into my room Doctor Perez is still there.

'Can I ask you something?'

'You can ask.' She half smiles.

'Is Jem okay?'

She nods slowly.

'Only, I'm worried he's going to hurt himself.'

'What makes you say that?'

'He's always getting injured. And he seems so—'

'Angry?'

'No. Well, yeah. But also sad.'

'I'll look in on him after I've finished here, okay?'

'Thanks.'

At the door, she turns. 'I've asked Gabe not to mention anything about this, but it will be recorded that I've been here.'

'I'll say I had stomach ache and felt sick. True enough.'

True enough for this place anyway.

'Oh,' she says. 'But what about the blood on your clothes and the towels and the pads?'

'I can't get them clean using my water ration in here. Can you get me a laundry duty?'

'I'll try. Remember to keep quiet about this, Calico,' she says. 'It's important. Choice can be taken away.'

'No shit,' I say. If this place has taught me anything, it's that.

28.

Four days alone in my room. Upset stomach being the lie, I had to isolate. Not the best, being stuck here with period pain and Jem's Remembering Book, reliving his anguish, missing Asha, trying to work out how to speak to her, to hear her. It's been bleak. But today I can go to resocialisation. I stuff Jem's book in the waist of my trousers and pull on a top to cover it. I really need to talk to him.

Only Veda and Shimmy are here though.

'Where are the boys?' I ask.

'Working out with Earl,' Shimmy giggles. 'Getting pumped up for us.'

Veda rolls her eyes.

'Is Jem okay?'

'Yes. He was here yesterday. A bit quiet.'

'Thankfully,' Shimmy says. 'Where've you been, sugar?'

'Oh, I had stomach ache. Doctor Perez said I couldn't mingle.'

'But you're okay?'

'Yeah. A weird ache, that's all. Bit like period pain.' Shit. Why did I say that?

They're both silent till Veda clears her throat.

'I don't know what that feels like,' she says. 'I never had a period. But you did, Calico, back before you were frozen?'

'Yeah.'

'Ugh,' Shimmy says.

'Cryogenic suspension causes infertility,' Veda says. 'So even if you menstruated before, you won't now.'

Veda says this like it's a fact, but I know she's wrong. It makes me uneasy. What else has she told me that isn't true?

'I used to have them, but not since—' Shimmy says. 'Well, not since I've been here, thank the lord. Disgusting messy things.'

'But . . . you weren't a *Chosen*?' The look on Veda's face – somewhere between horror and awe.

It scares me.

'Oh no, sugar. One thing my daddy took care of at least.'

'What's a Chosen?' I ask.

'A girl who's able to have babies,' Shimmy says. 'They make 'em pregnant and keep them in these special facilities.'

Cold stalks through me. 'Like battery chickens?'

'What's that, sugar?'

'They call them breeding programmes,' Veda says. 'I did an assignment about it at school. There's a lot of birth deformity and miscarriage from pollution. Not that many healthy live births. But they keep on impregnating them.'

'What happens to the babies?'

'They're taken away. Sold off to rich Infertiles. The fertility crisis is worldwide, but the breeding programmes are only in the Americas. Their record on reproductive rights is abysmal.'

I'm chilled to the bone. 'But who would agree to do it?'

'There's a lot of money involved. It's big business. The girls don't really have a choice.'

'So they're paid to have babies?'

'No. But someone is.' Veda's face is grim. 'Basically, Calico, fertile girls are a commodity. Some parents actually sell their own daughters to the programme. And there are these bounty hunters who track girls down. They're worth a lot of money.'

This is what Doctor Perez meant. The lack of resources in this place. I'm something Fates could make money from. She's trying to protect me.

How bad is it there's a place I could be that's worse than here? A place where I'd have even less choice. Fear and rage fight inside me.

'Honestly, I'm glad it happened,' Veda says.

'What!' I'm stunned.

'Oh, no, not the breeding programmes.'

'Thank God.'

'No. I meant the fertility crisis. There were too many people on the planet – that was part of the problem in the first place. And now women are not chained to reproduction, there's more equality. For most women, anyway.'

Shimmy sniffs. 'I'd still like to have a baby though, you know. A baby girl, to take care of.'

'Oh yes, I can imagine it,' Veda says. 'Shimmy and her daughter dressed identically. You obsessing over how fat she is, how pretty.'

'No – I wouldn't be like that at all. I'd teach her to stand up for herself and be strong and not let anyone tell her how to live her life.' Shimmy's blue eyes glaze with tears. She curls in on herself.

I go over and rest my hand on her satiny shoulder. 'What is it, Shimmy? What's wrong?'

'I was pregnant once.'

'Oh,' Veda says.

'I lost the baby.'

'Oh, Shimmy.' I wrap her in a hug. I don't even hesitate. Fuck the rules. Not being able to touch anyone takes away something that makes me human, that makes me, me. In this moment, I choose to break the rules. I choose to hold on to Shimmy.

'Left me with this great big empty inside,' she says.

I know that feeling.

The hollow.

Veda joins us on the sofa. Sits next to Shimmy's tiny feet. 'I am so sorry, Shimmy,' she says. 'Truly.'

Shimmy looks up. Even crying she's beautiful. 'I'm sorry too, sugar. I'm sorry too.'

The three of us are wrapped together on the sofa. A hum starts up in my head. Mum's favourite folk song. The words flutter from my mouth.

Blood and breath and bone,
threaded through with love and light.
Always in my heart and mind.
I'll carry you through deepest night.

'Oh,' Shimmy says. 'I know this.'

Her voice is higher than mine, rich and soaring. She takes Asha's part. Bittersweet. We sing it over and over, and Veda picks up the words and tune and joins in. It's not the same as being at home, with Mum and Asha. But it's something. Something warm in the coldness of this place. Something connecting me to these two girls. From different times, different places.

'What the hell's going on?' Earl's bulk fills the doorway.

We pull away from each other.

'Oh, Earl.' Sweet, bright Shimmy switches on. 'You're so kind to worry about us.'

He raises an eyebrow.

'Think I may have the same problem as Calico,' she says.

'Stomach pains? Yeah, there's a lot of it about,' Earl says. 'Taylor's done a deep clean of the kitchen to be on the safe side. Let's get you back to your rooms. You're first, Veda.'

Shimmy snuggles against me. She smells like a fresh peach. 'I'm glad you're back. Thought you'd gone off to get your surgery,' she says.

'No.' I don't have the energy to tell her again that I'm not having surgery.

'Well, when you do, I need you to give Nick this note from me.' She giggles and pulls a small square of folded paper from her vest. 'It's a love letter.'

I take the note, warm from her skin. 'The surgeon bloke?'

'Yes. He's the sweetest. And gorgeous, too. He's my saviour. Made me all neat and tidy again.'

'You mean you're scar-free and you have massive tits and a peachy butt.'

'No, I mean, you know, down there.' She points between her legs.

'What?'

'He put me back together down there.'

What the hell happened to her?

'Made me good as new.' She pulls back, smiles at me.

I see it in her eyes though, that stain behind the smile. Pain. She can't hide it.

'He's waiting for me. When I get out of here, we'll live a perfect pretty life. Me and him.'

'What about your family?'

A shadow crosses her face. 'I don't even know if they're alive, but Nick is. And he's gonna be there for me,' she says. 'So, you'll do it? Give him the note, when you get your appointment.'

'Okay,' I say. Another lie.

Gabe's standing in the doorway, messing with his

hair. How long's he been there? Did he see Shimmy give me the note? I hide it in my sleeve.

I walk back to my room with Gabe; he keeps glancing at me but we don't talk. My hand's against my stomach, so Jem's Remembering Book doesn't slip out.

Back in my room, I put the book under the mattress and Shimmy's note inside my pillowcase.

How did I get here? Lying. Hiding things for other people. Things that are important to them. Taking care of other people's secrets, when I should be looking for Asha.

29.

asha

reach out

surely
you cannot be
the only one
lost
and wondering
what it is
you need to do.

Perhaps
you are not
imprisoned here,
perhaps
you're not
constrained,
by anything
but yourself.

can you reach out, asha?
reach out

30.

Calico

'Okay, kid. Cleaning today.'

'Thought I was getting laundry?'

'Not yet. That's for the best behaved.'

'What have –' I start to ask, but then – they have my Remembering Book. They know it's my fault Asha died. They know about my list.

Jem's in the day room, sweeping the floor. The hollow shrinks a little when I see he's all right.

Earl talks me through the chores I have to do. Once he leaves, Jem immediately drops his broom and goes to the gym corner.

His head twitches, but he doesn't speak to Stan. Or me. His mouth's a grim line while he lifts weights.

I go over to him. 'Hey, are you okay?'

No answer.

'How come you love the gym all of a sudden?'

He keeps lifting the weights. 'Good for the mind.'

'Right.'

'And I don't like being manhandled by Earl.'

'So you're going to fight him off next time?'

It's half a joke, but Jem stares at me, dead serious. 'Seen *Terminator 2*? Sarah Connor doing pull-ups on her bed frame? So she'd be ready when the time came?'

'Yeah, I saw that. She was in a psychiatric hospital.'

'Exactly.'

'You think we're in a psychiatric hospital?'

He nods. 'Either that or we're in hell.'

His theories haven't changed then. My heart sinks. Wish he was in a better mood. But then, this is Jem. Maybe it's as good as it gets.

I clear my throat. 'I've got your Remembering Book.' I pull it out from under my top. My bloody fingerprints are still on the cover.

The weights thud on the ground. Jem grabs the book off me. 'Why d'you take it?'

'You left it in the resocialisation room. Didn't think you'd want Earl or anyone finding it. I didn't show it to anyone.'

'So, why've I had Perez banging on about depression and shit? Trying to inject me with nanomites?'

'Sorry. I didn't show it to her. Told her I was worried about you, that's all.'

'You were worried about me?' His face softens.

'Yes.' Moths flit through the hollow.

He flicks through his Remembering Book, like he's checking none of his words or drawings have been stolen.

'It wasn't your fault.' It comes out quieter than I want.

'What wasn't?'

'Stan. Dying.'

It's like I've punched him.

'You read it?'

I nod. 'But only 'cos—'

He's right in my face. 'Well, now you know what a monster I am. And why I'm the last person my mum would save.'

I put my hand against his chest. His heart beats fast against my palm.

'Jem—'

'I was starting to think you got me.'

'I do. I'm trying to help you.'

'I don't want your fucking help.' Rage twists his face. He shakes, vibrates with anger, like he did the other day.

'Calm down, Jem.'

He turns his back on me, goes to the door. He punches it, shouting and screaming and swearing until Earl arrives. With his needle.

I messed that up. Big time. I should not have read Jem's Remembering Book. Stupid. Stupid. Should've waited till I saw him again and asked him about Stan then. How they communicate. Could've told him the truth about Asha first, so he'd trust me. But no, I had to rush in.

Whatever. Now Earl's got to him again with a tranquilliser, and it's all my fault, Jem's not going to trust me any time soon.

He was right about one thing though.

I do get him. I do.

And he's wrong, too.

He's not a monster.

He's a messed-up boy I spend far too much time thinking about.

142

31.

Fates is in my room. Gabe's with him, eyes hiding behind his mess of hair. He pulls out the chair for Fates to sit, then stands behind.

'I've brought back your Remembering Book.' Fates hands it to me. His icy fingertips touch mine. I shudder. 'Interesting reading,' he says.

'I thought it was private.' God, I'm a hypocrite.

'Generally, the Remembering Books are. But you have a disinclination to follow the rules, don't you, Calico? I told you: I have eyes and ears everywhere.'

Gabe rubs at his hair.

What has he said?

'So, you have something to share with me, Calico?' Fates says.

Shit. Doctor Perez's warning. What Veda said. The Chosen.

My voice dries in my throat.

'Well?'

I shake my head. I'm saying nothing.

'Why do you always have to be so stubborn, Calico?'

'I – I'm not.' I force the words out. 'I don't know what you want me to say.'

'Search the room,' Fates says to Gabe.

What? No. The stuff Perez gave me is hidden under my mattress. There's a pile of bloody clothes and towels under the bed. Big clanging clues leading to the Chosen. 'Wait,' I say. 'Tell me what you're looking for.'

'The note that Shimmer Spires passed to you.'

Oh.

For a moment I think of denying all knowledge, but Gabe's already finished going through the clothes on my shelves.

'Here.' I pull Shimmy's note out of my pillowcase.

Fates takes it from me. 'You've read this?'

'No.'

'Why not?'

'It's not for me. She wanted me to give it to someone else.' There's a twinge of guilt at how easily I grassed on Shimmy, but I've no intention of meeting this surgeon guy. He sounds like a total sleaze.

'Who did she want you to give it to?'

'Um – Nick? She said he's a surgeon.'

'Ah, of course.'

'I only took it to make her feel better. I wasn't going to do anything with it.'

'But why would she give this to you?'

'She seemed to think I'd be having surgery.'

'Ahh.' Fates nods. He reads the note. 'If anything like this happens again, you must report it immediately. Is there anything else you want to tell me?'

'No.' I daren't look at Gabe.

'We should get goin', sir.' Gabe helps Fates up.

'Yes. On to our next visit. Ms Spires.' Fates sways, unsteady on his feet for a moment. 'Goodbye, Calico.'

He goes out first. Gabe turns to me and mouths: 'Sorry.' And then they're gone.

I sit on the bed, shaking. What have I done? They're going to Shimmy next. Will she be in trouble about the note? And what the hell's Gabe up to? Can I trust him or not?

32.

asha

search

how thick and sticky
this limbo is,
how tough and tricky
to move
to sense
to reach
beyond yourself.

but there *are* others here.
you have been catching
the subtle scratching
of soft souls searching

reach out, asha,
reach out.

33.

Calico

I guess I did something right. Finally, laundry duty. I bring my dirty washing with me wrapped in a grey towel. The acrid smell in the corridor is stronger inside the laundry. Like matches and eucalyptus. My eyes water.

Taylor hands me a cloth mask to cover my nose and mouth.

'Thanks.'

'It's the lye,' he says, 'used to make the soap.'

'Thought this was supposed to be the most desirable place to work.'

Taylor's eyes smile above his mask. 'Yeah, well, that's because of this—' He beckons me to follow.

I dump my dirty washing on the counter and go past deep stone sinks and some ancient-looking mangles.

'Here.' Taylor opens a door with an actual handle and apparently no lock.

Outside! I rush past Taylor, joy surging.

Heavy heat hits me but I don't care. I pull the mask down, breathe outside air for the first time in forty-five years.

A square yard is framed by towering concrete walls on all sides. There's no escape. Washing lines criss-cross the space. Stiff sheets and towels hang unmoving in the breezeless air. Above, there is sky. Cloudless and brilliant blue. It's bright up there, but not down here in the yard. It's still dull, the same as the rooms inside.

All these feelings rise up inside me. I can't tell whether I'm going to laugh or cry.

'You okay?' Taylor asks.

'Yeah, it's just—'

'Overwhelming?'

'Yes.'

'Stay out here for a bit if you like. I'd better get on with the laundry.'

'Oh no, I'll help.' I pull up my mask and hurry in to stop him getting to my pile of bloodstained clothes.

But he's already sorting them.

He looks at me. 'Are you okay, Calico?'

'Yes. It's grim, I know. It's from when Jem had his nosebleed. Got everywhere and I didn't want anyone else to have to deal with it.'

Not sure Taylor believes a word. I hate lying to him. He's been nothing but kind to me.

'We'd better soak these while we get on with the rest. Cold water's best for dried-in blood.'

I fill a deep sink with icy water and put the clothes in. Taylor shakes chalky powder over them.

'You up for a workout?' he asks.

We stand at two vast sinks next to each other. One sheet goes into hot water with the eye-stinging soap. Taylor shows me how to agitate the water with a wooden paddle. Then we have to inspect every bit of the sheet

148

and rub more soap on any marks. Together we twist it, squeezing out as much water as we can. My arms are throbbing already. I look at the mountain of towels and sheets on the workbench.

'No wonder you're so buff,' I say.

He blushes and laughs.

We dunk the sheet into the clean water of the second sink. Taylor swishes it around to get the soap out while I start the whole process on the next sheet. We carry on agitating, scrubbing, wringing.

'Have you seen Jem since the—' Taylor gestures at the bloody washing.

'Only once.'

'How was he?'

'Not good,' I say. 'The same as he was that time. Wild, out of control. Earl had to—' My voice catches in my throat. It's my fault Jem got like that.

'Did Earl sedate him again?' Taylor asks.

'Yeah. What is it, do you think? With Jem?'

'I reckon it might be post-traumatic stress. I mean, I don't know for sure, but he's told me some stuff about his first life that makes me think he wasn't doing well mentally, even before—' Taylor points at the walls. 'Like he went through a lot of trauma.'

Guilt jabs me. I know about that too. But not because Jem told me. Because I read his Remembering Book without asking.

'I feel like they could do more to help him here,' Taylor says.

149

'Not sure Jem would let them. He's so suspicious.'

'True. But my pop had PTS after the war and therapy really helped. I mean, it was before I was even born, but Mom says it was good for the whole family. We do a lot of talking about feelings, and hugging it out.' Taylor smiles.

The hollow yawns inside me. He knows his family are there waiting for him. I don't even know whether Mum's alive.

'Earl's tried to do some anger management with him,' Taylor says. 'But I think Jem needs more than that. I've said so to Doc Perez but she says it would affect the outcome of the research or something.'

'Great.'

'Yeah, I know. Seems unfair.'

I scrub away at the bloodstains. Wish I could wash away my guilt so easily.

'Time to mangle!' Taylor says.

He shows me how to thread the sheet between the rollers and then gets me turning the handle. I feel again like I've gone back in time, instead of into the future. The squeezed-out water goes into buckets, that go back into the sinks for the next load. A never-ending cycle. It makes me feel even more trapped.

We hang the sheets on the washing lines, but even being outside doesn't make me feel any freer. It's such a little scrap of air, of sky. It's not enough.

Lost Days

34.

Calico

I wake up running. Soaked in sweat. Heart's beating too fast.

My feet tangle. I stumble. Fall.

And lurch awake.

Not running but dreaming.

A dream about rows and rows of sheets hanging. When I pull at the sheets, behind them are faceless girls trapped in cages. I sprint up and down, trying to find something, only I don't know what it is.

My breathing slows. Just a dream. I'm awake now. Aren't I? The dark is so thick, so silent, it's hard to tell which way is up. I get out of bed and stand with the backs of my legs against it. The floor's solid beneath my feet. The bathroom door's in a straight line from here. Six shuffling steps and I reach it. Press my hand against it. Nothing happens.

I work my way along the wall to the other door. The way out. It doesn't open either. I shout for Earl, Doctor Perez, Gabe. Hammer on the door. I shout for Jem. He heard me before. But there's no reply. Must be because my door is closed.

No one answers. No one comes.

Panic thunders in my chest; fear tendrils from my heart to my throat. The dark presses in on me.

Maybe I'm dead.

Except death is nothingness.

And my body is pumping blood, I can feel it thud thud thud. And my arms and back and shoulders ache deeply, from doing the laundry.

I step back to the bed and sit still.

Maybe it's dark like this every night and I never noticed.

No.

Maybe this is part of the research – to see how we react under pressure or something.

Maybe the facility has run out of money and left me here to . . . no.

Or maybe Fates hasn't paid the bill, and they've cut the power off.

Shit.

You can't even open a door in this place without power. What the hell's going to happen? I'm trapped here without light, or food, or water.

Oh, shit.

If the power's off, what happens to the frozen?

What happens to Asha?

35.

No idea how long I've been in here. Hours or days.

The dark is just the dark, and I'm not afraid of it. Sat up enough nights next to Asha listening to her little bird breaths.

The silence scares me, though. Not being able to hear another living thing. No one breathing but me. And waiting for that to stop. The breathing. My breathing.

Maybe I'm not in a room at all. Maybe the hollow inside me got so big it swallowed me. Maybe I'm in a coffin. Under the earth. Maybe I'm already dead.

But then, why do I need to pee?

I feel for the water jug. Empty. For now.

Somehow, I wee in it.

I'm not going to drink it.

Yet.

36.

Maybe Jem's right. Maybe this place is hell. An endless dark, a never-ending silence. An eternal version of Grandma's naughty step.

'ASHA!' I shout. 'ASHA!'

The silence shatters. I hear something.

It's singing.

Mum singing.

It's not real. Can't be.

But still her voice seeps into me. I close my eyes and let it fill me up. I hum the harmony. The words whisper around me. *Blood and breath and bone, threaded through with love and light. Always in my heart and mind. I'll carry you through deepest night.*

I left Asha. I left Mum. Broke my promise. I'm as bad as Fates.

Tears thicken my throat, but I push them down and sing anyway. I reach for more than the first verse, but it floats beyond me.

37.

Did I sleep? Was that a dream? No, a memory. Asha in the ITU. Mum singing over her. And here's another one.

I only saw Mum cry once.

I was with Grandma and Grandad waiting to get into the Children's Ward at City Hospital. I'd never been there before. All I wanted was to be with Mum and Asha.

A tall black man dressed in pale blue scrubs and white shoes greeted us. He talked in a soft voice over my head to Grandma and Grandad. Photographs of children lined the walls. Some of them didn't have any hair. Something cracked inside me.

'Calico.' Grandma tugged at me. 'Grandad and I are going to see Mummy now. You stay here with the nurse.' They walked away.

The tall man smiled down at me. 'Let's go in here.' He took me into the visitors' room. There were toys and books. 'Calico,' he said. 'That's a pretty name. I'm George.'

'Where's my mum?'

'She's along the corridor,' he said.

'With Asha?'

'Yes, with Asha.'

'I want to see them.'

He nodded. 'They want to see you, too. I'll take you in a minute.'

'I want my mum.'

'Calico, your mum's a bit upset right now.'

Then Grandma's voice prickled down the corridor like thorns in the air. I ran out of the visitors' room towards her, got near enough to hear her say, 'You've brought this on yourself, Ruth. Two children out of wedlock. Different fathers. God's punishing you.'

There was sudden shouting, screeching. Mum. 'That's all you've got to say? You foul old witch. Get out of here. Get away from me ... Get away from my kids ...'

Grandma and Grandad stalked into the corridor.

I skirted past them, away from their spiky fingers, towards this sound, this awful sound, like the world was ending. I lurched through the doorway. Asha was on a bed, tubes going into her. And on the floor, in a puddle of dress, was Mum, crying.

George knelt beside me. 'Calico,' he said. 'You need to be brave, now. You need to be strong for your mother.'

I sniffed back my tears. No crying now.

I have to be the brave one. I have to be the strong one. I have to take care of Mum and Asha.

I don't know how, but after a while, Mum actually forgave them, the shitty grandparents. Maybe it was because she needed their help. Or maybe it's because she's the kind of Christian who actually lives the good bits – like turning the other cheek, and loving your neighbour, and treating others how you want to be treated – all that. Grandma was more the type who spent her time banging on about all the stuff you're not supposed to do, like having sex outside of marriage. She was obsessed with sin and pointless rules. Miserable woman. What a waste of energy. A waste of life. A waste of faith.

38.

I'm not Asha's sister here. Not the sister of the dying girl with the beautiful voice. Not the daughter of full-of-love, full-of-life Ruth. I'm just me. Calico.

I can be who I am, who I really am. The me without Asha.

And who is that?

The hollow girl.

The girl who does things that hurt people. Reading Jem's Remembering Book. Grassing up Shimmy.

What's happened to me?

39.

No idea how long I've been here in the dark. But I drank my own wee. That's what this place has done to me. And now I sweat it out again. I'm going to dehydrate to death in this dark, silent shithole. Still, maybe it's a better option than what else is on offer. Sold to the Chosen. Forced under the knife of a Perfection Surgeon. Tortured for some tenuous study. Murdered by a paranoid boy.

No. Jem's not paranoid. Just thinking of him makes me feel less hollow.

He's damaged. He's grieving. Like me. He feels guilty. Like me.

Asha. And Mum.

I feel far away from them. My whole life – my first life – all my memories are full of them. But now here I am, in this second life, and I'm making friends, growing feelings for people they don't know, making memories without them. What if, one day, the new outweighs the old?

Don't know why I'm thinking like this.

One day? I don't know if I even have another day.

I lie down, and will whatever's coming next, to come.

40.

asha

sea of souls

this limbo
is a sea of souls.
swimming,
not flying like angels.
floating,
not sinking like devils.

part souls
lost souls
half souls
waiting.

their wisdom
somehow seeps
into you
without words.

asha, you are
half a soul
not fully alive
but not yet dead,
for a reason
only you can know.

41.

Calico

Something wakes me. Is the darkness less? Low light seeps through the bulbs in the ceiling. I run to the bathroom. The door opens at my touch. I turn the tap. Water splutters and then gushes. I gulp it down. Splash my face.

'Calico?'

I go back into the bedroom. Gabe stands there, shoulders up to his ears, forehead creased. His shoulders drop when he sees me. He smiles.

'What happened?' My voice is rusty.

He brings over a tray with food on it. Same old crap. 'Earl's gonna tell you later. Eat up now. And that drink there's to rehydrate you. Um, get a shower. I'll be back in a little while to fetch you.' And he's out of here.

Weirdly, I'm not hungry, but I force the food down. And the drink. And take a shower. Not to do what I'm told. Not to be a good girl. But to be alive. To be strong. To be ready. Like Jem said. Sarah Connor ready. For when the time comes. For whatever's next. Because all the time the power was out, the question pounded in my head.

What's happened to Asha?

I take out my Remembering Book and write down what happened while I was in the dark. I tuck it in my waistband, cover it with my baggy jumper. All my memories, all my thoughts, are staying with me.

Found Days

42.

Calico

Gabe's back to get me. He won't answer my questions as I follow him to the resocialisation room.

Jem and Taylor are here, on the sofa. Their heads close, they talk in whispers. They're holding hands.

Taylor smiles at me. 'See, Jem, here's another one.'

They both stand. Taylor hugs me. He's trembling.

Jem watches. His eyes are lined with red. 'You okay?' His voice is raw.

I nod. He spoke to me at least. Has he forgiven me for reading his Remembering Book?

Gabe comes back, pushing Veda in a wheelchair. She's connected to a drip that rolls alongside them. Her brown skin is tinged with grey.

Taylor sits next to her. 'Are you okay?'

She nods. 'Dehydrated.' Must be bad if they have her on a drip.

We sit in uneasy silence. I need to talk to Jem about Stan, about Asha. I don't want to set him off again, but it's urgent now. This place is falling apart.

Earl bustles in. 'You lot feeling all right?' he says. 'Never heard it so quiet in here.'

'Where's Shimmy?' Taylor asks.

'She's gone.' Earl runs a hand over his tattoos.

'What?'

'Came to the end of her two-year contract, kid.'

Ohmygod. She's out of here? Gone off to live her perfect life with sleazy Nick?

'Oh,' Taylor says. 'But we didn't get to say goodbye.'

'We don't do goodbyes here, tends to be unsettling for the folk left behind.'

'Yeah, right,' Jem says. 'Seems a bit of a coincidence that she left during the power cut.'

And right after Fates took her note from me.

'The two things are unrelated, kid. But I got to admire the way you make a conspiracy out of everything.'

'What caused the power outage, Earl?' Veda asks.

'Some of the solar panels on the roof got damaged in a storm.'

There was a storm bad enough to damage the roof. I didn't hear anything.

'Anyway, it's passed, and the panels are on their way to getting fixed.'

'How long were we without power?' Veda asks.

'Four days.'

'What about the frozen?' I blurt.

But Earl's wrist vibrates and he turns to go.

'Earl!' I follow him into the day room.

He looks back at me, shakes his head, and leaves.

What does that mean? Is Asha okay? Or is she – gone?

The hollow wails inside me. I keep my mouth closed so it doesn't escape. I won't let it out, the dread that, after everything, she's dead again.

Maybe one of the others knows something.

Veda and Taylor talk in soft voices. Jem paces, his beanie pulled low. He mutters into his shoulder.

'Do you know what happens to the frozen in a power cut?' I ask.

Taylor and Jem shake their heads.

'No, I don't know,' Veda says.

'Can you ask your friend?'

'Who do you mean?'

'Shimmy said you had a friend in the lab.'

'They don't work here any more,' Veda says quietly.

'Oh. Sorry.'

The room falls silent. There's a Shimmy-shaped hole.

I go over to Jem. 'You want to sit down?'

'No, I've had enough of sitting down and closed doors. At least if I'm over here by an open one, I can pretend this isn't a prison.'

'It's not a prison,' Veda says. 'Can't you see any good in what they're doing here?'

Jem turns away. He doesn't say anything else, not even to Stan.

It's a relief when Gabe finally arrives.

'Can I go back first?' Veda says. 'I'm exhausted.'

He pushes back his hair. 'Sure.'

Taylor goes with them and I'm left alone with Jem. He keeps his back to me. I need to make things right with him. It's even more important now to find out how he talks to Stan so I can try, however slight the chance, to talk to Asha.

169

'I'm sorry I read your book.' And I am. Really didn't like that Fates read mine.

Jem doesn't reply.

'I didn't do it to be nosy, or to grass you up. I wouldn't tell anyone what's in there. I won't, I mean . . .'

He turns to face me. Double head jerk.

'I had a lot of time to think about everything. In the dark,' I say.

'Yeah, me too.' He steps closer.

'I read it because of what you told me about Stan.'

Jem flinches. 'You some kind of freak?'

'No. I wanted to find out about Stan, because—'

'You think I'm crazy. Paranoid. Like everyone else does.'

'No.'

He snorts.

'No, really, Jem. I don't.'

'I'm pretty fucked up, y'know.'

'This place'll do that to you.'

He does the grimace-smile. 'Think it happened long before I got here.'

'If it'd been the other way round, my Remembering Book, I mean. Are you sure you wouldn't have read it?'

'Oh, no. I'd definitely have read yours. But then, I'm a monster.'

'If you're a monster, I am too.'

'No. You're not.' Jem comes closer to me, lifts his hand as if he's about to touch my face. The hollow inside fills with the flutter of moths.

His head twitches. 'I – it's – I feel like you and me get each other. You're not like the others, always defending Fates and the shit that goes on here. You ask questions. You don't buy every line they feed you.' His voice drops. 'And – and when you saw what was in my Remembering Book, I thought you wouldn't want anything to do with me. Knowing who I really am.'

'I do get you, Jem. And what I read, it means I get you even more.' I rest my hand on his arm, take a deep breath. This is hard to do. 'I have to tell you something.'

Someone clears their throat. Gabe, lurking again. *Eyes and ears.* 'Time to get back to your rooms, guys.'

'No,' Jem says.

'You can't make us.' I need to talk to Jem.

He and I could take Gabe, get his key, find the Cryostore—

But Jem's vibrating. 'I'm going nowhere,' he says.

'Oh, man. Don't do this. You're gonna get me in trouble.'

Jem is sallow, slimy with sweat. His eyes are glazed, the brown turned black, staring at something I can't see. Breath crashes out of him, wave after wave, louder and louder.

'Oh, shit, man. Stop it.'

'Gabe, get a paper bag – he's having a panic attack.'

'Um—'

'Go on.'

He runs off. 'He'll – get – Earl,' Jem says. 'Nee – dle.'

'No, no. It's okay. I won't let him hurt you.'

Jem slides to the floor, crouches over.

'Breathe,' I say, and breathe myself, slow and deep, even though my heart is going crazy. I sit with him, and whisper: 'You're okay, you're okay.'

It won't help him, I know. I only ever had one panic attack and it was like being in the sea during a storm, flung against rocks, reaching for air. The waves pulled me under time and again, filling my ears, my eyes, my nose with water. Couldn't see, couldn't hear. Couldn't get air into my lungs.

But I wasn't in the sea. I was in the hospital. It was Asha's second diagnosis.

I'd spent five years praying to God to keep her well. Said my prayers when I woke up. In a specific order. Word perfect. If I caught myself making a mistake, I'd start again. No matter how many times, until it was right. Same again at breaktime, and lunch. No wonder I didn't have any friends. And again when I got home from school; before I went to sleep. If I broke the pattern, it wouldn't work. Asha would die. And yet there I was in a room in the hospital hearing the news that she was ill again, and everything I'd done meant nothing.

Gabe pounds up the hallway. He shoves a brown paper bag at me. I hold it round Jem's mouth and nose. The bag crackles. His breathing slows and he takes hold of it himself.

We sit, his clammy arm resting against mine. He stares at the ceiling. And breathes.

The counsellor said I was trying to control

everything with rituals. So many things I was trying to control. No one could. Not even God.

That's when I turned my back on church. And fell in with science instead.

Although maybe science isn't the answer either. Look at Lucas Fates, playing God. Manipulating things to suit his needs.

'Come on, guys,' Gabe says.

Jem tenses. 'I can't go back in that room.'

'Oh, you got to, man.'

'What if the power goes off again?' Jem says. 'What if we can't get out?'

'Not gonna happen.'

'How d'you know?' I say. 'It was terrifying being shut in there. Like being in a coffin and buried alive.'

'I get it. But, guys, you have to go back in your rooms.'

'Can't you leave us your key?' I say.

'Are you kiddin'? More than my life's worth to give you that. The keys don't work when there's no power anyway.'

'Fuck,' Jem shouts. His fingernails press into his arms.

'Jem,' I say. 'Calm down.'

His breathing is loud, louder, fast. 'I – can't . . .' he says.

'Gabe! We need to do something!' I say.

'Oh, man.' He runs his hand through that stupid hair. 'Okay,' he says. 'Okay. I know, I've got to fix some of the solar panels up on the roof. You can come with me for—'

Jem leaps up, drags me with him.

'Outside?' I say.

'For a little while. Then you got to go back to your rooms, okay?'

'Yeah,' I say.

Jem nods, his breathing still ragged.

And we follow Gabe along the corridor. The other way. The way we've never been before. The way that leads outside.

43.

Another corridor. 'What about cameras?' I ask Gabe.

'What cameras?'

'The ones that spy on us,' Jem says.

Gabe shakes his head. 'There's no cameras. I'm just gonna check no one's about though. Wait here a minute.' He goes round the corner.

'No cameras,' I whisper.

'You believe him?'

'Don't know.'

Gabe's back. 'Okay, let's go.' Round the corner, he opens a door, and behind it there's a ladder going up.

He leads the way. Zaps at a hatch above his head with the remote key. The hatch slides back.

A square of light.

I climb quickly up behind him, feel Jem rattle on the ladder below me, and then I'm on a flat roof. Outside. Blinking in the dusty daylight.

'Here you go,' Gabe says. 'Top of the world.'

Top of the world? There are rows and rows of solar panels below, and then, as far as I can see, there's dirt. No buildings. No trees or plants, people, animals, cars. No birds, no butterflies, no bees. Nothing on the horizon, only sky, gunship grey. The air is heavy. My hair's damp with sweat already. It sticks to my neck.

Jem pulls his beanie off.

'I got work to do.' Gabe points to the rows of solar panels behind us. 'Stay here.'

'Not like there's anywhere to go.'

The deserted land sprawls below us. I wanted to get outside, see the earth, the sky, something other than those walls. To feel there's still a world for me and Asha. But this vastness, this nothingness, it's as much a prison as the walls and locked doors.

Jem steps away from me, closer to the edge of the roof. He looks down.

The words from his Remembering Book whirl in my head. My heart's a hummingbird. This was a stupid idea.

'Jem, what are you doing?'

'Seeing how far down it is.'

'Why?'

He turns back to me. 'I was thinking I could go,' he says. 'Escape. Get out of here.'

'How?'

'Jump, maybe?'

Shit. 'It'd kill you.'

'Maybe,' he says. 'Would you come with me?'

I'm silent for too long.

'Forget it.' He turns away.

'No, wait. It's not – I can't leave.'

'Wasn't serious about jumping. I'll find another way out.'

'That's not it.' I take a deep breath. 'I can't leave here without my sister.'

His eyes examine my face. 'That's who you asked

176

me about? The first time we met.'

I nod.

'You still think she's here?'

'Yeah. Or at least she was, but with the power cut, I don't know if she . . .' The words catch at my throat. 'If she's still frozen.'

'That's fucked up.'

My legs feel weak. I drop down to sit on the roof.

Jem crouches next to me. 'How do you know she was definitely here?'

'She died just before me.' Not a lie. 'And it was all arranged . . .' I don't tell him how it happened, the detail, that I forced Mum to give consent. He wouldn't like that. I don't like that about myself. 'They won't even talk to me about her – all their stupid rules.'

He nods.

'Something I heard made me think she was in the Cryostore.'

Jem sits facing me, beanie in his hands.

'Anyway,' I say. 'That's why I can't leave. Because Asha's still here.'

'You can't leave *yet*.'

'Yes. I can't leave yet. When you told me about Stan, that you could hear him even though he's dead, I wanted to ask you about it. *How* you talk to each other, but I didn't get a chance, and then I thought maybe something in your Remembering Book might help me. That's why I read it. I'm sorry.'

We sit in silence for a while. The only sound is

Gabe bashing away at something out of sight.

'It's okay,' Jem says at last. 'I'm sorry about your sister.'

'Thanks.'

'It doesn't always feel like a good thing when I hear Stan, y'know. And I don't know how it happens. He only talks to me when he feels like it.'

'Oh.'

'Usually giving me advice I don't want.'

'Could you ask him, next time he speaks to you, about Asha?'

He nods. 'I'll try. But he kind of doesn't like it when I talk about you.'

'Oh.'

'Yeah. He keeps reminding me – well, you read it – about Zach.'

'That must be hard.'

'Yeah, it is.' He rubs his face. 'All seems unreal still ... Anyway, have you talked to Earl about your sister?'

'No. Not since the first day. I talked to Fates though.'

'What did he say?'

'He won't let me see her. Says if I tell anyone about her, I'll mess up the study. There'll be no money to find a cure for her.'

'Bastard.'

'So, don't say anything, will you?'

''Course not.'

'If they'd only let me see her. I know she's frozen, but it would make me feel . . . I don't know. I'm not used to being away from her. If I can see her – even if she's in a cryopod, I'll know at least she's safe.'

'I get it.' He reaches out his hand to me. And I take it. His skin's warm.

'There's something else.' I look down at our hands. 'All that time on my own in the power cut, I got to thinking. You know, if your mum had you frozen, maybe Stan's frozen too.'

'Fuck.'

44.

Jem leaps up.

'Wait.' I scramble after him. 'What are you doing?'

'Finding Fates. Get him to tell me if Stan's here.'

I hold on to his arms. 'No. Please. Don't.'

Jem pulls away from me. 'It's my brother!' He walks towards the ladder.

'They won't tell you, Jem.'

He glances over his shoulder at me. 'I'll make them.'

'How? You can't.'

'FUCK!' He stops walking.

'And if you ask Fates, he'll know I told you about Asha, and he'll never find the cure for her. He'll never let me see her.'

Jem's head twitches.

I hold on to both his hands. 'We'll find out about Stan. And Asha, okay? But we have to be careful.'

I hear Gabe clear his throat, and I step away from Jem automatically. But it feels like we're somehow still attached.

Gabe walks round the end panel. He waves us over. Passes Jem a beer.

'And for you.' Gabe hands me a bottle slick with condensation. 'Peace offerin'. For that thing.'

'What thing?' Jem asks.

'He grassed me up to Fates.'

'Had to give him somethin'. He's always askin' me.'

'Did you give him my Remembering Book, too?'

Gabe messes with his hair. 'Yeah. But he told me to do that. And I didn't read it.'

My face flushes.

Jem snorts.

'Did you tell Doctor Fates anything else?' My heart speeds up.

Gabe looks right at me. 'No.'

My mouth's dry from the heat, from lies and half-lies and secrets. I gulp some beer. It fizzes in my throat, then hits my stomach.

'So how d'you like your little taste of freedom?' Gabe asks.

'Freedom?' Jem's voice is quiet, small. He's trapped again. Like me, trapped here by hope. And I did that to him.

Gabe brushes his hair off his face. 'Yeah, well, guess no one really feels free in this place. Can't quite lose the feelin' of bein' a prison. 'Specially when the chief nurse used to be an inmate back in the day.'

'What? Earl was a prisoner?'

'I thought he was a soldier.'

'Yeah, that too. Fought in the war – always relivin' his glory days. But then he got in trouble and was sent here.'

'No way.'

'Yeah. Studied to be a nurse while he was in here. Then stayed when the Foundation bought the buildin'.

He totally loves the doc. Reckons he saved his life, showed him the light or whatever.' Gabe takes out a tobacco pouch and cigarette papers. 'Earl acts like the doc's God or somethin'.'

'Guess Fates is. In his own mind anyway.'

'Well, he brought you all back to life, didn't he?' Gabe rolls the cigarette. 'Anyways, Earl practically runs the place now.'

'How come?'

Gabe licks the cigarette paper, sticks it down and lights up. 'The doc's either shut up in his lab workin' on some special project, or in his office writin' bids for investors. Needs the money ever since the family trust fund ran out.'

'Who'd want to invest in this shithole?' Jem says.

'All sorts have in the past. Government. Medical. Military.'

'Does he ever get funding any more though? I mean, look at the place. And what's he got left to sell?'

'Nanomedicine and – other stuff.'

Other stuff? My muscles tense. To sell? What Perez said. And Veda. *Fertile girls are a commodity.*

Gabe swigs his beer. 'Earl won't hear it, but the doc's on his last legs, I reckon. He's old, real old, tired, sick.'

'What's wrong with him?'

'Not exactly sure. Somethin' bad though. He has to take this serum every day.'

The beer sours in my stomach. Fates is ill. What if he dies? How will I find out what's happened to Asha?

My insides plummet like I've fallen off the edge, of the roof, of the world.

'You want another?' Gabe waves his beer bottle at us.

'Where d'you get them from?' Jem asks.

'There's a brewhouse here, can you believe. Plenty of grain and yeast. I brewed it myself. Doesn't taste the best but it does the job.'

'Yeah,' Jem says. 'I'll have another one.'

I shake my head.

Gabe disappears behind the panels again.

'If I've got to be shut back in my room, don't want to be sober,' Jem says.

'Here, have the rest of mine.'

Jem knocks it back. 'I still don't totally trust Gabe.'

'Yeah, well, as has been said before, you're paranoid, Jem.'

'I am paranoid.' He nods. 'But I'm not delusional paranoid. I'm realistic paranoid.'

'I think you're pissed paranoid.'

'No.' He waves the empty bottle at me. 'There's something about him, I dunno, maybe it's his eyes, but I don't trust him.'

'You don't trust anyone, Jem.'

'I think I trust you.' His voice is quiet, serious.

It makes me feel warm, and I smile, before I remember all the half-truths I've told, all the stupid things I've done.

The smell of cigarette smoke, and Gabe's back with more beer.

I'm not sure about him either. He took my Remembering Book. He told Fates about Shimmy's letter, but he did say sorry for that. And I know from experience how Lucas Fates can make you do things you don't want to. Gabe didn't say anything about my period. And if he gets caught with us now, he'll be the one in trouble.

We all sit on the roof. Gabe looks out over the desert.

I can't talk to Asha like Jem talks to Stan, and if Fates really is ill, I need to get on with finding her. Make sure she's safe in her cryopod. And then work out how to keep her that way. Being nice to Gabe might be the way to do that.

'Where'd you get the tobacco from?' I ask.

'Found it in an outbuilding. Reckon it's some old con's stash.'

'Are there lots of outbuildings?'

'Yep. Not that I get much free time, but I like to go have a look around. Got to be some perks to being an unpaid intern.'

'Unpaid? How did you end up working here?' I ask.

'Um. My dad – died.' Gabe swallows. 'Took his own life.'

'Oh, I'm sorry.'

Jem twitches next to me.

'Anyways, things got screwed up at home so I guess I came here to figure stuff out.'

'Well, the level of screwed-up-ness in this place does put everything else into perspective,' Jem says.

Gabe nods. 'Yeah.'

'So, you do think there's something weird about the facility?' I ask.

He shrugs. Messes with his hair.

'Look, I know you don't want to give us a key, but could you let us in somewhere?'

His eyes squint in the smoke. 'Where you thinkin'?'

'The Cryostore.'

'Can't get you in there,' Gabe says.

Shit. 'Do you know how it works though? The Cryostore? I mean – what happened to it during the power cut?'

'I don't know. Earl tried explainin' it all to me once, 'bout the gases they use and the frozen bein' kept upside down in their pods, but I didn't really get it. Anyway, I can get in most places. But not the Cryostore, or the Records Room.'

'What's in the Records Room?'

'Everybody's files. All the people in the study.'

'They're not on computer? Or stored in the cloud?' Jem says.

Gabe laughs. 'Cloud? What's that mean?' He looks up at the sky. 'Dammit. Rain's comin'.'

He's right. There it is, in the distance, a darkness prowling this way. I can smell it coming for us.

'How do they store the records then?' Jem asks.

'On pieces of paper,' Gabe says as if we're the stupid ones. 'In cardboard cartons.'

'Are you kidding me?'

'Nope. You can't hack paper. It's cheap. And easy to destroy.'

His words crawl over me like tiny spiders.

'How d'you know that if you're not allowed in there?' Jem says.

'Saw Earl burnin' some one time. He said they were all old folk, who had no family left.'

'Did you believe him?' It slips out, I can't help it.

'Sure, why not?' Gabe says. 'They started freezin' folk back in the 1960s and they didn't reanimate any of 'em till the 2020s. So makes sense their families were all gone.'

'This fucking place.' Jem lurches to his feet, walks over to the edge of the roof. He sways there drinking beer and staring out across the dried-out earth.

'Jem,' I say. 'Do you have to stand right there?'

'Am I blocking your view?' He rocks on his feet.

'Jem! Don't!'

He steps back from the edge. 'Just testing.' The grimace-smile.

'Testing who?'

'Myself.'

'Did you pass?' Gabe asks. He sounds suddenly sober.

'Yeah.' Jem sits down again, the warmth of him close to me. 'Not going anywhere,' he whispers.

There's a rumble, like a boulder rolling down a mountain. A flash of lightning scars the sky.

'Man,' Gabe says. 'Seems like there's another full-on storm headin' our way. I should get you back.'

'Can't we stay and watch?' I love the feel of rain on my skin.

'Nope,' he says. 'You get struck by lightnin', I'll definitely be in trouble.'

Jem's silent and still. I take his hand.

'I can't be shut in there again,' he says.

'You have to, buddy.' Gabe walks over to the hatch.

'I'm scared to be on my own,' Jem whispers to me.

'Come on, guys!'

Thunder growls again. A flash of white. Closer than before.

'We don't want Gabe to get in trouble,' I say. 'Maybe he'll bring us up here again.'

Jem turns his gaze from the far distance and back to me. I squeeze his hand.

We go over to Gabe. I hold tight to Jem. Somehow, I feel I'm his tether, and he's mine.

Gabe's already gone down the ladder.

'You first,' I say to Jem.

He nods and goes through the hatch.

Lightning etches the heavy sky again.

I turn my back on the desert, the dust, the heat, and climb down into the underworld.

45.

asha

riptide

the sea souls show
that you are caught
in a riptide,
that's why
it's hard to move.
forwards is not
the way out.
look
to the sides
and look behind.
listen
for echoes
of your past,
and you will find
your path.

46.

Calico

Jem and Gabe wait for me in the dark hallway.

'What's happened? Is it another power cut?'

'No,' Gabe says. 'They shut down the power in sections where it's not needed.'

'They turned it into night,' Jem says.

'Yeah.' Gabe nods. 'And the nights get longer and longer.'

Ice slithers down my spine. They're controlling time in here? I'm counting days in my Remembering Book, but what *is* a day in this place? How will we know when our two years is up?

We walk past the silent day room, along dark corridors. Closer to our cells. Jem is on vibrate next to me.

Gabe stops, activates the key. Jem's door and mine slide open at the same time. Jem twitches.

'Go on, now,' Gabe says.

'Can we go outside again? Another time?'

'Sure.'

'Tomorrow?'

'Yeah. Maybe.'

'Hear that, Jem?' I turn to him. But he's got his back to us.

'What. The fuck. Is that?' he says.

Something pale floats through the dark. A ghost?

'Get in your rooms,' Gabe says.

The pale thing is coming closer. Damp-mouthed, heavy breathing. It shuffles past, with a flutter against my face like a cobweb. The powdery smell of old paper, old people.

I flatten against the wall between our doorways.

'Jem, get in your room, man.'

A low moan echoes along the hallway. There's another one coming. And another.

'Shit, how did they all get here?' Gabe takes out his walkie-talkie, presses a button.

'Who the hell are they?'

'End Stagers.'

There's a cry, so sharp, so sad. The sound pierces me.

'Earl's comin' and you need to be in your rooms,' Gabe says. 'If you get caught, there'll be no more trips outside.'

Jem edges towards his doorway but I'm mesmerised by the drifting faded beings. Three more sweep along together. Colourless eyes in melting faces. One stops by Gabe, strokes his face. 'Angel boy,' she whispers. 'Angel boy.'

I'm shaking.

'Get in your room,' Gabe says over his shoulder. 'Earl's on his way.' He turns back to the End Stagers, the key in his hand.

Jem backs into his room.

And I follow him in.

The door slides shut behind us.

We stare at each other. My heart's on fast forward.

'Now we're in a zombie apocalypse?' Jem says. 'What the . . . ? God. That was creepy as fuck.' He falls back on to his bed, hands over his face, and laughs.

First time I've heard it. A real laugh. I am filled with warmth and light. I laugh too, even though I'm half waiting for Gabe to drag me out. But nothing happens. I press my ear against the door.

'You can't hear anything like that,' Jem says. 'There's a tiny gap at the bottom of the door. If you lie down with your ear right next to it, you might hear if someone's screaming really loud.'

'Do I want to know how you discovered that?'

He grimace-smiles. 'I was lying on the floor one time, and I heard you screaming.'

'When I hurt my hand.'

'Yeah. Thought they were taking you against your will.'

'No. I did it on purpose,' I say. 'At least, I tried to stop the door closing. And then when it broke my hand I got to go to the hospital wing and see if Asha was there.'

He nods and looks at his pieced-together portrait of Stan on the wall above him. 'But you didn't find her.'

'No.'

He sits up, touches the picture.

Thoughts of Asha suddenly crowd my mind – all the fears and worries and questions. The hoping to know and the needing to not know. It's a constant scratching inside my head. Is it bad that sometimes I wish it would switch off?

I perch on the edge of Jem's bed. 'Tell me something about Stan. Something good.'

'Okay.' Jem closes his eyes. 'He laughs a lot, a big loud laugh that pulls you in. He's exhausting to be around. Constant enthusiasm about everything, always wanting an opinion on things I don't even care about, and then telling me why I'm wrong.' Jem smiles. 'He was sort of like the soundtrack to my life. Like if I was in a movie. He's always been there making a lot of noise. I'd shut myself in my room sometimes to get away from him. Kind of ironic now. Here I am shut in a room and I can't get away from him even though he's dead.'

Jem's smiling. A proper smile I've never seen before.

'You know how people say someone's larger than life? That was him. Maybe he's larger than death, too. That's why he's still around, spilling over into my life now.' His voice goes quiet. 'Only, he doesn't laugh any more. He brings everything back to that night. I don't know, sometimes I think he's punishing me.'

'Maybe you're punishing yourself.'

Jem shakes his head.

'Maybe he's like your guardian angel, watching over you or something.'

'Ha. I'm not worthy of a guardian angel. Not that I believe in any of that shit. Stan would be worthy though. He could do anything he wanted and be good at it. Top grades, got a place at a top uni, loads of clever, beautiful friends. Wanted to be a doctor like Mum.' He shakes his head. 'I keep thinking of all those lives he would've saved . . .'

'Jem, don't go there.'

'Yeah. Anyway, the more I think about it, the more I think he might be frozen like you said. I mean, his funeral and everything happened while I was in the coma.'

Should I have given him that sliver of hope? What if Stan isn't frozen? What if he died in the accident and that was that?

'Or maybe he's already been reanimated,' Jem says. 'He could be out there in the world doing his stuff right now.' He takes hold of my hand, strokes it slowly with his thumb.

Tiny sparks dart over my skin.

'When we got out after the power cut,' he says. 'Sounds bad, but I was so glad that everyone else had been locked in as well. They've done it to me before. Loads of times. But not for as long. I really thought this was it. I was going to die. Again.' He looks at me. 'Only this time I didn't want to.'

The moths swoop through the hollow.

He shuffles over towards the wall and brings me with him. I lie down, my head on the pillow next to his.

'Tell me something about Asha,' he says.

'She's always singing. On her own. Or with Mum. Or the three of us together.'

'She's like the soundtrack to your life as well.'

'She's my *whole* life. I've spent so long looking after her, don't know who I am without her.'

The lights dim into night-time mode and our voices drift in the dark. We tell each other all the things about Stan and Asha. The good, and the bad, and the pain. The weight of it, and the light. Until I don't want to talk or think about Asha any more.

We're so close, me and Jem, his breath is warm on my cheek. I turn my face. It's too dark to see him. My mouth finds his. Our murmurs merge into kisses, sweet and silent and safe.

47.

asha

the sea teaches you
how to soul reach.
you must be a wave
seeking through the
shale and sand and shells,
searching
for the echoes
that will lead you
back to shore.

48.

Calico

I dream of rain soaking my hair, splashing on my skin. But when I wake I'm not outside.

The facility walls surround me.

My room is back to front though.

Not my room, Jem's.

The hollow inside me is hardly there.

Jem steps out of the bathroom in boxers and smiles at me. His face is so alight, alive. I sit up with the sheet wrapped round me, smiling back. But the bedroom door slides open, and Earl is suddenly in here.

'What the hell!' he thunders.

I try to get out of bed, but my legs tangle in the sheet, and Earl is already on Jem, dragging him from the room. I scramble up, but they're gone.

Shit. Shit. Shit.

49.

My hands shake as I get dressed. I make the bed. Sit and wait.

It's Doctor Perez, not Earl, who comes for me. Her eyes are tight. She takes me back to my room.

'What were you thinking?' she says.

'I—'

'Intimate contact with other reanimates is forbidden. You know that.'

'Is Jem okay?'

'Calico, listen to me. The rules are for your own protection.' Her voice drops. 'It's likely that you're fertile, as we've discussed.' Her fingers go to the cross. 'You cannot risk a pregnancy. I won't be able to help you then.'

'There's no way I want to get pregnant.'

'Did you have intercourse with Jem?'

'That's none of your business.'

She sighs. 'I should do a pregnancy test. And it's not only pregnancy you need to worry about.' She shakes her head. 'You know so little about the world now, about the diseases that exist and the danger they bring.'

'But Jem and I have been shut in here for decades. We haven't been in contact with any of these new diseases.'

'You need to take me seriously.' She lifts the crucifix

to her lips for a moment. 'I'm going to share something with you, Calico.'

'Please, not your religious beliefs about premarital sex and abortion. I don't believe in God.'

She looks shocked. 'Neither do I. I'm a scientist.'

'You wear that cross.'

'It was my sister's. I wear it in memory of her.'

'Oh,' I say. 'Sorry.'

'I want to tell you her story, but can I trust you not to share it?'

More secrets. But she's keeping one of mine. 'Yes,' I say. 'You can trust me.'

'Maria was older than me. Bold, beautiful, a fighter. You remind me of her actually. When she was sixteen, she started to menstruate. We kept it quiet, she, my mother and I. Didn't tell my father or brothers.'

'Because of the Chosen?'

'You know about them?'

'Veda told me.'

'It was a similar organisation, state-run.'

'Why did you keep it from your dad though?'

Doctor Perez doesn't answer.

Nausea rises into my throat. I remember Veda saying that some parents sold their fertile daughters.

'Someone found out about Maria when she was at university a few years later. She was given notice that she must join the National Breeding Programme, that it was her duty. But she didn't want to. She was passionate about protecting the planet. That was what she wanted to do.'

'What happened?'

Doctor Perez looks at me, tears in her eyes. 'She had a backstreet hysterectomy. Sterilisation was illegal at that point, and anyway, could be reversed. This was the only way she felt she could be valued as a person in her own right. To remove her womb, her ovaries. Think about that. Having to make that choice.' Doctor Perez wipes her eyes. 'She lost too much blood, got an infection. She died in agony a few days later.'

'I'm . . .' The horror of it silences me.

'So that is why I wear this cross. Not to show faith in any god, but to remember my sister and what I believe in. All lives are equally valuable. I am pro-choice. Pro-people. Pro-planet. But not everyone is. So you need to be careful, Calico. You must protect yourself.'

'I'm sorry,' I say. 'I'm so sorry about your sister.' I'm sorry that the only choice she had was no choice at all.

'So, I'll ask you again, Calico. Did you and Jem—'

'We didn't do anything that could lead to pregnancy or disease, okay? We were freaked out after being locked in during the power cut, and didn't want to be on our own, that's all.'

'Well, you'll both be on your own now. You and Jem will be kept apart.'

I have to hold it close to me, my night with Jem. I don't want it stripped away. I don't want to lose it. This new warm memory I have. A new part of me. Something precious and bright in all this darkness.

Doctor Perez does her tests in silence. Taps into her

nanocom. 'Doctor Fates will want to see you soon,' she says. 'Please be careful what you say to him. The facility is short of money and, as I hope you now understand, someone like you – a fertile girl – is very valuable.'

Her words clang, a warning bell. 'Why do you work for him? He's so—'

She sighs. 'He was once at the forefront of life extension science. Highly respected. I came here to work on a project – not cryogenics, something else. But it soon became obvious that the cryogenic part of the facility had problems – the lack of funds, the accelerated ageing. I put my project on hold to help him, to help the patients.'

'You put your own life on hold to help everyone else?'

'What else could I do? I'm a doctor first and foremost. I took an oath.' She grasps the crucifix, shakes her head. 'I shouldn't have told you all this. So unprofessional. Please keep it to yourself.'

After she goes, I'm left reeling. The Chosen feel too real, too close.

It was a stupid thing to do, go into Jem's room, kiss him, sleep in his bed.

How was any of that being a good girl, following the rules?

How was any of that going to help Asha? I've put her in danger. Again.

And Jem. I can still smell him on my skin. What will Fates do to Jem?

50.

'You wanna brush your hair, kid?' Earl says.

'What are you now, my stylist?' The jangle of nerves makes me mouthy. I haven't seen him for days. Or anyone else. Apart from Gabe silently bringing my meals.

Earl's craggy face is stern. He hands me a hairbrush. 'Smarten yourself up a bit. You got an appointment.'

'Who with?'

'Doctor Fates.'

I shudder. 'What's it about?'

'What d'you think?' Earl steps out into the hallway. 'You knew the rules, kid.'

The hollow is back, scratched open and raw. Oh God. Is this it? Has Fates found out? Are the Chosen here for me? I can't be taken away from here, from Asha, from Jem. How will I save them?

Earl leads me a way I've never been. Down some dusty stone stairs with a rickety wooden handrail. It's darker, cooler, quieter. I brush away the sensation of cobwebs catching at my skin.

'Where are we going? This isn't the way to his office.'

'You'll see.'

On the next landing there's the Records Room. We pass it and carry on down. There's no paint on the walls here, just bare stone. It's glacial, damp.

'Here.' Earl stops to unlock a door. It's labelled: Cryostore.

At last. Am I going to see Asha? A parting gift from Fates before he sells me to the Chosen? The hollow fills with moths reaching for the light.

The Cryostore is a long hallway with small rooms off it. This used to be death row, Veda said. I shudder. There are no doors on the cells. I guess they used to be made of metal and that's all gone now. The rooms are empty.

'Where are the cryopods?'

Earl doesn't answer.

Hope sinks lower with every step, every empty room. At the end of the hallway, there's a closed door. Earl knocks.

'Come,' Fates says.

Earl lets me in.

The moths are a frenzy inside the hollow.

Fates sits at a desk, in a pool of hazy light. The soft focus doesn't hide the new creases in his face. He's writing. Doesn't look up, doesn't speak. The chill seeps into my bones. Does he feel it too? 'Cos that hand of his is shaking.

'Where are all the cryopods?' I ask. 'Did they stop working in the power cut? Where's Asha?'

He ignores me.

'Please, Lu – Doctor Fates,' I say. 'Just tell me, did the power cut—' I can't say it.

He puts down the pencil. 'Cryogenic preservation does not rely on electricity or any other form of power.'

The moths swoop.

'You don't remember from when I explained the process?'

'No.' Had other things on my mind at the time. Like imminent death.

'But you do remember what I told you would happen if you stepped out of line? If you broke the rules again?'

'Yes,' I whisper.

'Is your sister's welfare not important to you?'

'Yes. You know it is.'

'I don't believe you, Calico.'

'Saving her is the most important thing in the world to me.'

'So you say, yet you jeopardised Asha's future for one night of – what – passion? With that ridiculous boy?'

'Please, don't hurt her.'

He's silent for a long time. The moths crawl through the hollow, into my throat, my mouth.

What have I done? What have I done to Asha? Me, being selfish. Trying to block her out with something for myself. Like the party all over again.

'We have rules for a reason,' Fates says. 'Breaking them could have a hugely detrimental impact on the study. And by extension, on Asha's outcome.'

'I know. Please. What can I do to make it right?'

'I'm glad you ask.' A dry smile.

Can't help but feel I've trapped myself again.

'Come.' He slowly stands.

An arched opening leads from the room. Shelves

line the walls, with lanterns. Metal and blue glass. No candles or bulbs, although there's something inside the lanterns. Faint light, moving, like tiny opals tumbling. Mesmerising. I reach out to one as we pass.

'Don't touch,' Fates says.

'What are they?'

'Doctor Perez calls them Soul Holders.'

An ice-cold finger runs down my spine.

'I fear Sophia is something of a poet. This was her project. As materials used for traditional cryogenic storage are in short supply now, we're always looking for other methods to extend life using fewer resources. Instead of preserving a whole human, she devised a method to transfer consciousness, holding it until a time when an artificial body, or some other vessel, will be available. It's called TOC – Transference of Consciousness.'

'There are people in these jars?'

'In a manner of speaking, yes. The essence of a person, their knowledge, their consciousness – or soul, if you like.'

Goosebumps prickle at my neck. This can't be real.

'It's a beautifully simple process. Modified neuromites are sent into the brain to harvest information from the neurons.'

I stare at the opals spinning behind the blue glass. They are beautiful. Magical.

'Unfortunately the project stalled. We have other priorities now. Come.'

The passageway leads into a small stone chamber. It's empty, apart from me, Fates and a single cryopod.

Asha! I fly to it. The metal cylinder is upright. I reach out.

Don't know what I expect. To feel a massive surge of Asha? A connection anyway, however tiny. But there's only icy metal against my palms. I rest my forehead on the cryopod. *Asha? Asha, are you here?*

No answer.

I go around the pod, checking for a window so I can see a part of her, know for sure she's here. At the back, a handwritten label on faded card. *Doctor Isabella Fates.*

Not Asha.

Not Asha.

My bones melt away. I drop to the damp floor. The hollow inside me splits wide open and howls. 'Where's Asha?'

Fates shakes his head.

I drag myself up and lurch back out to the Soul Holders. Is this where she is? I turn one around. A label. Another name I don't recognise. And another, and another. I move through them faster and faster, the glass clinks as they knock together, one falls over and rolls to the shelf edge, teeters there, opals spinning.

It drops.

Someone's soul. Someone's sister.

I catch it, hug it against my chest.

Fates is beside me. He takes the Soul Holder, places it back on the shelf.

'You're not going to find your sister here, Calico.' His hand tremors as he gestures through to the cryopod. 'That's the only one left.'

The hollow howls again. 'No! Where is she? Where's Asha?'

His eyes are steely. 'She's not here. She never was.'

51.

The hollow fills with fire. Red heat burns through the moths. 'Where. Is. She?'

'Calico—'

'TELL ME.' She's dead. She's dead. 'WHERE IS SHE?'

'Russia,' he says.

It hits me hard. 'What?'

'Asha is in cryogenic storage in Russia.'

'You lied to me.'

'No,' he says. 'No. I told you she was in cryostorage. Which she is.'

'But not *here*. Why?'

'Let's sit down.' His icicle fingers are on my arm. He leans on me as we go back to the desk and chairs. 'It's simple economics,' he says. 'We knew Asha would need to be stored for longer than you, because of her disease. Cryogenic storage is cheaper in Russia. They use group cryopods there, rather than individual.'

'How do I know any of this is true?'

'She's definitely there. Your mother—'

'Mum?' The smell of roses in the rain, her soaring laugh, wrap around me. 'She went to see Asha?'

'Yes. She visited the Russian facility herself to verify that Asha was there. At my expense, I should add.' Like he did her a favour, when we'd never be in this situation if it weren't for him. But then, without him, Asha would be dead and buried. No hope left. All options gone.

'Did Mum come to see me too?' The question slips out.

'Oh, yes. She was very persistent, Ruth Brown. I see where you get your tenacity from.'

'When was she here?'

'A year after you were frozen.'

'But that was over forty years ago. She hasn't been back?'

'No.'

I want to ask if she's still alive, but I don't want to know the answer. And anyway, how can I trust a word he says?

'How do I know Asha's still in Russia?'

'I have documentation from the facility.' He takes a cardboard folder from the desk drawer. Passes me some papers. They're in Cyrillic.

'I can't read it.'

'There are photographic records too.' He hands me a paper wallet. I slide out two faded photos.

Asha. There she is. A little blue bird on a bed of ice.

The other photo is of her being lowered, head first, into a cryochamber. Another body is in there already, much bigger than her, and there are two smaller ones.

I look at Fates.

'The Russians store humans and animals together.'

'There are animals in storage with Asha?'

He nods. 'Interesting that people preserve their pets

in the hope they'll one day be reunited. The human capacity for love always astonishes me.'

'What the hell do you know about love?'

'Ahh,' he says. 'Everything.'

He knows everything about love?

'All of this –' he gestures above us – 'is built on love.' His voice quivers. 'The last remaining cryopod – it contains my mother.'

His mother.

His mother is frozen.

Isabella Fates.

Lucas closes his eyes. 'I never met her. She died in childbirth. My father had her cryogenically suspended. And I've worked my entire career to find a way to reanimate her. So, you see, my life's work, everything we do here, was born out of love.'

'That's not love. It's obsession.'

'Is it? We're the same, you and I, Calico. The lengths we'll go to for someone we love.'

No.

We're not the same.

Are we?

52.

Fates dabs at his face with a handkerchief, but when he looks at me again his eyes are dry. 'Unfortunately, the primitive techniques used in my mother's suspension mean that we are unable to use our current process to reanimate her. In addition, her cryopod is becoming compromised by age and there are no materials available to replace it.'

'Why don't you ship her off to Russia?' The words spew out of me.

His face is like an iced-over pond cracking. He sinks into the chair. 'She would not survive the transfer,' he says.

'What about the cryopod I was in? Can't you put her in that?'

'Ah, no. That was also compromised. We were lucky to get you out when we did.'

I suck in a deep breath of frigid air.

'Why don't you drain her soul and stick it in one of them?' I point to the Soul Holders behind us.

'Oh, Calico. Because I'm like you.'

No. Why does he keep saying that? I'm nothing like this bastard.

'You and I, we want the whole person back. I want my mother, all of her. I want to be held by her. Hear her voice. Feel her touch.'

Nausea curdles in my throat.

'And so, now we arrive at the consequences of your little escapade with Jem,' he says. 'Your punishment for breaking the rules.'

Oh God. I can barely breathe. Is it the Chosen?

Fates tilts his head to one side, blinks. 'We need more funding to continue our research. Then we can repair Mother's cryopod. I simply want you to speak with some potential investors.'

Veda said the Chosen would pay good money for a fertile girl. 'Talk to who?' I ask, heart thumping.

'The Protection Services.'

Doesn't sound like a breeding programme, but I have to make sure. 'What's that? Like social services?'

'No. They're companies involved in the outsourcing of private militia. The cryogenic process is perfect for their needs, they just don't know it yet. My hope is that at least one of the Protection Services will fund a project with us.'

'I don't get how *me* talking to them will get *you* money.'

'Well, Calico. I want you to tell them about your experience post-reanimation. How you've had no physical or mental side effects, how you've healed so well, so quickly.'

'Um, don't you think that might be because there was nothing wrong with me in the first place?'

'Of course. But that's not something you will share with them.'

'So you want me to lie?'

'I want you to avoid telling them the circumstances of your death and cryogenic processing. As Doctor Perez intimated, my approach to you and Asha wasn't strictly ethical, although it was legal at the time. You should focus instead on the story of your reanimation and recovery.'

'What happens if I get caught lying?'

'Don't get caught.'

Great.

I don't want to do this, but I'll have to. For Asha. Even though there's no proof she's still in the Russian Cryostore. Those photos were decades old. I hate doing it though. Having to lie for Fates, having to sell myself for him.

Like Doctor Perez's sister. The only choice is no choice at all.

And now I have to make another deal with him too. I *am* as bad as him. I'm a hypocrite.

'If I do this for you, lie for you,' I say, 'there's something I want in exchange.'

His face is frosty. 'Of course there is.'

'If I get you the money, I want to use some of it to go to Russia. Make sure Asha is where you say she is this time.'

'Oh, Calico. You can't go anywhere. You're legally dead.'

Icy daggers stab at my chest.

'You don't have a passport or any identification

because you – as a person – Calico Brown – simply don't exist in your own right. You're research material. Property of the Fates Family Foundation until your time here is up and the relevant paperwork can be completed. By me.'

Shit.

'However, I will agree to this,' he says. 'If you convince one of the Protection Services to invest in the cryogenics project, I'll arrange for your sister to be transferred here. I will use some of that money to do so. I think that's more than generous.'

I can't trust him, with his fake smiles and all the lies. He's made promises before. But still hope leaps inside me. And do I even have a choice anyway? What will happen if I don't do it?

I won't risk Asha again.

I have no choice.

And he knows it.

'What do I have to do?' I ask.

Fates smiles. 'We have a series of meetings arranged, with representatives of the various Protection Services. The first one is in a month.' He taps his wrist. 'Earl will be here shortly. He'll explain the detail to you. In the meantime, we'll need to do something about your physique.' He looks up and down my body.

I want to rip his eyes out. 'I'm not having surgery.'

He laughs. 'No that's not an option. You can't afford it. You'll have to do the work yourself. Earl will provide a training programme.'

Working out? I can do that.

'The future of the facility,' Fates says sternly, 'of my mother, of Asha, rests on your shoulders, Calico.'

The weight of it presses down on me. What if I fail? 'There must be other ways to raise money.'

He nods. 'Of course, but none as humane.'

I shudder. The Chosen? And what other schemes has the world come up with while I was sleeping?

A knock on the door. 'Come,' Fates says.

Earl's huge bulk blocks the light from the hallway.

'Miss Brown has agreed to my proposal, Earl. You can commence her new training programme immediately.'

'Yes, Doctor Fates. Come on, kid,' Earl says. 'Let's get going. There's a lot to do.'

I walk next to him through the damp corridor, passing the empty cells.

'You know who's in there?' I ask. 'The last cryopod?'

'Sure. But we don't talk about it, right?' he says. 'You know that. Keep it zipped.'

'Not like I've got anyone to tell.'

'If you hadn't got yourself caught up with Jem, I'da been happy to let you go to resocialisation.'

God. Jem. 'Is he okay?'

'Sure.'

'You haven't hurt him?'

Earl stops and faces me. The bristles on his chin are at my eye level. 'Why would you say that? Only person hurting that kid is himself.' He sets off again. 'Case you haven't noticed, we're not in the business of hurting folk here. We're in the business of saving them.'

Not sure I believe that. Saving a select few, maybe. 'Can I see Jem?'

'Nope. The two of you need to learn to follow the rules. Take it from me, it's the only way in the end.' He stops at the day room. 'And you can get started with a weights session right now.'

53.

It's been a week of intense training. Earl's walking me back to my room. 'We'll have to fit in another session later,' he says.

'You are shitting me. Two a day's enough.'

'How many times, kid – language!'

'Oh yeah. Sorry.' But I'm not sorry. That's how I talk. It's like he's trying to crush the last tiny bit of who I am.

He comes into the room with me.

'I was going to shower.'

'That can wait. You need your serum.' He takes the brown bottle from his scrubs pocket.

Forti-serum.

'I don't want it.' Topping up my testosterone levels to make me more toned, burn more fat, like I'm some Olympic athlete.

'You ain't got a choice, kid. Orders of Doctor Fates.'

I know it's for Asha but I have to force the oily serum down.

'Good,' Earl says. 'Now I want to talk you through what you're doing and why – *again*. Seeing as you can't follow the basic rules.'

He doesn't respond to my eye roll, starts banging on about the military again, reliving how amazing it was. Telling me how disciplined I'll have to be, follow orders without question. I'm not very good at that, apparently. No swearing. Not great at that either.

'Being a soldier now is different to back in the day—'

'Back in *your* day.'

He nods. 'But the discipline's still the same. Not many folk want to be in the military any more. So the ones that join up get good pay and perks.'

'And Fates reckons offering to freeze people is a perk?'

'*Doctor* Fates. Yeah, it's a perk. Encourages people to sign up. You got any questions?'

I pick up one of the tatty brochures I'm supposed to read for research. 'Why does it say Protection Forces, not Services, on here?'

'It's an old brochure. They changed it to Services.'

'When?'

'A few years back.'

'But they still do the same thing? Private militia. Security.'

'Yup. I'll leave you to it. Back later for that training session.'

Great.

I take a lukewarm shower. The water ration is never long enough.

The brochures are still on my desk, reminding me of what I've got to do. The lies I've got to tell for Fates. The hollow seethes. I'm doing this for Asha but it's hard.

I got us into this though. It's all my fault.

Asha. I need to think about her. I take out the

Remembering Book. I go to write the day – 39. Shit.
My period must be due again any day now.

Don't think about that. Think about Asha.

<u>Day 39</u>

I can see Asha, head bent over paper. Humming
while her pen swirls and spirals. Left-handed.
Lucky leftie, Mum calls her. It started that day,
years and years ago, before Asha was ill. Picnic tea
up on the common. The sweet smell of grass and
chocolate cake.

'Come on, we have to get home,' Mum says.
'I've got a student soon.'

'No, wait,' Asha says. 'I'm going to find a four-
leaf clover.'

'That'll take forever!' Mum starts to pack the
stuff away.

But Asha squats down, searching the grass,
in her bright pink top and her blue kick-pleat skirt.
'Ah, here it is.' She twirls a perfect four-leafed
clover.

Mum gasps, laughs, picks Asha up. 'Only you,
Asha. Only you. Lucky little leftie. You're going to
be so lucky in life.'

54.

asha

Clover

echoes reach you.
calico, mum.

you'd found the clover already,
four green hearts
with a whisper of white.
you kept it hidden, careful,
in your hot little hand.
surprised them with it
like you were a magician
or a wizard.
made calico smile.
you're the luckiest girl in the world, mum said.
the luckiest girl in the world.

55.

Calico

Doctor Perez insists I have a break. She says I'm exhausted. And I am. Double or triple training. Today I can go to resocialisation. I'll see Jem. Moths dance in the hollow.

Gabe takes me. He doesn't say a word. Hides his eyes behind his hair. Guess he got into trouble for letting me in Jem's room, even though it wasn't his fault. Over two weeks ago now.

Only Taylor and Veda are in the day room. They hug me.

'You're getting all buff,' Taylor says.

I smile.

'We've been so worried about you,' Veda says.

'I'm okay. Where's Jem?'

'We haven't seen him.' Taylor's face is serious. 'Don't know what the hell he did, but he's in isolation a long time this go around.'

That's my fault. My fault. I close my eyes and see him teetering on the edge of the roof that night Gabe took us up there. What he wrote in his Remembering Book. What he's been through.

I sit close to Taylor and Veda on the sofa. Makes me think of when I was here with Veda and Shimmy that day. How we've only known each other such a short time but it seems like forever.

'So,' Veda says. 'What did Jem do?'

'Broke some stupid rule,' I say. 'We both did.'

'Ah.' She smiles. 'I thought as much.'

It didn't feel like breaking a rule. Felt right at the time. Slipping into his room, his bed, his arms. It was easy, an escape from all this. But the consequences of it are not so easy.

'What did you do?' Taylor asks.

'Gabe took us up on the roof. We're out in the middle of nowhere, did you know? Miles and miles of nothing.'

Veda nods.

'You got caught up there?' Taylor asks.

'No. When we came back down to our rooms, there were these ... ghosts or ...' A flicker of moth wing on my neck. I shiver at the memory. 'Gabe called them End Stagers.'

'Not ghosts,' Veda says. 'They're Agers. It comes right before they die. They get up and wander, trying to go home.' There are tears on her eyelashes.

I put my arm round her. With everything I'm doing for Fates, he and his no-touching rule can sod right off.

'It was so sad,' I say.

'But not what got you in trouble.'

'Um, no. That was me getting caught in Jem's bedroom the next morning.' I can't help a little smile slipping out.

Taylor laughs, then Veda starts, and I join in. Warmth spreads through the hollow. A lightness, a brightness.

'So, you've been in isolation too?' Taylor says.

It would be easy to lie. I'm not supposed to tell anyone anything, as usual, but they're my friends. 'I've been getting in shape for something I have to do for Doctor Fates.'

'This the meetings with the Protection Services?' Taylor says.

They already know. 'Yeah. Do you have to go to them too?'

'Apparently, we're on standby,' Veda says. 'I expect it depends how things go with you.'

'No pressure.' Taylor smiles.

'Shit. Do you think they'll make Jem go?'

'God, no,' Taylor says.

'Not a chance. Can you imagine what he'd say to them?'

We're laughing again when Gabe arrives to fetch Veda and Taylor.

I'm left alone and the warmth slips away from me. I curl on the sofa. A hint of Shimmy's peach scent lingers. I close my eyes, see Fates, his face skull-like in the half-light, a faded ghoul, the keeper of souls.

He said all this came from love. He said we're the same, me and him. We're not, we can't be. I don't want to be.

But it's there, in my heart, a little splinter of truth.

I'd do anything to save Asha. Always have. I took on God, and doctors, and lawyers, and even death, for her.

But none of the things I did hurt other people. Not in the way Fates has. The Agers, the End Stagers. They're all people he experimented on, and things went wrong. He didn't care about hurting them as long as it would save his mother.

Would I have done what I did for Asha if I'd known other people would get hurt?

The answer scares me.

The answer is, I don't know.

56.

asha

threads

soul reaching
for more echoes,
you find a song of
blood and bone and love

a silken whisper,
washed in sadness
and shame.

mum?

pictures play
like a movie screen.
mum's showing you
what you haven't seen.

oh.
the threads unravel now.
before you can
go forward
you must find
your calico
and tell her
what she
doesn't know.

57.

Calico

<u>Day 49</u>

I dreamed of Asha again.

It's raining. We're in the den, me and
Asha, under the climbing frame in our back
garden. The chickens potter about — Chikita
and Henrietta, and Kevin the Cockerel. Asha
named them. The piano thumps inside the house,
one of Mum's less talented students. It's the
summer holidays before Asha starts school. Her
favourite game is hairdressers. She has a plastic
basket with clips and combs and brushes, and
a pink hairdryer that makes a noise but doesn't
dry anything.

She takes a tissue and tucks it into the neck
of my T-shirt. Lifts a strand of my hair.

'What are you doing to me today?' I ask.

'Checking your hair for woodlice.'

'Head lice,' I say. 'Not woodlice.'

'Oh, no,' she says. 'It's woodlice you got.' She
comes round and opens her hand, and there's a
woodlouse, curled in an armoured ball.

We laugh. She brushes my hair and pretends
to cut it with her blunt plastic scissors. I close my

225

eyes and let her fingertips and the rhythm of the rain soothe me.

'Uh-oh,' she says.

'What?'

'Grandma.'

I peer across the rain-misted garden. Grandma gesticulates from inside the French windows. 'Teatime,' she mouths.

'I'm not hungry,' I shout back.

Not sure what she's saying now but she looks pretty cross.

'Why can't we have tea in here?' Asha says.

'Yes! Let's go and get it, bring it back here.'

Out on to the wet grass we go. I turn my face to the sky and let the rain sprinkle on my eyes and cheeks, open my mouth to taste it.

The French window slides open. 'WHAT ARE YOU DOING?' Grandma yells. 'You're getting your clothes all wet!'

But who cares? It's only water. Asha and I twirl together in the rain, laughing, singing. Until Grandma comes out in a see-through mac and cream wellies, drags us in. She roughly towels Asha down. 'You'll catch your death,' she says.

And she says it again. Only it's not her voice. It's Lucas Fates.

You'll catch your death, he says.

I hit the punch bag. Jab, jab. Hook, hook. Last set of the circuits session. I think of Fates as I pound the bag. It's his face I'm smashing. The hollow inside me is emptier than ever. Still haven't seen Jem, although I relive our night together over and over. It's like a warm light in a dark tunnel. Something that's mine and his. I hope he's staying calm, not winding them up, not getting hurt. Not hurting himself. I push down the panic that he's gone, that he's disappeared like Shimmy did.

I follow Earl back along the corridor. There's music coming from somewhere. I stop, look around. A single voice. My pulse picks up. *Blood and breath and bone . . .* Mum's favourite song. Am I hearing things? *Asha, are you there?*

'What's up, kid?' Earl says.

The song disappears. Did I imagine it? 'Thought I heard singing.'

'You feeling light-headed?'

'Yeah.' I have been all week, tired from at least two hard training sessions a day. Plus I'm always hungry.

'Let's get you back to your room. Dinner and a good night's sleep.'

Dinner is a double portion of vegetable stew. Same as yesterday. It doesn't fill me up. My body craves steak, or sausages, or bacon. I lie down. Apart from that one resocialisation with Veda and Taylor, all I've done is eat, clean, train, hydrate. Eat. Sleep. Eatcleantrainsleep. And take the serum. Not sure what it's doing to me, but I haven't had another period yet.

Sleep evades me. Old bones rattle inside the hollow. I hear the song again. Mum's favourite. But she's not singing it.

And suddenly I know.

That voice I heard out in the hall.

It was Shimmy.

58.

Am I hearing voices like Jem does? Why Shimmy and not Asha then? Never Asha. I miss her so much. The hollow is wide open.

I sit at my desk, pencil and notebook ready, but nothing comes. I close my eyes. A song plays in my head, *the* song, and I open my mouth and join in. Let the swell of music wrap around me, keep all the demons at bay. I sing every song I've ever known, every song there's ever been. Lullabies and old songs, new songs ... even hymns. *Abide with me ...*

Mum's voice twines with mine.

Mum? Are you there?

A memory whispers back.

<u>Day 51</u>

Mum's ready for church, sheet music piled in her arms.

'I'm not going,' I say.

'We'll miss you in the choir.'

'Well, get used to it. I'm not going to church ever again. I don't believe in God any more.'

She puts the music on the kitchen table, takes me in her arms. She smells of roses. 'Don't hate God because of Asha's illness.'

I move away from her.

'You know what, Calico, I'm not sure I believe in God either,' she says. 'I was brought up with church being the big thing, and it's kind of in my bones, but I don't totally trust it. I don't buy that it's innately good. All that Eve tempting Adam rubbish. People spending all their time telling you what you're doing wrong, instead of just getting on with doing right themselves. But I do find a comfort in the rituals. I believe in being kind and loving my neighbour. And I know it's not true that the devil has all the best tunes.' She smiles. 'You'll find your own way, Calico. You'll find it.'

Find my own way.

My way has always been Asha first.

Saving Asha. That's my religion. That's my science. It's based on hope and love and not giving up. Ever.

But I don't know. Somehow, now, here in this place, not giving up on Asha means I'm giving up who I am. Like lying for Fates, like going along with what he and Earl tell me to, like not having the right to decide what happens to my own body. This excessive training, the serum.

Next morning, when Earl comes with breakfast, I'm still in bed.

'Come on, kid. Up and at 'em.'

'I don't feel well.'

'Let's take a look at you.'

I keep my head turned away, covered by the blanket.

'Come on, kid.'

'No. I want to see Doctor Perez.'

I hear him suck air through his teeth, but then he leaves.

'Calico? What's wrong?' Doctor Perez asks.

I turn around and sit up slowly. It's just me and her.

'Do you know about this serum they're giving me?'

She frowns. 'No. What is it?'

'Forti-serum. Supposed to be helping me lose weight, tone up.'

She taps her wrist a few times. 'There's nothing recorded. Anything like that should be monitored carefully.'

'I don't want to take it.'

'I'll discuss it with Doctor Fates.'

I get the rest of the day in bed, half-sleeping, dreaming, thinking.

About Jem, about Asha, about me.

59.

I wake with mild pain tugging between my hips. Period?

Earl brings in breakfast and a pile of clothes. 'Eat, and then put these on,' he says. 'And brush your hair.' He's still pissed that Doctor Perez got Fates to veto the forti-serum and that was over a week ago.

'The meeting's today?' I ask.

He nods. 'With EarthKnit.'

That doesn't sound very military.

'I'll be back,' he says.

I go to the loo. No blood but the pain is worse. I feel sick at the thought it could start any time. It could start while I'm in the meeting.

I drink the tea and force down lentil porridge.

The new clothes are pale beige, like something soldiers wear in the desert. Trousers and a T-shirt, tight-fitting, especially across my chest. My breasts look massive. I put a jumper over the top. I'm still trying to get the brush through my hair when Earl comes back in.

He's dressed differently too. A long-sleeved T-shirt under his scrubs covers his tattoos. And he's had a shave. No bristles on his chin and his head's so smooth it shines.

He points to the jumper. 'You'll have to take that off.'

'I don't want to.'

'The whole point of this meeting is for them to see how fit and strong you are, kid. You got to show off those biceps.'

It's like I'm a piece of meat.

I take the jumper off. Cover my chest with my arms.

'Here.' Earl passes me a small box. 'There's some cosmetics,' he says. 'Do what you can.'

God, I've never been into make-up. Could do with Shimmy right now.

'And don't overdo it,' Earl says.

'Yeah. How about I don't do it at all?'

'Lose the attitude and get on with it, kid.'

There's a tiny mirror set into the lid of the box. My eyes look back at me for the first time in months. I see my face in pieces. I'm still me. I brush mascara on to my lashes and draw lines round my eyes, rub some shiny stuff on my lips.

'Guess that'll do.' Earl looks me over with a scowl.

I want to punch him but – I agreed to meet these people, for Asha. To bring her here from Russia.

We step into the corridor.

'Where we going? Out of the facility?' It buzzes through me, a little thrill.

'No, course not. You can't go anywhere. You don't exist,' Earl says.

How could I forget.

We enter a part of the building I've never seen before. The walls aren't peeling here. There's a fresh-paint smell.

Earl's wrist vibrates and he glances at it. 'They're taking a little longer on the tour of the facility.'

'They're touring the facility?'

'Yeah.'

I can't believe it. They'll see all the stuff that's going on here.

'But what about the Agers?' I say.

'What about 'em?'

'Well, what if they see them?'

'They won't.'

'Or hear them?'

'It ain't your concern, kid.'

'It is, Earl. I'm going in there and lying to these people for Fates. I need to know what they've seen, what they know. What Fates has told them.'

'It's *Doctor* Fates to you. Show some respect. Stick to the script and you'll be fine.'

'But—'

'The Agers have been moved to soundproofed rooms. Okay?'

'I guess.'

'We're nearly at reception. You can wait there.'

'Aren't you coming to the meeting with me?'

'No. Doctor Fates'll be there though.'

'Shit,' I say.

Earl stops walking. His whole body bristles. He turns and he's so close to me, I step back but I hit the wall. He rests his hand by my head, his huge face right in front of mine.

'How many times? Watch your mouth.'

My heart hammers.

'And watch your mouth IN THERE. None of your deviant behaviour. You show you're strong, willing, and able to take orders – got that?'

I nod.

'And they're the ones asking the questions – not you. Right?'

'Yes.'

His nanocom buzzes right by my ear. He moves away. I don't feel strong, willing and able. I feel small and weak and alone.

Earl stops at some double doors and opens them, lets me through. I'm transported back to my old life, the world I used to live in. It's a reception area like at City Hospital. The doors shut behind me. Earl's left on the other side.

Straight ahead there are glass doors. And beyond them is outside. It's different to the dry, dead landscape I saw from the roof. There's a bit of neat garden. Grasses; green, black, red, and silver. A cactus with a purple flower. There's even a tree. A single tree. Broad enough that someone slight could be sat leaning against the trunk out of sight. Writing poems and singing. I rest my forehead on the glass. *Asha. Asha, are you there?*

60.

I know Asha isn't there. I turn away from the outside.

There's a light wood reception counter to the left. My chest thrums. Maybe there's a phone. I go round to the desk. No phone. I rummage through the drawers – not much in them except the bottom one. I close my fingers around a smooth object, shaped like a plectrum but thicker. A jolt of joy. I know what it is. A key. Like the one Gabe has. I'll be able to leave my room whenever I want. I'll be able to see Jem. I'll be able to get to Asha – when she arrives here. I crouch, slide the key into my sock. It rests there, like a pebble under my foot. A reminder that there's still hope. A way out.

Under the desk, there's a brochure. A photograph on the front. A group of people. It's us. Taylor, Veda, Shimmy, Jem and me.

Not quite right, though. Taylor's more pumped in the picture. Pretty sure he'd like it. Veda's hair is long, gleaming, instead of the pixie cut, a grin on her face, not her usual thoughtful frown. She doesn't have any crutches. She has two whole legs. What the hell is this?

The me in the photo is smiling, and I don't do much of that any more.

Shimmy is perfectly Shimmy. All sleek and satin. Except for her baby-blue eyes. They're empty, dead, like the life's been airbrushed out of her.

And Jem isn't Jem. Not Jem enough. It takes a moment to work out why.

His scar is gone.

Spiders scuttle up my spine. I reach to touch Jem's face. Have they really done that to him? Forced him under the knife? Injected nanomites into him?

'Calico?'

I jump and drop the brochure.

A tall black woman with close-cropped hair smiles at me.

'Yes, I'm Calico.' I walk round the desk and take the offered hand.

'I'm Cynthia, CEO of EarthKnit,' she says. 'I'm so pleased to meet you.'

I am suddenly conscious of my sweaty palms.

'Are you all right?' Cynthia asks.

'Bit nervous,' I manage.

'Just be yourself.'

Stick to the script, Earl says. *Be yourself*, Cynthia says.

Fates doesn't want me to be myself. And I don't even know if I have a self any more.

No Asha. Legally dead. Research material. Piece of meat.

The door is marked *Governor's Office*, but inside it could be my grandparents' living room. Patterned carpet, dark wood, heavy old furniture.

Fates is here. He's shrunk in the month since I last saw him. It's shocking. The armchair dwarfs him. His skin is yellowed like the pages in my Remembering Book. He *is* ill. Gabe was right that time up on the roof. And that was ages ago. I need to get things moving. If Fates dies, there'll be no one left who can help Asha. No one else knows anything about her.

'This is Calico Brown.' He introduces me to the rest of the room.

They're not what I expected, EarthKnit Protection Services. Sitting on the sofas and comfy chairs. No uniforms. Loose linen clothes. Three men, three women. All of them smiling at me.

'Welcome, Calico,' Cynthia says. 'We appreciate you taking the time to speak with us.'

I sit in a chair near her. There's a spasm in my lower belly. I press my thighs together in the pale trousers. Really hope my period is not about to start.

'I have to tell you,' Cynthia says. 'One of the reasons I'm so excited to meet you is that we share a birthday. We were born on the same day. In the same year.'

Oh.

I gaze round the room. They're all late fifties, early sixties. Older than Mum when I last saw her. This is what I'd look like now if I hadn't been frozen. They could be kids from my year at school, all grown up.

Fates clears his throat.

A red-haired woman is looking at me. Did she ask me something?

'I think Calico may be a little overwhelmed,' Cynthia says.

They all nod, serious.

'Of course,' a man with a moustache says.

Everyone smiles. Reassuring. Except for Fates.

'Sorry,' I say to the woman. 'What did you want to know?'

'I asked about your family,' she says.

Stick to the script. 'They're all dead.'

Her face falls. 'Oh, I'm so sorry.'

The others mutter condolences.

The hollow inside me shrinks a little. Maybe the world's not as bad out there as it is in here.

I glance at Fates. His mouth is thin, pressed tight. But it's going to be hard for me to stick to the script if the others don't know their lines.

They're all still looking at me. Drinking me in. It's weird. 'Um, did you want to ask me something?' I venture. 'About the – process?'

'That's Pete's area,' Cynthia says.

The white guy with a moustache leans forward. 'I think we're pretty much decided based on what we've seen already,' he says. 'But I guess it'd be good to hear your experience. What do you remember of reanimation?'

'Um. It was weird.'

Fates frowns.

Off script. My breath speeds up. 'It was like – I suddenly came back into myself. I had physical sensations, like pins and needles. I could hear the voices of the doctors. I was a bit confused, but then I remembered what was happening.'

239

'Right from the start?'

'Pretty much. Yes.'

'Astonishing.' Moustache man shakes his head.

'But then I was unconscious again—'

'The first phase of physiological rehabilitation is performed under sedation,' Fates says. 'It means that the reanimate gets back to a good level of physical fitness very quickly.'

'And how long from reanimation to what we see here?'

'Two months,' he says. 'In this case.'

Pete nods. 'Extraordinary. Still, the resources required are huge – metals, gases, drugs.'

'Worth it though, surely,' Fates says. 'To preserve your soldiers.'

'Protection Officers,' Cynthia says crisply. 'Warfare is rare these days. Fighting the viruses and mending the planet are the primary focus. Our ethos is to protect people and the earth, restore what we can. And as part of that, what we're concerned with is preserving knowledge, human wisdom. Now that technology is so sparse, so fragile.'

This fills me with a lightness. A hope for the world outside, for me and Asha when we get out of here.

'But you still need soldiers –' Fates shakes his head – 'peace-keeping forces, whatever you want to call them. And surely they'd welcome cryogenic suspension as a benefit of their employment.'

That's how he sold this to me.

But Cynthia's not buying. 'I think perhaps you've been shut in here too long, Doctor Fates. The world outside has changed a great deal.'

Fates looks over to Pete, the military moustache man. But he is nodding in agreement with Cynthia.

'I assume you've arranged meetings with the other main Protectors,' Cynthia says. 'Amplify, EcoHeal, etc. They'll tell you the same thing. Preserving knowledge is key.'

'Full cryogenesis is the best way to do that. We—'

'I disagree.'

Fates's voice crumbles away.

'Doctor Perez's Transference of Consciousness project is much more appropriate to our needs,' Cynthia says.

Fates waves a dismissive hand. 'Sophia has stopped work on TOC.'

'Yes, but Doctor Perez and I discussed the reasons behind that decision, and I'm hopeful that with the right support she'll be able to return to the project.'

'Sophia—'

'Doctor Perez, you mean. She has a double doctorate after all. Medicine. And ethics.'

The word hangs in the air.

'I suppose I'm rather avuncular towards her,' Fates blusters. 'She's still so young, not much experience of the world.'

'It's young people who get things done, Doctor Fates. Think what would have happened without Global

Eco President Thunberg. She started when she was a young girl.'

'Like all of us,' Pete says. 'The Green War was won by the young.'

'Experience is important, of course,' Cynthia says, 'but energy, and new ideas, and open-mindedness are driving forces too.'

'Surely there's a place for cryogenics in some form?' Fates almost whines.

'Perhaps,' Pete says. 'But the strengths of the TOC project over full-body cryogenics are clear. It requires far fewer resources. The extraction and storage processes are already pinned down. And the storage vessel is impervious to viruses, unlike the human body.'

'Yes,' Cynthia says. 'The next stages of the research, to access and engage with that store of human knowledge, are what we're interested in.'

Fates is silent. He somehow seems even smaller. Like Cynthia is the sea, eroding him. A wave of hope surges inside me. But it crashes when I think of Asha. We need the funding for cryogenics to save her.

'Let's move on,' Cynthia says. 'Brad, you had something?'

'Sure.' Brad radiates well-being. 'Hi, Calico.'

'Hi.'

'May I ask you a personal question?'

'Yeah.'

'Are you fertile?'

Oof. That wasn't in the script. 'Um, not as far as

I know.' Not really a lie, I tell myself. Despite the dull ache in my belly.

'I run the Motherhood,' Brad says.

'A breeding programme?' Fates asks.

A sharp spike of panic.

'A Reproduction Protection Programme,' Brad says. 'I thought perhaps some of your cryogenic subjects might be a possible source of reproductive materials. We could harvest from those who were frozen before fertility rates plummeted.'

My breath is coming too fast. I will it to slow.

'With consent, of course,' Brad says. 'I must stress we do not support the Forced Breeding Programmes. Our approach is wholly different.'

'Well, it's something we could consider looking into,' Fates says. 'With appropriate funding.'

But there aren't any more frozen people to harvest from. Not here, anyway. Only his mother. Oh. God. That's grim. A load of Lucas's siblings running round the planet.

'Well,' Cynthia says. 'I think we have all we need for now.'

'Gabe will see you out.' Fates stays in his chair.

I stand, hoping my period hasn't started while I'm wearing these pale clothes.

Cynthia shakes my hand. 'It was a pleasure to meet you, Calico. If I can be of any assistance to you after your time here is done, please do get in touch.'

She seems so kind, so real. I want to tell her about

Asha being in Russia. Ask her to help me. But Fates is too close. *Eyes and ears.*

I follow them to the reception area. Gabe is waiting by the external doors. He's wearing a shirt and trousers, his hair slicked back. I watch as Cynthia and co. go outside and through the garden. Will my key open that door? They climb on to a truck with *Fates Family Foundation* painted on the side.

'Come back in here, Calico,' Fates calls. 'I think we need a little chat.'

I make myself go into the office.

'That could have gone better,' he says.

'I did my best.'

'Did you?'

'Yes. They didn't seem that interested in cryogenics,' I say.

He stares at me with flinty eyes.

Another spasm in my belly. I squeeze my thighs together.

'We have to make them interested, Calico. *You* have to try harder.'

'I will,' I say. Anger churns in my chest. Despite the key pressing against my foot, I feel so trapped.

Fates slowly pulls himself up out of the chair and pauses a moment, straightening a little.

'Still,' he says, 'there may be an opportunity in that motherhood scheme.'

My heart stalls. Does he know? Is he going to sell me off to the Chosen?

'Not sure it would bring in much money,' I say, dry-mouthed.

He's reached the doorway. 'I only need enough to save my mother.'

'And Asha,' I say. 'And Asha.'

But he's already gone.

61.

asha

treading water

you have been
in the sea of souls
too long
treading water,
unfinished business
keeping you from shore.

time to cast your net, asha,
to send out threads,
to catch your sister
before it's too late for her.

62.

Calico

Waiting in this stupid reception area, I'm tortured by the outside being so close. Knowing the key is in my sock, but I daren't risk trying it in the door. Clammy with sweat in these stupid too-tight clothes. Period pain tugs at my guts. The meeting murmurs in my head. What does it mean for Asha, for me? Wish I'd had a chance to talk to Cynthia on my own. She was not what I was expecting from the training. None of them were.

At last Earl appears on the facility side of the reception doors. He beckons me through. I take one last look at outside and go to him. His tattoos are uncovered again. The clocks without hands. The crucifix that trails into a dagger dripping with blood.

I follow him along the hall, feel the key beneath my foot.

'Hope you behaved yourself in there,' he says.

'Tried my best.'

We're back in the peeling-paint corridors, a herd of Agers ahead. Gabe's there, encouraging them along from behind. There's a constant low grumble, moaning, crying. The sound of fading humans.

Fading humans. Fates. What he said after the meeting. The Motherhood. I'm not safe. Asha's not safe. But also, the world doesn't seem to be what he thinks it is, either. Things have changed, and he hasn't kept up. Maybe there will be another way—

Wait. What was that?

Weaving through the low rumble of the Agers. A laugh, like coins falling.

Shimmy?

I push past Earl, but he grabs my arm, pulls me back the way we've come.

'Was that Shimmy?' I ask.

'Shimmy's gone.' He drags me round a corner and along the corridors until we're at my room. When we stop I yank my arm away from him.

'Earl,' I say. '*Was* that Shimmy?'

'You need to forget about her.' He pushes me through the doorway.

My breathing slows. It was Shimmy. I'm sure. Her laugh. And I don't want to forget about her. I only actually know a few people now, and she's one of them. I want her to be okay.

I rip off the meeting clothes. No period, which is a relief in one way. But the low grumble in my belly means it'll be arriving at some point soon. It's more stressful not knowing when. The key falls out of my sock.

I leave it on the edge of the sink while I shower off the stress sweat of the meeting. Once I'm dressed I take the key, put my finger on the indent. The top divides into two, like a stag beetle opening its wings. Underneath is green on one side and red on the other. I touch the green and nothing happens.

No! Please!

I tap the green again and my bedroom door slowly opens.

Freedom. The urge to go out there and run and run spurts through me. But no. I need a plan. Can't waste this. I touch the red and the door slides shut.

For once, I'm in control.

I put the key straight back into my sock. Safe.

Gabe brings me dinner.

'You okay?' he asks.

First time he's spoken to me since that night on the roof.

'Yeah,' I say. 'You?'

He messes with his hair. Nods.

'Sorry if we got you in trouble, me and Jem.'

'Earl'd find trouble for me to be in whatever. Don't worry about it.'

'Thanks. Have you seen Jem? Is he okay?'

'He's bein' very . . . Jem.' Gabe smiles.

'That's good.' I think.

'Anyways, you got another meetin' next week,' he says, 'so you're back to trainin' tomorrow.'

'Great.'

He smiles again. 'That bad?'

'It's just boring.' I bat it away. Shouldn't give him anything to tell Fates. Need to be on my best behaviour until I've managed to get this money in and get Asha here.

But, yes, that bad.

63.

I double tap the key. The door opens straightaway. I pause outside Jem's room, rest my head against the door. But, no, not yet. First, Shimmy. I have to see if she's still here.

The hallways are quiet and dark. In the hospital wing the lights are on low. I sneak into the ward. A lifetime's passed since I came here looking for Asha. There are fewer patients in here now. What's happened to them all? Still and silent mounds in some of the beds. Except for one, in the far corner. There's a lamp on, someone half-sitting.

'You come to visit with me, sugar?'

Goosebumps, ghost bumps. 'Shimmy?'

'Who else?' The copper of her voice has turned to lead.

I make my way to the bed.

Her peachy skin has creased into crepe paper, the bones beneath pronounced, like her skull's forcing its way out.

The hollow inside me wails. Shimmy is an Ager.

She pats the side of her bed. There's plenty of room; she's smaller than ever. I push away the flash of Asha. Tiny, dead bird.

'How do I look?' Shimmy smiles. Her eyes are bright blue, huge in the hollows of her face. But her front tooth's missing.

'Pretty,' I say, too slow.

'Liar.' Her laugh's rusty. 'Never was pretty.' She holds up her hand as I protest. The skin wrinkles at her wrist like a sleeve pushed back. 'You can paint pretty on the outside of anyone. I never was pretty, not underneath.'

'That's not true,' I say. However much she wound us up, she brought something to those shut-in rooms, to all of us. A warmth, a light. 'We've missed you,' I say. And that's not a lie.

'Oh, sugar.' She pats my hand. 'Sweet of you to say. I missed you, too. Now all I got is silence and waiting to get better.'

There's a spark of hope inside me. Maybe that drip in her arm is full of anti-ageing nanomites or something. Maybe they can cure the accelerated ageing now.

Her bony fingers pluck at the blanket. 'My head's been so messy,' she whispers. 'Like it's filled with tangled ribbons. I can't get unwound. More I try, tighter the tangle. Keep seeing stuff that happened before, or maybe not. I don't know any more.'

'What kind of stuff?'

'There's this man keeps asking me questions. Who I am, when's my birthday. *I* don't know. Been lying about that for years. He's got this book, says it's mine. Asks me if I remember what I wrote in it.' Her gaze drifts to the ceiling, her mouth open. Drool pools and drips on to her chin.

I reach forward, wipe it away with a corner of the sheet.

'Oh, thank you, sugar,' she says. 'Where was I?'

'You were saying about the man and your Remembering Book?' Because I'm pretty sure that's what it was. And now I understand why they make us write in it. The control in an experiment. So they can see if our memories have deteriorated.

'The man, yes. He's got this voice like ice. Freezes you.'

Lucas.

'Doctor Fates?' I say.

She nods. 'That's him. He asks me if I know what happened to me. How I died. And I tell him car accident with my family. And he says no, that's not what happened, that's the lie you tell.' She drifts again. Blue eyes blinking at nothing.

'Shimmy?'

'The man says, they're all alive, your family. "What about Bobby?" I ask him. His head moves, ever so slight. "Your brother?" he asks. "No, my dog," I say. And you know what he says then, sugar?'

I shake my head.

'"Ah. No," he says. "Your dog *is* dead."' A tear slips down her creased cheek.

'Oh, Shimmy, I'm sorry.'

'Daddy makes more money out of me dead.'

Sadness leaches from her.

'Better for them if I'm dead, or frozen, or getting treatment in a facility. They'll be playing me on the radio all the time.'

I don't know what to say. Her own family wouldn't want her dead or living like this, would they? But then, if they're so rich, why's she still in here? She wouldn't have needed to sign up for the study in lieu of payment like I did.

Shimmy sighs.

'You still have Nick.' I want to make her feel better, give her hope, but as soon as I say it, I know it's wrong.

Her eyelids droop. 'Nick's not gonna want me now.' She pinches the sagging skin on her arm. 'Pretty sure he only does perfect.'

'But if he loves you . . .'

'I might look naive, sugar, but I'm not.' She rests her head on the pillow, closes her eyes. A tear slips out. 'I overheard them once. Him and that doctor man. I was a perk of the job for Nick. I painted pretty on that, too. Turned it into a romance. But I was payment for services rendered, that's what the doctor said. He didn't care about me.'

There's an angry drumbeat in my head. Fates 'owns' us, thinks he can barter us, sell us, use us to further his own agenda. He's taken away our right to choose, to consent. Jem was right about that all along.

'Well, you have me, us – we're your friends,' I say.

'Aw, sugar. That's sweet. I just wish Bobby hadn't died. He loved me, that dog did, like no one else.'

'I'm sure your family love you,' I say.

'Maybe they did once. But money warps love.'

253

'How d'you get so wise, Shimmy?' I want to make her smile, but it doesn't work.

'The world don't want people like me going round being wise. They only want me for what I can bring 'em.'

There's a question pressing at me. I don't know how to ask, not sure I want to know the answer, but: 'How long have you been in the facility, Shimmy?'

'I don't know, sugar.'

'More than two years?'

She nods. 'That must've passed a long time back.'

Her words drop heavy on my shoulders, a sudden certainty that none of us is getting out of here after our two years. Or maybe ever. Fates has lied to us over and over.

Shimmy shuffles down till her head's fully on the pillow.

I go round to turn the lamp off.

'Leave it on,' she says. 'I don't like the dark.'

'Okay.' I lean in, kiss her forehead. 'Night.'

'What's your name, sugar?'

Ice-cold spiders walk up my neck.

'Calico. I'm Calico.'

64.

asha

echo

an echo of calico
finally comes
on the shimmer
of a butterfly wing.

the lightest touch,
it takes you back
to when you were small.

calico drawing
with her finger
on your bare skin.
you had to guess
what the picture was.

you never guessed right
the first time.
didn't want your turn
to end,
that shiver on your skin.

65.

Calico

I walk back along the dark hallways. Shimmy didn't know who I was. The Ageing's not supposed to happen to teenagers. But it's happened to her. Are the rest of us going to get it, too? My heart speeds up. That's what the Remembering's about. Keeping track of our minds to see if we're sliding into dementia. I shudder. And how long ago was Shimmy reanimated? How long has she been here? Are we all trapped here for the rest of our very short lives?

I breathe deep. No. I have a key now. I'm not trapped. Not by locks and doors and walls anyway. Only by love.

But. Oh God, Shimmy's sad, loveless life.

Whatever else was wrong, Mum always loved me. Yeah, she was stressed and messed up sometimes. But that was because she loved us so much. What happened with Asha tore her into tiny pieces, and she hadn't patched herself back together.

Maybe Shimmy's right; maybe money warps love. We never had much of that so I wouldn't know.

Or maybe love just gets warped sometimes.

Like, Fates – all this horror out of love for the mum he never even knew.

And me. What I've done for Asha. Thought I was giving her another chance, more options, a choice.

And Jem. He loves his brother so much, blames himself for his death, and it's eating him up.

Jem.

I stop outside his room. Moths skip through the hollow. I knock on the door, slide the key in two and press the green.

Jem's on the bed, curled like a woodlouse, his back to me, bare and bruised. He's so still, so quiet. So un-Jem, not twitching or muttering, that I'm scared to go over to him.

'Fuck off,' he says.

Relief makes me laugh. 'Is that addressed to me or someone I can't see?'

He unfolds, turns. 'Calico?'

'That's my name.'

'Are you real?' He's up, coming to me.

'Yes, I'm real.'

'How did you get in here?' His hands on my shoulders, he examines my face. 'Are you okay? Did they hurt you?'

'I'm okay.'

He still has his scar. They haven't changed him. I touch it with my fingertips. 'You all right?' I keep it light. I see the shadows behind his eyes.

'Feel like I'm going mad,' he says.

'Madder?'

He grimaces. 'Yeah, madder.'

'What did they do to you? Did someone hit you?'

He points at his right shoulder. 'I did it to myself. Tried to break the door down. Couldn't stand the silence.'

'Stan not talking to you?'

He shakes his head. 'I can't hear him any more, Calico. What if they've killed him? Because of what we did.'

My heart twists. Now he's blaming himself twice for Stan's death. And that's my fault. I put the idea in his head that Stan might be frozen. And I slipped into his room that night, his bed, his arms . . .

'Jem, he's already dead.'

'You said – you said he was frozen—'

'Might be, I said he might be.' I clear my throat. 'I've found out a lot of stuff since I last saw you.' I take his hand and we sit on the bed.

I tell him about the creepy meeting in the Cryostore, the Soul Holders, about Fates's mother, how she's the only frozen left here. How Asha is in Russia, and Stan *could* be too. Handing out hope like Smarties. I tell him about the key, and the Protection Services meeting with EarthKnit.

I stop talking.

He shakes his head. 'Worse even than my paranoid little brain imagined.'

'Yeah.' I lean into him, his skinny warmth. His scent of salt and soap.

I can't tell him about Shimmy. It's too much. It's too hard. I don't want to weigh him down with what's going to happen to us all. He's my only escape.

Jem kisses gentle, touches like a question, soft and sweet. We're not supposed to do this. We're not supposed to be together. But I don't want to stop. It's the only thing that brings me any peace. He's the only thing that brings me peace.

My face is wet. Jem's crying.

'What is it?' I say.

He wipes his eyes with the heel of his hand. 'Thought I'd lost you. Thought I'd fucked everything up.'

I stroke his hand. 'No. No, you didn't.'

'I spent more time thinking about you than Stan.'

'And you feel guilty?'

He nods.

'Me too.' I do feel guilty. About these moments with him that melt Asha from my mind. That, Fates said, *jeopardise* her.

But still, I want to wrap Jem up, somewhere soft and warm, somewhere safe.

We lie back, holding hands. I can hear Jem breathing. It's like the sound of the sea.

We used to play a recording of the sea to help Asha sleep. After the first hospital stay. She was only small. When she got home from months in the hospital, she didn't seem to know how to fall asleep any more.

Asha's face from back then is so clear to me. Her big eyes, drooping into sleep as the room filled with the sound of the tide coming in over sand, like the earth breathing. Even when she'd drifted off, I'd leave it on. Calming, somehow. Reassuring. Life. Breath.

'What you thinking about?' Jem says.

'Asha.'

He turns, pulls me close to his chest. His heart flutters like a trapped bird. And I get another Asha flash.

She sits in a hospital bed, folding paper into swans. Origami. She found a book on it in the hospital school room. I was crap at it. No patience, fingers too fat, too fast. Asha would sit for hours, the patient patient, creating something out of nothing at all.

The Asha image slips, changes into Shimmy. Small, ancient, wise, in a pool of light, because she's scared. But she shimmers like a candle in the darkness of this place.

66.

asha

message

copper-tinged,
a part-soul brings
a message:
her wings
have brushed
against calico

and asha,
you must follow
her gossamer trail
towards the truth.
your truth.

67.

Calico

Perfect timing. My period finally arrived yesterday and today's the meeting with EcoHeal. I tried to wear my long jumper over these ridiculous pale trousers but Earl wouldn't have it. I am so stressed the blood will leak that I barely take in what's being said until I hear Fates ask about breeding programmes. EcoHeal call theirs the Redistribution of Fertility Resources Department. Fates has a lot of questions about it. I sit tense throughout, my whole body squeezed tight, nausea rising with every word.

Finally, they move on. They're not interested in Doctor Perez's Transference of Consciousness project. Nanomedicine seems to be their thing. Fates taps his nanocom and after a while Veda swings into the room on her crutches, with Doctor Perez walking behind.

Shit. I hope EcoHeal haven't seen that brochure.

'Perhaps you could tell us about your disability, Veda? Were you born with it?'

'I wasn't born with it, no. My leg was damaged during cryogenic suspension and amputated when I was reanimated.'

I didn't know that. Fates must be desperate if he's telling EcoHeal about it.

'Tissue fracture can occur during cooling, although it's rare,' Doctor Perez says. 'Veda's experience is unusual.'

'And you aim to regrow the whole leg?'

'Yes. We harvest cells from Veda's bones, muscles, arteries, etc. for tissue regeneration.'

'How does it feel, Veda?'

'The harvesting's – unpleasant. It's tiring, so we have to limit how much we can do at once.'

'We'll soon be at the point where we can stop harvesting,' Doctor Perez says. 'The cells are multiplying and forming new structures in our lab. Eventually we will "grow" a new leg.'

'How long will that take?'

'The timescales are not clear currently,' Doctor Perez says.

Fates coughs. 'Thank you, Sophia. Perhaps you could accompany the girls back to their rooms.'

We drop Veda off first.

'Are you all right, Calico?' Doctor Perez asks. 'You look pale.'

'Just stressed. My period started yesterday and I've been shitting a brick I'd leak blood while they're talking about breeding programmes,' I say. 'Why these trousers have to be such a light colour—'

'Oh, I didn't think about that.'

'Can you get me some more pads?'

'I'll try.'

God knows what I'll do if she can't.

We pass the hospital wing. The groans of the Agers echo from the walls.

Shimmy's face drifts into my mind, an old lady with baby-blue eyes.

I turn to Doctor Perez. 'Can I ask you something?'

'Of course.'

'Is there anything you can do for the Agers? A cure? A way to hold it back?'

She frowns. 'Not at the moment.'

'So, there's no hope.' It drips away like melting snow.

'Eventually we may be able to reverse the damage, but it's keeping them alive until then that's the issue. They fade so fast. If we had the facilities, we could re-suspend them at the first sign of it.'

'You could freeze them again?'

'Theoretically.'

We walk in silence for a while. Shimmy's face hovers in my mind. Maybe there's a sliver of light. And another reason to get this funding.

I wait awhile after Doctor Perez leaves me and then go to see Jem.

He's not here.

His drawing of Stan's been ripped from the wall, pages scattered about the place. Blanket and sheet crumpled on the floor. I swallow down panic – the night of the party. Asha, gone when I got back, her room in disarray. Is this my fault too? Have they been monitoring us?

I pick up one of the pieces of paper. Stan's eye stares

up at me. I fold it. And then again, until it is sort of an origami swan. It's wonky, rubbish, not as good as Asha used to do. I leave it on Jem's pillow.

Back in my room, I strip off the pale khaki outfit, shower, get into my soft worn clothes. It's disturbing that they have the comfort of home.

No. This is not home. Asha is home. Mum.

Jem, maybe.

Where is he?

Shimmy was here one day and gone the next. Falling fast into the Ageing. What if, what if that happens to Jem?

The hollow yawns inside me. It'll never go away. I can never fill it up.

I dream of Asha, in sepia. She holds out her hand. Not to me, to someone at the side of her, out of shot. Asha's smiling. She doesn't look sick or scared. She looks strong.

68.

Earl batters into my room like a bad-tempered storm, slams the breakfast tray down on the desk. He has a black eye.

'What happened to you?'

'Not your concern.' He scowls. 'Eat up. Doctor Fates wants to see you.'

There's news already? From one of the Protection Services?

We pass Gabe with some Agers. I check them over out of habit but none of them is Shimmy. Maybe I can make a deal with Fates. Maybe with funds coming in he can re-freeze Shimmy like Doctor Perez said. Maybe there's still time to save her.

We're at the staircase leading to the Cryostore. Is Lucas down there all the time now? Has he moved his office here deep in the earth? The chill seeps through my clothes and into my bones.

He's waiting for me, hunched behind the desk. Through the archway, I see the Soul Holders on their shelves, opals tumbling behind blue glass.

'Thank you, Earl,' he says.

'I can stay, sir.'

'No, no, that's quite all right. You're not going to be any trouble are you, Calico?' Fates smiles, but his eyes stay glassy and hard.

'No.'

'Behave yourself, kid.'

Me and Lucas Fates alone together again. It rarely ends well. But I've done what he asked this time. Stuck to the script.

'We have an offer of investment,' Fates says.

Butterflies rise inside me.

'Unfortunately, it specifically excludes anything related to cryogenics.'

My guts tumble. 'So, Asha's not coming?'

'No. Not yet.'

'Can't you siphon off some money for your mum and Asha?'

'That would hardly be ethical, Calico.'

'Since when has that stopped you?'

He has the grace to incline his head. 'Unfortunately, EarthKnit have chosen to bypass me, and Doctor Perez has control of the finances. Apparently her ethics are unquestionable.'

So Cynthia doesn't trust him either.

'Still we have one last chance. There's a final meeting for you to attend, with Amplify. You must get them to agree to the funding specifically for cryogenics. My mother's life depends upon it.'

And Asha's.

I swallow down anger and exhaustion. 'How? How am I supposed to convince them when I couldn't with the others?'

'Ah. This time, I want you to tell the truth.'

'What?' Is this some kind of trap?

'Tell them what you did for your sister. Tell them about Asha, how you're waiting for her to be cured and then reanimated but the funding's run out.'

First, I have to lie, now tell the truth.

'Have you told them about your mother?' I ask.

'No. I need to be seen as scientific, objective, not emotionally involved. Whereas you – well, I've seen how our visitors responded to you at the other meetings. They seem to warm to you. They seem to like you.'

'Not enough to give us the funding.' *Us?* He's got me thinking like him now. Wait. Maybe there's a way I can use this.

'So, you want to use *my* story, my sister's story, to get the money to save *your* mum.'

'You could put it like that.' His smile is empty.

'There's something I want in exchange. Something extra.'

'Still developing the negotiation skills, I see. And what is it you want?'

'Shimmy. I know she's still here.'

The smile slides from his face.

'I know she has the Ageing—'

'Who told you?'

'No one. I heard her, and then I saw her.' Not lies. 'There must be something you can do to help her.'

Fates is silent. He stares at the desk so long I think he's fallen asleep. Then he looks at me. 'Come,' he says.

He gets up shakily. His walking has got slower. We

pass the Soul Holder shelves and go through into the chamber with his mother's cryopod.

He points to the corner where another dented pod is propped against the wall. 'It's not functional yet,' he says.

'What – how – where did you get it?'

'Gabe discovered it in an outbuilding.'

'Are there any more?'

'Sadly not. They were all sold. And this one needs repairing. But it *will* be functional. The question is, Calico, who should occupy it? Shimmy? Or your sister?'

His words thud into me, bullets of ice.

'Asha's not here,' he says, 'but she *is* safely suspended in Russia. Shimmy is rapidly deteriorating, and she's here. Shall I save the pod for Asha when she eventually gets here? Or shall we preserve what's left of Shimmy now? You know, I'm tired of making all the decisions – this one's on you.'

I have turned to stone. Can't move. Can't think.

'Come on. The choice is yours,' he says.

No, no.

It makes me sick to admit it, but he's right. Asha's already safely suspended. Shimmy's fading fast, right here, in front of me.

'If you freeze Shimmy –' the words grate in my throat – 'how long will it be till you can reverse the Ageing and reanimate her?'

'I honestly don't know.'

'And the cure for Asha?'

'There's still no treatment.'

He's giving me a choice, but it's impossible.

I don't know why I'm even asking these questions. There's only one answer for me. And he knows it.

'Asha,' I whisper. 'Keep it for Asha.'

He nods with a sickly smile. 'See what you'll do for love,' he says. 'You're no different to me.'

69.

My mind rages all night over the choice I made. Asha over Shimmy. It makes me sick that Fates is right. I *am* like him. One half of me screams: how could you have chosen Asha? She's safe, in Russia. Shimmy's not safe, and she's got no one taking care of her. And the other side of me repeats: she's my sister, *my sister!* What else would I do?

Earl brings breakfast in. 'You look awful, kid.'

'Thanks.'

'S'pose it might get you a pity vote.'

I can't eat. I sip at water.

At least I don't have to wear the light khaki clothes for the Amplify meeting, or put make-up on.

It's me and one other person. No one else in the room. I could tell him anything, the old man with glasses who sits and listens quietly to my story about Asha. When I finish, he says the world has changed fast over the last few decades, and Amplify's priorities are the planet and virus control. The needs of the many outweigh the wants of an individual. He tells me everyone has lost someone, everyone has sacrificed something, and I have to get used to life without my sister. That's the way it is.

Earl takes me to Fates. What the Amplify man said replays in my head. Little splinters of truth. My selfishness, my hypocrisy – guilt over what I've done to Shimmy. Me, saving Asha, at the expense of another. Am I only thinking about what I want, and not what the world needs? Am I like Fates? Is that who I am now?

'Well?' Fates breaks into my thoughts. 'How did it go?'

'I tried my best.'

'Let's hope it was good enough.'

Hope. That's all we have.

70.

I'm untethered, drifting through the hallways behind Earl. Bodiless, ethereal. Like part of me has dislocated. My mind's full of mist. What have I done to Shimmy? Who have I become? Have I lost myself?

Jem's voice breaks through the fog. Loud, disturbed. I'm at the day room and Earl has gone.

There's another bruise on Jem's face. And his hand's swollen. He's so agitated, he doesn't even notice me. Or perhaps I'm invisible now. His head jerks about and he's speaking too fast for me to catch what he's saying. Taylor holds his arms, looks right into his eyes. 'Calm down, Jem.'

Veda nods at me. 'Stan's back,' she says.

Oh. There's a double stab in my heart. Jem's got Stan back. But I still can't hear Asha. Stan is back with Jem. And that takes Jem away from me.

It's what I deserve. If he finds out all the things I've done, he'll hate me anyway.

The edges of the hollow peel away until I'm inside out.

Jem's voice gets louder. He thrashes against Taylor. 'Stan's right. It should've been me.'

'No, Jem.'

'Always knew I'd die young. It was meant to be me.'

His pain's so raw, so real. I move closer to him. But

he doesn't see me. His eyes are glazed. His scar is vivid on one cheek, the bruise spreading purple on the other. What the hell has Earl done to him this time?

'And then Stan had to go and die in a really fucking stupid way, and it's all my fault and—'

'Shut up about Stan!' Taylor shouts.

Jem steps away, suddenly silent.

'You talk about him all the time. But Stan's dead.'

Jem's head twitches.

'He's not here any more.'

'He *is*. I can fucking hear him.'

'You spend all your time talking to him, *about* him, comparing yourself to him. How he was so clever and attractive and good at everything. And how you aren't—'

'Yeah, exactly,' Jem says.

'But you're different people. Good at different things. You're not only his younger, not as clever, not as good-looking brother. You're you. Bet he couldn't draw like you.'

'Maybe not,' Jem mutters.

'And you look good to me.' Taylor clears his throat. 'Least, when you're not all battered. And I absolutely, totally, know this about you, Jem: no way you'd have gotten into a car stoned and driven your friends to their death.'

Veda gasps. Jem reels like Taylor punched him. His fists clench.

But Taylor stands his ground. 'Which makes you

a better person than Stan,' he says. 'A million million times. So next time you compare yourself to him, think about that.'

'I should've stopped him,' Jem says.

Taylor slumps on to the sofa. 'I've got older brothers,' he says. 'Stan would not have listened if you'd tried to stop him. Probably would've made him drive even more wildly. You'd likely be dead, too.' Taylor gives a sad smile. 'Well, you know what I mean. I like you, Jem, for who *you* are. Stan's a *part* of your life, but not all of it, not all of who you are. And you're wasting this life, this second chance, thinking about him all the time.'

'Taylor's right,' Veda says. 'Who your brother was, what he did, doesn't define you. You can go and be whatever, whoever, you want to be.'

Jem is still and quiet.

It's like Taylor took hold of me and gave me a shake.

Jem's sense of who he is, that's all tied up with Stan. He can't see who he is, who he could be, separate from his brother.

Is it the same for me and Asha?

I drop on to the sofa next to Taylor.

It was always me and Asha together against the world. Dickhead disappearing dads. Overworked mum. Stupid strict grandparents. Asha's 'friends' who drifted away, stopped coming round to see her. Mine, who didn't ask me to do things any more because I'd said no so many times. But what did they know about anything? They didn't have to deal with the illness, the treatments, the puking, the bone-deep exhaustion, the always looking on the bright side, talking to doctors and solicitors and . . .

Not their fault. And I'm glad my friends never had to deal with all that. Watching someone you love fight and fade, over and over.

Still, it made me and Asha different. Special.

And maybe I lost sight of who I was, other than being Asha's sister. Even stuff I loved like running was put on hold to get her through the next treatment.

Here, in this weird place, I'm just me. And I'm still messing it up. Doing a shit job at being me.

The room sways, or maybe it's my body.

'You okay?' Taylor puts his arm around my shoulder.

The world blurs.

Jem kneels in front of me. 'Calico,' he says. 'You don't always have to be so strong. It's okay to cry.'

And I do.

I cry for Asha, and for Mum.

I cry for Jem, and Stan.

I cry for Shimmy.

And I cry for me.

71.

asha

diamonds

tears
like diamonds,
hard and bright,
echo through
to you.

made in the
deep dark
earth of denial,
dug from
the mine
of her mind
at last.

calico is crying.

treasure
for you, asha.
breadcrumbs,
stepping stones,
a path.
your path.

72.

Calico

<u>Day 66</u>

No more memories. I need to be in the now. I'm all cried out. Tired. Tired of all the secrets, the lies. My own and everyone else's. I'm tired of having no control. Tired of being this version of me. The me this place has made. But I've got a plan now. To find out more. About Asha, Stan, Shimmy. There must be a way to save them all.

I wait until it's dark and go to collect Jem. We walk hand in hand. The kind of thing you'd do in normal life, but we never have. I feel him twitch, a pulse in his fingers. The hallways are dark. We pause at every corner. But no End Stagers haunt the halls tonight, and there are no staff about either.

The stairwell has a dim light. We go down to the next level and stop at the Records Room. Chill air curls around us from below. The Cryostore. Death row. I shudder.

'You okay?' Jem whispers in my ear.

'Yeah.' I'm not though. Still haven't told him about Shimmy, and the guilt, the shame, lurks inside my hollow. I'm worried about what we'll find – or not find – in here too. Maybe Earl already burned our records.

I get out the key, slide its smoothness apart and press the green.

The door to the Records Room opens.

A light turns on as we walk in. The air tastes stale.

It's as Gabe said, that time up on the roof. A narrow room. Wooden shelves with cardboard boxes. A concrete ledge sticks out of the wall, overflowing in-trays on top, papers waiting to be filed. Waiting a long time by the look of the dust, thick as velvet.

My heartbeat quickens but there are hardly any actual files inside the boxes. Not for me or Asha, anyway. And not for Stan. But Jem has one.

I hear him swallow as he opens the cardboard folder. He lifts out a single sheet of paper. 'Fuck,' he says. 'So, she did do it.'

He shows me the cryogenic consent form. It's signed by his mother.

He walks over to the wall, slumps to the floor.

'That's good though, right?' I ask.

He looks up at me, scowling.

'I mean because *she* did it, your mum, not someone you don't know. It's like Shimmy said. It's what a mother would do.'

He sighs. 'Maybe.'

I smile at him.

There are still the papers on the ledge to check. Flicking through, name after name, my eyes itch. Dates of death, dates of reanimation, dates of re-death. All completed in messy doctor scrawl. But causes of re-death, all those boxes are left empty.

Re-death.

I get a flash of Shimmy, ancient and frail.

Jem's head rests on his knees.

There's nothing of any use here. It's a dead end.

Fates has *my* file, I know it. He took the photographs of Asha from it. Asha dead. Asha in Russia.

Like I've conjured him, Fates speaks out in the hallway. His voice is the sound of ice cracking. Doctor Perez is with him, soothing, melodic. I hold my breath. Jem cringes into the corner as they pass by the Records Room. Their footsteps echo in the stairwell. Down they go to the Cryostore. To Isabella Fates and the souls trapped in jars.

I open the door a crack and peep out. All clear.

'We going back?' Jem whispers.

'Not yet. I want to see what they're up to.'

'Calico—'

'You stay here,' I whisper.

I sneak out into the corridor, heart pounding. Jem catches my arm.

'What are you doing?' he mouths.

I shrug him off and slip softly down the stone steps towards the Cryostore. Jem follows me down, along the hallway and to the room at the end.

I take a deep breath. We should go back. We can't get caught. Can't risk losing the key.

But then I hear: 'You're so kind to bring me here, Sophia.'

They must be in the small chamber with his mother's cryopod. I pass the Soul Holders. Jem is just behind me. Fates says something about running out of time.

'I'm concerned about your health, Doctor Fates. You shouldn't wander around by yourself.'

Is he that ill he can't walk unattended?

'I wanted to see Mother.' He sighs. 'The pod's not going to withstand much more patching, is it?'

'No,' Doctor Perez says.

'Will we get the funding in time?'

Funding? He said there wasn't any for cryogenics.

'I'm doing all I can. But they're only partway through their due diligence,' Doctor Perez says. 'We may not be approved.'

'We must be, Sophia. What can I do to make it happen?'

'You could talk to Earl.'

'Earl?'

'The boys—'

'He's trying to help you prepare for Project C.'

Project C? What's that? Some other hideous thing they've come up with. Or – oh. The Chosen?

'I don't need his help.' Perez's voice is sharp.

'Earl means well, Sophia.'

'I disagree. What he's doing is verging on physical assault. I can't stand by and let that happen to my patients. Jem in particular does not respond well to coercion.'

'Ha,' Fates says. 'Indeed.'

I look at Jem.

He raises his eyebrows at me.

Doctor Perez is speaking again. 'Jem's already suffering from post-traumatic stress, and you know how I feel about the delay in giving him counselling. It is ethically dubious at the very least. And if word gets out about Earl's behaviour, the reputation of the facility will be damaged and that would be catastrophic for Project C, and any future plans.'

'But still,' Fates says. 'Earl has a point. It might speed things up.'

'It's not worth jeopardising the project.' Her voice is firm. 'If you won't stop Earl, I can take the project elsewhere. Cynthia has offered a purpose-built lab.'

'No need for that, Sophia. I'll talk to Earl again.'

'Thank you, Doctor Fates. I'll leave you to have a moment with your mother, but we should go back soon. It's nearly time for your serum.'

Jem and I tiptoe to the hallway, up the stairs and into the Records Room.

We wait silently, so close I can hear Jem's heart beating.

Fates coughs as they pass by. My whole body tenses till they've gone. 'What did Earl do to you, Jem?' I whisper.

'Don't want to talk about it.'

I touch the bruise on his cheek. 'You can tell me. What did he do?'

'He came for me with a bloody great syringe.'

'Like before?'

'No. It was bigger. And he was trying to put it in my eye.'

'What the—?'

'Yeah. I know. I freaked and punched him. He went for me again, but Fates called him off.'

'He was there?'

'By then he was. Gabe had run off and got him.'

'Gabe was there too?'

'Yeah. He's not so bad. He really doesn't like Earl either.' Jem sniffs. 'Anyway, I can't sleep, knowing Earl could come for me in the night, sedate me and do something I don't know about. Can't eat, in case he's put something in the food to knock me out.' He shakes the piece of paper. 'And my fucking mum signed me up for this.'

I wrap my arms around him. He presses his forehead to mine.

'And there's nothing here?' he says. 'About Stan?'

I shake my head.

Not a thing about Stan, or Asha, or Shimmy.

73.

asha

blue souls

the diamond tears lead you
to a strange and secret place
where blue souls are trapped,
by a fractured man.

angel saviour devil ghost,
there was love in him once,
but now he's like
a putrid pear,
core rotted away.
what made him
who he was,
gone bad.

calico echoes
all around this space
but soul reaching
shows you
she's not one of
the blue.

your sister's
still alive,
but she's trapped too.
she's in a kind of limbo
just like you.

74.

Calico

My room feels empty, like the hollow inside.

We found out nothing that night in the Records Room, except that Earl's nearly as batshit as Fates, and Jem's mum did do the thing he thought she never would. At least Jem has an answer. He knows something he didn't before. I still don't know if Mum's alive, or if what Fates told me about Asha is true. Whether she is, or ever will be, safe or well. I'll only know that if I can get to her in Russia. But how? Another country. I don't have a passport. I don't exist. That's what Fates said. I'm legally dead.

What if none of his money-making schemes come off? What if his mum's cryopod fails? What if he dies and we're left in the hands of Earl? What if it's the Chosen for me?

All day, every day, everything spirals and loops in my head like one of Asha's doodles on fast forward. Asha. Mum. Jem. Shimmy. Stan. The Chosen. The Ageing.

Weeks of kitchen duty, cleaning, laundry, resocialisation, sweet sleeps with Jem, have drifted by while I've been lost in my head.

It's no good. I need to *do* something.

'You okay?' Jem asks me as Gabe takes us back to our rooms.

I nod. 'Tonight. We'll try Fates's office,' I whisper.

'Okay.'

Maybe there'll be other files there. Some kind of document. Anything that'll help us.

It's the last place I want to go. But I'm running out of options.

I wait until after the lights fully fade and open the door, check for End Stagers. I don't like to disturb them. They're fixed on a route, to a destination they see in their own minds, but which is somewhere in their past. They'll never reach it, but they'll never know that. They don't scare me any more. But becoming one does.

I let a few moments go by and no one passes. No one coming from either direction. I knock for Jem. He stands there ready.

The smile falls from his face. 'Fuck,' he says.

There's a waft of air behind me, the hairs on my neck shift, goosebumps, ghost bumps. Jem pulls me behind him.

'No,' he whispers. 'Shimmy?'

Shit. I move out in front of Jem.

There she is. Shimmy. Ancient. Or a ghost come to haunt me for what I've done to her. She drifts to a stop, leans against the wall. Her hair is silver, face so pale. Skin drapes from her tiny frame, like she's melting away. Her blue eyes are glazed with white.

'Jesus,' Jem says. 'What the—'

'She's an End Stager,' I whisper.

I go over to Shimmy.

She touches my face with papery fingers. 'Where's my baby girl?' she says. 'I've lost my baby girl.' Her voice is low, slow, like a breath that's running out.

'It's okay, Shimmy,' I say.

'What the fuck?' Jem says. 'This is not okay.'

Shimmy cowers against me.

'You're scaring her,' I say to Jem.

'She's the fucking scary one.'

No. I am. I let this happen to her. I made the choice between her and Asha.

Shimmy sucks back saliva. Tremors run through her body. She slides down the wall till she's a tiny heap on the floor.

I sit next to her.

Jem paces the hallway, muttering. Head twitching.

I hold Shimmy's hand in mine, stroke the dry leaf skin, the bones like twigs. 'I'm sorry, Shimmy,' I whisper. 'So sorry.'

'Be here awhile with me, sugar.' Her head droops forward like the words wore her out. And then she starts to hum. Makes me shiver. I close my eyes. Shimmy's breath wavers, and I take up the tune, and then the words spill out. *The Lord's my shepherd . . .*

I swore I'd never sing a hymn again, but there's comfort in it for Shimmy. I see Mum back in the ITU, singing over Asha. My heart is breaking.

Shimmy's head rests on her chest. When I finish the song, she twists her face to me, tears on her cheeks.

'The angel,' she says. 'Baby girl. No. Devil. Angel,' she pants.

'Shimmy, it's okay.' I stroke her face.

'Don't . . . trust . . .' Breath rattles in her throat.

'Don't trust who?' Jem stands in front of us.

She turns to him.

He crouches beside her. 'Who shouldn't we trust, Shimmy?' he says, softer.

'The angel,' she whispers. Her head droops again, a silver flower.

Jem sits on the other side of her. She rests against him.

'Sing, sugar,' she sighs.

My voice cracks on the first word, but I keep on with the hymn. You can't sing if you're crying.

Jem stares at me, his dark eyes full of questions.

I keep singing until Shimmy's hand goes limp in mine and she slips into silence.

We wait. I don't know what for.

'Is she—?' Jem whispers.

I slide my finger along Shimmy's bony wrist. She's warm, but there's no pulse. The hollow inside fills with snow. I have to swallow down my shame. 'She's gone.'

Jem rubs his hands over his face. 'Fates lied. She never left, she got the Ageing.'

'Yeah.'

'You already knew.' His voice quivers.

I nod.

'Why didn't you tell me?'

288

'I – I – don't know.'

He stands up and his foot catches Shimmy. Her body crumples. A low groan escapes from her.

'Fuck.' Jem backs away.

I reach over, hands shaking. 'Shimmy,' I whisper. But there's no breath. No pulse. No life. 'She's dead.'

'No shit.' Jem paces the hallway. 'And we're all gonna die too. We're all gonna get the Ageing and die. In here. Like that. You should've fucking told me.'

'I—'

'So busy trying to save your dead sister, you didn't think this was worth mentioning to your real live friends, to me?'

'It's not like that. I didn't know how—'

'You didn't think I had the right to know. Didn't think I deserved to see the whole picture so I could make my own decision. That it? You're as bad as Fates.'

'No!' But it's there again, that tiny splinter of truth. I stand up. 'I didn't know *how* to tell you. I can't save you – us – from the Ageing, but I could save you from knowing about it. From the fear of it.'

'Like I don't already live in fear every second of every day in this place. I was ready to go, you know that. I only stayed for you. To be with you.' He shakes his head. 'Can't believe you hid this from me. Who the fuck do you think you are?'

It's like he's body-slammed me.

He walks away, takes a slow deep breath. And another.

When he comes back, the twitching's stopped. 'Okay,' he says. 'I get that you were maybe trying to protect me and the others. But you don't have to do that. You don't have to do everything by yourself. You could've told me. Or don't you trust me?'

'I don't know.' The words fall out. I don't know if I trust anything, or anyone, or if I ever have.

'This is it now, Calico.' Jem's voice is strained. 'I don't want to spend what's left of my life in this shithole waiting to disintegrate. We have to find a way out of here.'

'I can't. Fates is bringing Asha here.'

'You don't still believe that, after this?' He points at Shimmy. 'Asha's not coming! Fates lies about everything. You have to face it. You can't save her. You need to save yourself.'

We stare at each other.

In the pause between us, voices echo along the corridor. Gabe and Earl. I press the key to open our doors, and Jem and I go into our separate rooms.

I look back at Shimmy. She's a pile of rags and bones on the floor. In the morning, when they let us out, we'll have to pretend we don't know anything about it.

This place, making liars of us again.

'What else haven't you told me?' Jem whispers as the doors slide shut.

75.

asha

truth

truth
is not
a solid thing.
time wears rock
paper thin.
the tiny breeze
from a
butterfly wing
melts mountains
into sand.

76.

Calico

What else haven't I told Jem?

So many things.

How I died.

Why I died.

The deal I made with Lucas Fates.

Why Asha died. (Because I left her.)

That I wished for half a second she was already dead. And then she was.

I haven't told him about the Chosen.

How they might come for me.

That I'm starting to think maybe I deserve it.

But if they take me away from here, I'll never be able to save Asha.

And I'll never be able to see him.

I didn't tell him that Stan's not frozen. He's properly dead.

Most likely anyway.

I wanted Jem to still have hope, to keep him alive. For himself.

And for me.

I didn't tell him about Shimmy because I was scared.

Scared of getting the Ageing.

Dying, again. Re-death.

Not being able to save Asha.

And I didn't tell him that I could have saved Shimmy, but I chose Asha instead.

The hollow roars, wild waves crashing in a cave. I'm drifting, alone, in a small boat, on a surging sea. The direction I want to go has always been the same. Asha. But now there are these currents, pulling and pushing me around. Jem. Shimmy. Sending me off course. Confusing me. Exhausting me. Scattering me like driftwood on the shore, stabbing me with splinters of truth.

And every time I close my eyes, instead of Asha, I see Shimmy, the ghost Shimmy, searching for her dead baby.

She's the same as me. Trying to get to the one she loves. Trying to get home.

77.

asha

copper-wing

the copper-wing,
no longer
half a soul,
comes by.
set free,
she breezes
sweetly past,
on her way
to those
who wait for her:
a baby
and a dog.

78.

Calico

I've been shut in my room. I guess they had to sort out Shimmy. Oh, God, Shimmy. Tiredness is etched into my eyeballs, into my bones. I'm a zombie walking along the corridor next to Gabe. He doesn't talk anyway. His face was grim, eyes red-rimmed when he arrived this morning. He and Earl must've found Shimmy. I want to reach out, tell him she died peacefully, with her friends by her side. But I can't. Not even sure it happened. I haven't slept, but it feels like a dream. A nightmare.

Jem's voice bounces out of the resocialisation room and along the hallway. Banging on about how he's getting out of here. Right now. I glance at Gabe, but he's off somewhere in his head. He drops me at the door. Jem's talking intensely at Taylor and Veda. She gives me a troubled smile.

'Shut up, Jem,' I say.

'Don't tell me what to fucking do.'

'They can hear you down the end of the corridor.'

'So?'

'If they find out about the key, no one's getting out of here.'

'You've got a key?' Taylor asks.

'Yes. But I don't even know if it opens the external doors.'

'What happened?' Veda gestures at Jem. 'Something's set him off.'

'I can hear you,' he says. 'I'm right here.'

'We're well aware.'

'Shimmy died last night, all right?' Jem's scar is livid on his face.

'What?' Taylor sways like someone's thumped him. 'H-how d'you know?'

'Fates lied about letting her go,' Jem says.

Veda reaches for my hand. 'No, no.'

'She had the Ageing,' Jem says. 'And Calico knew and didn't tell us.'

'What – I—' Veda is shaking all over, reaching for air.

'It's true,' I say. 'We were with her when she died, me and Jem.' My voice is weirdly calm. Separate from the turmoil inside my head.

'Oh my God.' Taylor hides his face in his hands.

Veda's tears fall thick and fast. I wrap her in a hug.

'It's s-stupid,' she says. 'Shimmy used to irritate me so much.'

Even Jem's quiet while Veda and Taylor cry. He doesn't look at me. But I watch him. The twitching is back, and his mouth moves silently. What is Stan telling him?

'So, this is why you want to leave, Jem?' Veda says at last.

'Yeah. We're all going to get it. I don't want to die in here. I want to go.'

'How are you planning on getting out of here?' Taylor says.

'Calico's key.'

'Will you shut up!' I say. 'Anyone could hear you.'

Jem turns, paces the room, muttering to Stan.

Veda sniffs back tears. 'I don't understand though, Jem. Why do you want to leave if you think you're going to develop the Ageing? At least here there's the possibility of a treatment.'

'You're so deluded; you still believe this place is about helping people.'

'Jem—'

'They don't care about us. Any of us. You didn't see Shimmy. What it's like when it's someone you know. Someone you care about.' He rubs at his face. 'We should all get out of here. Taylor, you'll come with me, right?'

'No. I don't have long left anyway. My parents signed me up for this because they couldn't afford to pay. I don't want to get them in any trouble. And like Veda said, if I get sick, I'd rather be here. They might find a cure. And if they don't, well, I wouldn't want my folks to see me like that, how the Agers get. Better for them not to know.'

Jem groans. 'You're so fucking pious it makes me puke.'

'You could ask Doctor Fates to release you from the study early,' Veda says.

'Like that's going to happen.' Jem stops in front of me. He kneels like he did the day I cried. 'Come with me, Calico. We can find them. Go to Russia . . .'

'Russia?' says Taylor. 'Find who?'

'They don't know?' Jem says.

I shake my head.

'More lies. I can't believe I ever trusted you.' He gets up and turns away from me.

'Jem,' Veda says. 'We've all had a shock, hearing about Shimmy. We need some time to process—'

'There. Is. No. Time,' Jem shouts. 'We're all going to die. We need to get the fuck out of here.'

'Okay, kid, you win – you're out of here.' Earl marches in and grabs Jem. 'Gabe said you were kicking off. You never learn.'

'FUCK. OFF.' Jem lashes out a fist. But Earl catches it in his massive hand. He bends Jem's arm behind his back and drags him across the room.

Shit. This is no sparring session. This is assault – like Doctor Perez said.

I run after them. Some Agers scatter, crying and moaning.

I grab at Earl's huge arm, but he shrugs me off. I grab again. He slams Jem against the wall so hard, I hear all the breath shudder out of him.

Earl turns to me. 'Don't mess with me, kid. Get back in there, now.'

'No.' I push at Earl's chest. But he's so solid, he doesn't move. The veins in his thick neck pulse green, poison ivy on a tree. He grips my shoulders, squeezes hard. 'Don't. Mess—'

'Let her go,' Jem says quietly. 'Don't hurt her. I'll go with you.'

Earl releases me. He marches Jem off before I can say anything else.

Jem looks back, his scar like a slap mark on his cheek. Jem, who was so mad at me, angry, hating me for what I've done. Broken his trust. All the stuff he said. It's all true. So busy saving my dead sister, I didn't think about him. But he still put himself between me and Earl. He still helped me.

I run after Earl and Jem, past Gabe herding the agitated Agers.

'Hey, Calico, where you goin'?'

'To help Jem.'

Gabe catches up. Takes my arm. I swing round, shove him off. 'Don't touch me!'

He backs off, hands up.

'I have to help him.'

'I know,' Gabe says. 'I'm coming with you. We need to find Doc P.'

Taylor and Veda have come into the hallway.

'Can you keep an eye on this lot?' Gabe points at the stray Agers.

'Um—' Taylor says.

'Yes, of course.' Veda swings on her crutches over to a weeping woman and talks softly to her.

Gabe and I run.

'What's Earl trying to do to Jem?' I ask.

'You don't wanna know.'

'I do!' I yank at Gabe's arm.

He winces, stops running.

I see the bruises on his arms. 'Did Earl do that to you?'

He nods.

We set off running again towards the lab.

'What is it?' Doctor Perez says. Her hand flutters to the crucifix.

'Earl's taken Jem,' I say. 'He's lost his mind. He put his hands on me too.'

'And me.' Gabe lifts his T-shirt. There are black and yellow bruises on his stomach.

'Take Calico back to her room, Gabe.' She taps at her nanocom.

'No,' I say. 'We're coming with you. You won't be able to stop him by yourself.'

'Doctor Fates and I will deal with this. I want you safe in your room though.' She looks at me and I think of the things we've shared. I have to trust her.

'Come on,' Gabe mutters. 'Sooner she gets to Jem, the less damage Earl can do.'

79.

Gabe lets out a shaky sigh.

I'm jangly with adrenalin. The last thing I want is to go back to my room.

'Can we go up on the roof again?' I ask Gabe. 'I need some air.'

He rubs his hair. 'Um – I guess. Could use a smoke anyways.'

I follow him up the ladder to the roof, climb out into quiet dark, thick air, heat.

There's a grinding noise. White light flutters. Gabe's crouched, cranking an old wind-up lantern. The light's pure and bright. It silvers his hair, like a halo. He stops winding and sparks up a cigarette.

'Thanks for helping me,' I say.

'No worries.'

I peer through his cigarette smoke at the solid wall of darkness beyond the facility. There's not a single speck of light. No stars. No moon.

'You know about Shimmy?' Gabe says.

Goosebumps prickle over me. 'You found her,' I say. 'This morning.' Only this morning.

'Yeah.' His voice is a scratch. 'I – this place . . .'

'I know.' I go, sit next to him.

'And now Jem,' Gabe says.

'What? He hasn't got it, has he?' Panic shotguns my chest. 'The Ageing?'

'No, no. Far as I know, anyways.' Gabe pulls on the cigarette, sends smoke out into the air again. 'I meant, I heard Jem wants to leave.'

I don't answer. Paranoia's back. *Eyes and ears.* But then Jem was bloody shouting his head off about it earlier, so it's hardly a secret.

'You goin' too?' Gabe glances at me. The smoke curls around him.

'No.'

He hands me the cigarette.

I take it, suck in the smoke. Maybe it'll fill the hollow.

'There's somethin' between you and Jem?' Gabe asks.

'Maybe.' I sigh. 'There was. I messed it up.'

'No judgement,' Gabe says. 'Seen the way he looks at you, is all.' He takes the cigarette back. 'I wanna go, too. Get out of here.'

'Well, what's stopping you? You can leave any time you want, can't you?'

'I got reasons to go, and reasons to stay.' He grinds the cigarette stub into the roof. 'If Jem goes, I got one less reason to stay.'

Oh.

He gives me a shy smile. 'It's okay. He's not interested in me like that. He told me. I get it. It's you he wants. But I – care about him. And he cares about you – so, you know, I want him to be happy. Why won't you go with him?'

'It's not that simple.'

'You got more reason to stay here than to go? Somethin' more important to you than he is?'

I feel my heart pull apart.

'You can't find a way to do both?' he says.

The light from the lantern disappears and I'm left in the dark again.

80.

Back in my room, what Gabe said is whirling. *You can't find a way to do both?* Can I save Asha and still go with Jem? How can I *not* leave with him? I can't ever know for sure he's safe unless he's with me. Every time I see him, he's got new bruises. And there's the PTS, the sudden rages, hurting himself. I can't stop bad things happening to him if he's not with me. It's Asha all over again. I left her alone once and everything went wrong. All of this happened because of that one moment when I decided to go to the stupid party.

Doctor Perez comes in.

I sit up. 'Is Jem okay?'

She nods.

'Where is he?'

'In his room, asleep. He accepted some sedation after I promised him Earl no longer has access to your rooms.'

Is a Perez promise worth more than one of Fates's?

'What did Earl do to him?'

'Nothing. It's okay. Jem's exhausted. And so are you. Your last bloods were not as good as usual.'

'Oh God, the Ageing, it's started already?'

'What do you mean?'

'We're all going to get accelerated ageing, like Shimmy.'

Her fingers go to the gold cross. 'How do you even know about Shimmy?' She shakes her head. 'Never mind.' She sits on the edge of my bed. 'You're not going to get the Ageing – because you're a teenager. Neither will any of the others.'

'But Shimmy got it.'

'She wasn't a teenager. Even though she looked like one. Her father lied about her age for years. She'd had a lot of Perfection Surgery. She was a perpetual teen star.' Doctor Perez shakes her head. 'You don't need to worry about any of that. But you do need to get some rest now. Making yourself ill isn't going to help anyone.' She puts a cool hand on my forehead.

I close my eyes. 'Is Jem really okay?'

'Yes.'

'Why was Earl doing that to him and Gabe?'

'A misguided attempt to help Doctor Fates develop a new process.'

'What new process?'

'Calico—'

'Doctor Fates is ill, isn't he?'

She takes a deep breath in. 'Yes. Earl feels indebted to Doctor Fates. He credits him with turning his life around. He'll do anything to get what Doctor Fates needs, and that means money. So you must still be very careful, Calico. Remember: the Chosen would pay a fortune for a girl like you. Get some rest now,' she says.

Rest? *Right.* Like that's going to happen.

I have a choice. I could lie here and shut my eyes to

this world, but I'm not going to. There are things I can do. Things to take back some control.

I wait awhile after she leaves and then I go to Jem's room. He's sleeping, like she said. His scar cradles his cheek. I'll make peace with him tomorrow, and tell the others that we're clear of the Ageing. I can't be sure that Doctor Perez is telling the truth about it. But I'm making the choice to believe her. I'm choosing hope.

81.

asha

found

calico.
you have found her.
she's trying to
save the world
armed with only half
the information,
and heading straight
for the man
whose soul
h
a
n
g
s

b
y

a

t
h
r
e
a
d

82.

Calico

All quiet on the way to Fates's office. No End Stagers, no mad brutal Earl. I have a little twinge. It's an old feeling, a good feeling. I'm doing something productive. For Asha. And for the others. And for me. That bit's new.

I pass through all the doors using my key, until I'm in the lobby, outside Fates's office. There's a strange noise, like waves ranging over small stones, only not as rhythmic. I edge towards the office, slide the key's smooth sections apart, press the green.

Lucas is slumped across the desk; the sea sound is his breath. Bony fingers reach for a brown bottle. His flailing hand knocks it to the floor.

Run! My body turns away from him, but he whimpers, so small, like an injured animal. I can't leave him.

And now I'm in the room, picking up the bottle. The label says *Sano-serum*.

'Help me,' he mouths.

'You want this?' I hold up the bottle.

He nods, his fingers scrabbling for it.

I pull out the cork stopper.

'All of it?' I ask.

'Yes,' he mouths.

I help him sit back, hold his head and lift the bottle

to his dry lips. He closes his eyes and drinks. His skin is pale grey, like the walls. It's like he's seeping into the building. Three weeks since I last saw him and he's deteriorated so much. My blood thuds in my ears. What happens to Asha if Fates dies?

But already, he breathes steadier.

A few minutes pass.

'Well, Calico,' he rasps. 'We're even now.'

'Even?'

'I reanimated you, and you just brought me back from the brink of death. One life for another.'

I shake my head. 'No. We're not even. You still owe me Asha. When's she coming?'

He struggles upright in the chair. 'What are you doing here? How did you get out of your room?'

'Answer my question and I'll answer yours.'

'Your negotiation skills are really coming along.' He coughs.

'When are you bringing Asha here?'

He takes a sip of water. 'None of the investors are interested in cryogenics.'

'That's not my problem. I did everything you asked me to. And you said you'd bring Asha here.'

'I can't bring her here when there's no money to maintain her or to work on her treatment.'

'But the cryopod's waiting for her.'

'Ah. Not any more.'

Icy daggers in my chest. 'What?'

'Its parts have been used to repair my mother's pod.'

The hollow stretches into a scream.

'You forced me to choose between Asha and Shimmy and you've used it anyway.'

He nods.

'Were you ever going to use it for Asha or Shimmy?'

He won't look at me.

'So it was never a choice.' I should've known. Lucas Fates and his lies. There's a roar inside me, it echoes round the hollow. I should've left him fighting for breath. Or made a deal with him while I had that bottle in my hand. I should have let him die. He's a monster.

But doing any of those things would make me a monster, too. And I am not like him. I'm not.

There's one last thing I can try. 'What about Project C?' I say.

His head tilts; he glares at me. 'What about it?'

'They're doing their due diligence right now, aren't they?'

He lifts a finger, closes his eyes. Like Grandad used to, weary of me. Telling me silently to shut up. 'I don't know who you've been talking to—'

'No, you don't. You're not the only one with eyes and ears.'

'Gabe, was it?'

I don't reply.

Fates waves it away. 'The fact you have acquired this knowledge is of no consequence. It's not as if there's anything you can do about it.'

'You don't want their due diligence to reveal what's

going on in this place. I mean, assaults on minors by members of staff. Your own mother stored here. That's hardly objective and professional, is it? Study protocols corrupted. Rules broken left, right and centre. And what if they find out about the accelerated ageing? All those deaths you're responsible for.'

'Enough.'

'What if Project C doesn't go ahead? What if Doctor Perez takes it elsewhere? What will happen to your mother then?'

'Leave my mother out of it. She doesn't have anything to do with this.' He's shaking with anger.

'But this is all *because* of your mother! All this damage you've done.'

'I didn't set out to hurt anyone. Quite the opposite.'

'You told me all of this came from love, Lucas. Made me believe I was making the right choice, keeping Asha's options open, giving her another chance. You made me think you were a good person. Prove it now. Keep one of your promises and bring Asha here.'

He stares down at the desk for a long time. 'I can't.'

'You mean you won't.'

'No, I can't.' He rests his elbows on the desk, hands together like a prayer. 'There was an accident at the facility where Asha's stored.'

Frost creeps over my skin. 'What kind of accident?'

'A fire.'

There's suddenly not enough air. 'Is Asha all right?'

'No. No, she's not. The whole place was destroyed. No survivors.'

'When did this happen?'

'A long time ago.' He looks at me. 'Asha isn't coming. Asha is dead.'

His words slash through me.

No, no.

The hollow fills with water. It swirls through the empty cave of me. My frozen heart cracks. And darkness falls.

Lost Days

83.

Calico

Asha is dead.

Lucas Fates, skull-faced, staring down at me on the floor.

And then, out of nowhere, Earl, incandescent with rage, shouting, stripping off my clothes, searching for the key, finding it, taking it away from me.

Don't damage the goods, Lucas says.

But I'm already damaged.

Death is not the end, he said.

But this time it is.

I'm not Asha's sister any more.

84.

Gabe comes in and out, brings me food he has to take away again. I don't want to eat. Can't get out of bed. Asha's death has drugged me, weighed me down.

Doctor Perez is here. She tries to get me to sit up. 'You remember me telling you to be careful?' she says. 'Not really the best way to stay under the radar, was it? Breaking into Doctor Fates's office and picking a fight with Earl?'

There's another side to every story, but this one's spinning out of reach, scattered in the air like dandelion fairies. I can't get hold of it, can't catch the truth.

It doesn't matter any more. They can say what they want. Do what they want to me. That's my choice.

'Calico. You need to get out of bed.'

'Why? Nothing matters any more,' I say. 'My sister's dead.'

The finger flutter to her crucifix. 'I thought your sister died a long time ago,' she says.

'The first time she did. And now she's dead again. Fates told me.'

Doctor Perez shakes her head.

Sarah Connor. It's like Jem said. No one believed her either.

'Calico, are you depressed?'

'What do you think? How would you feel if you'd just found out your sister had died?'

316

'Empty,' she says. 'Sad and angry.' She squeezes my hand. 'I lost my sister, too. You know that. I understand how you feel. But you must carry on. She'd want you to.'

Would she? I don't even know what she'd want any more.

I turn away and close my eyes again.

All I want to do is sleep. Because when I sleep, Asha's in my dreams.

85.

Calico

My dreams are a movie montage of memories.
The scarlet robin-girl flits across the garden. The
Virgin Mary, with a blue tea towel round her head,
dropping baby cheese-us. Pass the parcel. Pretend
haircuts under the climbing frame, mud pies,
plaiting her hair. First time in a hospital bed, wires
and tubes. No hair. Origami birds. Poems, pictures.
Last time in a hospital bed. Asha's fingers drawing
on my back. Asha writing on my skin. A little
splinter of truth, working its way in.

> Relief.
> Guilt.
> Shame.

Asha? Asha, are you there?

86.

asha

stuck

calico cannot hear
or feel you.

and mum's sadness
hums in threads
that stretch across
the universe,
calling you
home.

you are stuck
between them, asha,
vibrating
on a silken string.

87.

Calico

I come out of the loo and Gabe's in my room, stripping off my bedding.

'Why don't you get a shower,' he says, 'while I finish this?'

I don't have the energy, want to crawl under the covers and sleep again.

'Here.' He hands me a pile of clean clothes. 'Go on. It'll make you feel better.'

I'm too weak to argue. Nothing matters any more.

I close my eyes, and the shower is rain. Asha and I dance in the garden, winding Grandma up. The next day it rains again, and Mum comes out and dances with us. Is Mum dead too? Maybe Asha's with her. That's a sort of comfort. But I want to be there too.

Gabe's made my bed. He's left me some dried fruit and bread. I climb under the covers, exhausted again.

88.

Maybe it's the next morning. Maybe it's the next month. Doctor Perez is here again.

'I think you should go to resocialisation today, Calico. Some company would do you good. Your friends are missing you.'

That's a lie. Who would miss me? I'm no one, nothing.

'I'm sure you'd like to see Jem.'

Jem. He's still here. He didn't escape.

'Calico?' Doctor Perez frowns.

'What?'

'You're dissociating for longer and longer periods. I need to run some tests.'

'No,' I say. 'No more tests.' Nothing. Nothing any more.

Time isn't real. But it must pass because Gabe's here again, coaxing me to eat an apple. 'I brought it for you specially. The delivery just came. Come on, Calico. I'm gettin' in trouble because you're not eatin'.'

'Stop bringing food then,' I say.

'I can't.'

Like Fates. I can't. You won't. I can't. Asha's dead.

'You okay?' Gabe says. 'You zoned out then.'

'I'm tired.' I hand him the apple core.

89.

The dreams, the memories are different now. Shimmy, back to how she was. Full of energy and light. And Jem, doing his grimace-smile or laughing, out of control, like that time after we saw the End Stagers. And his true smile. I only saw it once, how it made his face alive. I dream him angry, too, shouting at me when Shimmy died. No, he wasn't angry. He was scared. Scared of what would happen next. Accelerated ageing. Earl, tough but kind, until he went all tough and mean. And Doctor Perez, fluttering fingers, tired eyes. Doctor Perez who knows my secret.

No Asha at all. Asha is gone. She's not in my dreams. Asha is dead.

We should've left, me and Jem, when we had the chance. There's no key now. We're trapped in this place full of lost souls.

90.

I can't sleep any more. It's like I overdosed on it, and now I'm cold turkey. I curl on the bed, staring at the wall till the cracks blur. I hear the door slide open but don't turn around. I can't face Gabe or Doctor Perez trying to make me eat something. I'm sunk as a stone in a deep deep well. Don't ever want to be pulled out.

'Is she asleep?' A whisper. Definitely not Gabe or Sophia Perez.

A tentative touch on my back. I turn a little.

Jem.

Warmth and light.

Behind him are Taylor and Veda.

Taylor smiles. 'If you can't come to resocialisation, we'll come to you.'

I sit up, see stars. 'How did you get in here?' My voice scrapes.

'Good to see you too,' Jem says.

'I have a key.' Veda slots it into the handle of her crutch and sits on the chair.

'Where did you—'

'My friend gave it to me before they left. Earl found yours, I assume.'

I nod.

'Did he hurt you?' Jem asks.

Earl grabbing stripping searching. 'I don't remember.'

323

'What were you doing?' Veda says. 'How did you get caught?'

Jem sits on the corner of my bed. 'Calico? You okay?'

They're all staring at me. Did I zone out again? Get a grip. Get a hold of something.

'I went to Fates's office.'

'Why on earth would you do that?' Veda says.

'Trying – to help – trying to get some kind of information, or proof or ID—'

'Why?'

'So we could leave, get out of here. Jem was right. We should've gone.'

'You changed your mind?' Jem says.

'Yeah.' No. I don't know.

'No more secrets,' he says.

I stare at him. No more secrets? Is it that easy?

'Asha's dead,' I whisper. 'The facility in Russia burned down.'

Jem's arms are round me. I hide my face in his bony shoulder. Breathe in his salt and soap scent.

'I'm so sorry, Calico,' Taylor says. 'Jem told us about your sister.'

'I'm sorry too,' Veda says. 'How did you find out that she died? Was there something in Doctor Fates's office?'

'Yes, *he* was. He told me about the fire.'

Jem pulls back from me. 'Fates told you about Asha?'

I nod.

'And you believed him? After everything he's lied about?'

'I—' Wait. Why *did* I believe Fates? Has he ever told me the full truth about anything?

'Don't give up on Asha,' Jem says. 'Not till you've got one hundred percent proof.'

There's a tiny light in the hollow. That's the thing about hope. Even when you think it's gone, it's not. An ember, hiding in the ashes. It only needs the faintest whisper of a breeze to make it glow.

'She's drifted off again,' Veda says.

'No. I'm still here.' I take Jem's hands in mine.

'We've been talking – the three of us,' Veda says. 'You and Jem were right about some things. We're all in it now. It's better if we pool our knowledge and work together.'

'No more secrets,' Jem says again.

Eyes and ears. But that doesn't matter any more.

I tell them everything.

Well. Almost everything.

91.

'So, it's true about teenagers being immune to the Ageing,' Veda says.

'Yeah. Well, according to Doctor Perez.'

'Just because one thing Fates said is true, doesn't mean—'

'Yes, Jem, I know. Not everything is black and white. It makes our decision a lot easier, that's all.' She looks at Taylor.

He nods. 'Yeah.'

'What decision?'

'Whether to leave the facility before our contracts end.'

'We should all go together,' Taylor says. 'Everything we've been through, and then losing Shimmy. We're family now. We can go to my folks. They'll help us.'

Jem turns to me. 'What do you think?'

'Let's do it.'

But then the door opens.

Earl stands there, his huge bulk filling the frame. 'What the hell's going on?' he bellows.

Jem's body tenses next to me.

'How did you all get in here?' Earl's face is red. The vein in his thick neck stands out like a snake on a tree. 'Don't tell me there's another key?'

Shit. I don't turn to Veda. Don't give it away.

'Oh, um. My bad.' A voice from the hallway. Gabe shuffles in.

He's covering for us?

'Oh-ho. Let's hear it.' Earl folds his massive arms over his chest.

'Doc P said it'd be good for Calico to go to resocialisation. But she wouldn't go, and was gettin' down, and so I brought the others here instead.'

'Right,' Earl says. 'Making up the rules as you go along.'

'*Where* they are don't matter. It's the social interaction that's important.'

'Getting a little ahead of yourself, aren't you? You're not in charge yet,' Earl spits. 'Let's see what your grandfather's got to say about this.'

'Grandfather?' Taylor asks.

'What the fuck?' Jem's twitch is in overdrive.

Gabe pushes back his crazy surfer hair.

Icy spiders walk over my skin.

Can't believe I've been so stupid.

His eyes. They're not like the sea at all. They're like a clear cold lake. Frozen.

Shit.

Fates.

Lucas Fates is Gabe's grandfather.

92.

'Why didn't you tell me?' Taylor says to Gabe.

'It ain't important,' Gabe mutters.

'Are you fucking kidding?' Jem's vibrating.

I keep hold of his hand, tether him to me.

Earl presses his nanocom. His craggy face is one big smirk. 'We'll see what Doctor Fates has to say about all this.'

'He knows what I'm doin',' Gabe says.

'And what's that?' Taylor's lip quivers.

'Gatherin' information,' Gabe says. 'I'm doin' it *for* him, Earl. He told me to. What? You didn't know? He didn't ask your permission?'

Earl snarls.

I'm reeling. *Eyes and ears, eyes and fucking ears.* Gabe knows important stuff, secret things about me. And what else? What's he seen? Heard? Those times up on the roof, all cosy. That night when he came with me to save Jem. I thought he was helping us. But was he spying for Fates?

'He's bluffing,' Veda says. But I think she's the one bluffing. Her voice has a tiny tremor. Everyone looks at her. 'Well, there isn't anything to tell, is there?'

'I got plenty to tell,' Gabe says.

'Like what?'

'Like your night-time get-togethers,' Gabe says. 'With your lab geek when he was still here.'

'Don't know what you're talking about.'

'Like Calico bein' fertile,' Gabe blurts.

Veda gasps.

Oh no. No no no.

'What. The fuck. Has that got to do with anything?' Jem lets go of my hand. He's off the bed, lurches for Gabe. Earl gets between them. Shoves Jem away.

'You fucker,' Jem mutters at him.

Earl glares at me. 'Is it true?'

Shit. The Chosen, the Chosen. I don't answer.

'Doc P told me to keep quiet about it,' Gabe says.

Jem lunges again, but Earl holds him back. 'Is that right?' he says. 'So Doctor Fates *doesn't* know about this?'

'Yeah.' Gabe won't look at me.

'Perez told you to lie about it, so you did? What's your granddaddy going to think about you lying to him? And about this, of all things?' Earl gestures at me. 'Sitting on a fortune and knowing nothing about it.'

I'm an object. A commodity. I shrink into the bed.

'I didn't lie.' Gabe's voice is quiet.

'You know what this means,' Earl says. 'She could be the answer to all our problems.'

Bile rises in my throat. Everyone's staring. Veda shakes her head. No more secrets.

Earl's got everyone else back into their rooms. Gabe hasn't said a word to me. There are running footsteps. Doctor Perez appears. Her dark hair's fallen loose. 'What the hell's going on, Earl?'

'Could ask you the same question.'

'What?'

'The game's up, Perez.'

'What are you talking about?' Her gaze slides from me to Gabe. She frowns.

'Let's go see Doctor Fates, shall we?' Earl says. 'You, me, and Fates junior here. Calico can stay and think about her sins.'

'Fine,' Doctor Perez snaps. 'I'll meet you there.'

'Oh, no, you don't.'

She takes a deep breath. 'All right then, let me have a moment to check Calico over. She hasn't been at all well. Wait outside.'

Earl rolls his eyes, but he and Gabe leave the room. They don't close the door though, stand there looking in.

Doctor Perez puts her body between me and them. 'I'm sorry,' she says quietly.

'The Chosen?' I whisper.

'I'll do what I can.' And she's gone.

No more secrets, Jem said.

No more lies, he meant.

He gave me back hope, and now it's gone again. I won't be able to find Asha if I'm a Chosen. I won't be able to be with Jem.

Asha. Small and well. Early morning, in the misty garden. She's gone out to collect the eggs. She loves those chickens. Rushes out there every day to open the coop and hug each one. Their feathers warm and soft, fire-coloured on top and smoky-spotted underneath.

Asha turns her face to me. She's silent screaming. Blood on her hands.

The fox got them all.

It's Earl who comes for me with the scratch of a needle. *To keep you calm, kid.* But I am calm. There's no fight left in me. Nothing left of me. It's a relief, the slide into oblivion.

93.

asha

tarnished heart

the ghost man's there,
soul faded,
ripped and shabby,
tarnished heart.

there are others
with him now,
a ball of smoke and rage,
a soft golden light,
and someone
in the shadows
hard to see.

danger dances
around calico.
flames flicker,
reaching out
for her.

you need to
find a way,
asha,
to tell her
what she
doesn't know.

End Days

94.

Calico

There's something hard behind my back. My chest is crushed. I can't move. My arms are trapped, hips, forehead, ankles. I struggle against tight straps. Breath comes too fast.

Where am I? My eyelids half lift. I'm in a chair. A huge chair. My feet don't reach the floor. I can't turn my head. Cold air licks at my skin. There's a smell like singed hair. Opposite me is a window. Beyond it another empty room. I swallow down panic. The Chosen. What are they about to do to me?

I wrestle with the bindings. It's no use.

And then there's a voice. Ice creaking. Fates. Coming this way.

I close my eyes, will my body to be still.

Feet shuffle, laboured breathing, the tap of a cane on the tiled floor. The squeak of another set of shoes.

'You're quiet,' Fates says.

'Just takin' it all in.'

Gabe? What is Gabe – the traitor, the work experience kid, *Lucas Fates's grandson* – doing here?

'What the hell's going on?' My eyes spring open.

'Ahh, the sedation's worn off already.' Fates creaks over to me. 'I was hoping to get through this without any interference.'

'Get through what?'

Fates leans on his cane. Tired, grey skin. Death-is-not-the-end eyes peer into mine.

'Is it the Chosen?' I whisper.

He snorts. 'Oh, that was an interesting development. Finding out about your fertility – but no. You are far too valuable to sell off to the Chosen. Far too important to me.'

Not the Chosen, not the Chosen.

But what then? My heart plunges. 'What is this place?'

'Would you believe, Calico, this was formerly the prison's execution chamber.'

Nausea rises in my throat. 'Why am I here?' I whisper.

'To undergo a small procedure.'

Ice-cold prickles. 'What? What procedure?'

He turns away from me, to Gabe. 'Go see where Earl's got to. He's not responding to my nanocoms.'

'He told me to stay with you.'

'I don't need a nurse,' Fates snaps. But he does; he could crumple at any minute.

'I know.' Gabe looks unsure. 'It's just—' He gestures at me.

'I hardly think a girl in restraints is going to do me any harm. Go find Earl. I want to get started while my serum's working.'

Gabe brings a stool over for Fates to sit on, and then goes. Leaves me here. Alone with the devil.

Fates's breath stutters.

'What's this procedure?' I say.

'Ah, Calico. Always – so many questions.'

'I think I have the right to know what you're doing to me.'

Phlegm rattles in his throat. 'You have no rights. You signed them away.'

'To save my sister,' I say. 'That was the deal. And you didn't stick to your side of it.'

'I – always meant to reunite you – restore your sister – to health.' Coughing wracks his frail body. He pulls out a handkerchief, stained with blood. 'Now time is – running out – for me.' He coughs again. Blood and spittle spray over us both. 'I can't wait – any longer.'

'Wait for what?'

Fates shakes his head; one paper-pale hand grasps the arm of the chair. He gasps for air.

I thrash against the straps.

He touches my arm. So cold. I stop moving.

His coughing slows, quietens.

'What are you going to do to me?' I whisper.

'Transference of Consciousness.'

'You're going to put me in a Soul Holder?'

'No. Your body – will be the vessel for – another consciousness.' A cough rips through him.

Icy rivers run through my veins. 'What? Who?' I scream.

'My mother,' he says. 'It's my mother.'

95.

Yesterday, it didn't matter if I lived or not. Too many people I love, lost to me. But Jem came back. He relit my hope for Asha. Veda, Taylor. And anyway, it's my life. Lucas Fates doesn't get to decide when it ends.

I pull at the restraints. They don't give. All I can do is keep him talking.

'Have you done this before?'

'You can – rest assured, Calico – I wouldn't do this – to my mother – if I wasn't confident it would be successful.'

'But what's going to happen to me?'

'You'll be gone.'

I'm trapped. A piece of meat on the butcher's block.

He stares at me with his death-is-not-the-end eyes. But this time, it is the end. The end of me. And soon.

He picks up a syringe from a nearby trolley. His hand quivers.

'Wait,' I say. 'Can't you save my soul? Put it in a Soul Holder?'

'Yes. I could. But I won't.' He leans over me; his breath's curdled. 'I'm going to keep – a tiny part of you in your body – for my mother. Your fortitude. She'd like you.'

'You don't know what she'd like,' I spit. 'You've never even met her.'

A tremor passes through Fates. He grabs the armrest. The syringe drops on to my lap. My fingers flick it away. It skitters across the floor.

'That was foolish,' he says. Sweat beads on his skin.

The door opens. 'Where have you been?' Fates snaps.

'Had to help with some End Stagers. They were wanderin' the corridors.'

'Where's Earl?'

'Still dealin' with Doc P.'

What does that mean? What is Earl doing to Doctor Perez?

Gabe walks towards us. 'Earl gave me this. Where d'you want it?' He holds out a container to Fates. Metal and blue glass. The spinning opals inside. A Soul Holder full of neuromites. Isabella Fates. Isabella's soul.

Fates reaches for it but his hand tremors again. 'Put her on the trolley,' he says.

Gabe picks up the fallen syringe. 'You want this?'

'You'll have to do it,' Fates says.

'No.' I struggle. 'Gabe, don't—'

'And get on with it. I'm sick of her whining.'

Fates moves to the trolley and his mother's soul.

'Please, Gabe. Don't do this.'

'Relax,' he says. 'You won't feel a thing.'

Exactly what I'm scared of. Never feeling anything again.

The syringe comes closer. My bones, my veins are glass. I wait for them to shatter.

But there's no pain. The syringe is still full.

What's going on?

'Is she out?' Fates asks.

Gabe puts his hand over my eyes. 'Yeah, she's out.'

He hates me so much he wants me to be awake when this happens? Conscious, while my soul is ripped from me. Or is he trying to help me? I close my eyes.

Fates coughs. There's a thud. And that sound, like a stormy sea again. He's struggling to breathe.

'You all right, Grandpa?'

'I – need – more serum.'

'You sure? You've had your dose for the day.'

'Do – as you're – told – boy.'

I force my head to turn a tiny bit. Fates is on the floor. Grey-faced, he holds his mother's Soul Holder close to his chest. It's splattered with blood. Gabe takes a brown bottle from the trolley. *Don't do it. Don't do it.* He opens the bottle and lifts it to his grandfather's mouth. Fates can barely swallow. He lies there not moving. But his breathing calms. The tide coming in and out. Gabe helps him on to the stool. Like before, in his office, Fates rallies quickly.

'Now,' he says, 'where were we?'

Earl barrels in, pushing a gurney.

'Everything gone to plan?' Fates says.

'Yes, sir. Perez is contained in the Cryostore.'

Doctor Perez is trapped too. She won't be coming to help. And what has happened to Jem and the others?

Earl parks the gurney next to me.

'Who's that for?' Gabe says.

'Funny you should ask, kid.'

Earl grabs him. He jabs a needle into Gabe's neck and folds him on to the gurney.

'No!' I shout.

'Goddammit. She's not sedated?'

'Apparently not,' Fates mutters.

'Shall I put her out?'

'No, leave her. If she wants to remain conscious for the procedure, so be it.'

'The boy's all ready for you, Doctor Fates,' Earl says.

'Mother first. I want her to see me as I am, one time.'

Oh. My. God. They're doing it to Gabe, too? Lucas's mother into me. Lucas into Gabe. And it didn't sound like Gabe knew anything about it either.

I fight against the straps. 'Gabe!' I shout, but he's out of it.

'Hush now, Calico. Agitation is not good for the soul,' Fates says. His hands fumble with a narrow pipe.

'Let me do that.' Earl clips it on to Isabella's Soul Holder. 'Here.'

The chair I'm in suddenly flattens and I'm lying down, still trapped. Fates places the Soul Holder on my chest. The pipe moves like a snake towards my face. Needles protrude from it. And they're coming towards my eye.

I try to shake my head from side to side.

'Hold her, Earl.'

'NO!'

Earl looms over me. One massive hand goes round my neck, one on my forehead. I can't breathe. My body writhes, reaching for air.

'Stay still, kid.'

Closer, closer.

I scream, shake my head. Earl pushes harder on my throat, forcing me into silence. The needles press against my eyeball. Shards of glass explode inside my head. The scrabble of spiders' feet. Neuromites streaming into me. They spin their webs. The strings of someone else's soul fill me up, pictures of someone else's life. A baby cries. I'm stretched thinner and thinner, until only a tiny part of me is left, clinging to the corners.

No!

I push back.

'Don't fight it, kid.'

'Did you expect anything else from Calico Brown?' Fates says. 'She's a fighter. I want Mother to have some of that spirit, that strength.'

Fighting means I'm helping Fates? Fuck that.

I stop. I stop pushing back.

There's a scream from somewhere, like a hand slapping my face. 'Stay!' a voice says. 'Stay!'

The spiders stop spinning. In the silence, I hear – faint, distant – feet running.

'Goddammit,' Earl says. 'How'd they get out?'

Banging on glass. 'CALICO!'

Who's that?

Jem?

Too late.

I let go.

Of him.

Of everything.

And fall into darkness.

96.

asha

dead man walking

the dead man walking
grabs my sister's soul,
his own is tissue thin.

he never learned
that love means
sometimes letting go.

for him,
love's warped
into a thing
that binds
and blinds.

97.

Calico

Darkness, stillness, quiet.
    I float in a midnight ocean.
    No more screaming.
    No more pain.
    No more.

    Opals spin in the dark.
    A soul, someone's soul.
    Drifting towards me.
    Or going away.
    Mine?
    Or Lucas's mother's?
    Isabella's?
    No.
    One that brings the softness and warmth of feathers.
    Fingertip words whisper.
    A song weaves its way to me, into me.

> *Blood and breath and bone,*
> *threaded through with love and light.*
> *Always in my heart and mind.*
> *I'll carry you through deepest night.*

And who is the singer?

Asha?
Asha, are you there?
There's a sensation
like when we were small,
and she climbed into bed,
and clung to my back,
and sang in my ear.
Even though I have no back,
or ears, or nerves, or brain any more.
She's here with me.
I've found her.
Asha.

98.

asha

too late

oh no.
calico, already
half a soul?

you're too late, asha.
too late.

no.
you have to save
your calico.
tell her what
she doesn't know.

she must not die
for you.

99.

Calico

Disruption in the dark. Flickers of light on a
blank screen.
There we are, me and Asha. Sitting on
her bed.
I brush her hair.
But then I get up and go.
I leave her.
It's that night. The last night. The night it all
began.

asha

getting calico out
of the house
to the party
is so hard.
but she goes, at last,
because you ask her
to do it for you.

you sigh up to sitting
so tired,
but this is the last of it.

take out your notebook
and the purple pen
and write.
take your medicine,
and go to sleep.

Calico

I leave Asha and walk across the common,
pass the old oak tree, to the party, the lights,
and the smoke, and the music.

asha

and then mum is
home too early.
she stumble-slips into your room.
paper slides from its envelope.
silence
d
r
i
p
s
as she reads.

no, asha, no

recovery position,
her fingers
down your throat,

she sobs over you,
and washes Death away,
brings you
back to shore.

Calico

Mum has the phone on loudspeaker
nine nine nine
emergency
daughter, stage four
overdose

asha

you rest in the shallows
as mum sings her soft words.
the doorbell rings.
she

runs

out

runs

back

in

for the letters.
paper scrunches
in her hands.

why, asha?

and then all the
gentle brutality
of being
brought back
to life.

Calico

Asha left me a letter?
Why didn't Mum show me?
What did it say?
Asha? Asha, are you here?

asha

all these years
playing catch-me-if-you-can
with Death,
it's tiring.

sometimes you
just want to sit this one out.
or make up
your own rules.

but
people don't see
or hear you any more,
not who you are
or what you say,
only what disease
has made you.

asha, the weak,
powerless, voiceless,
choiceless.

I had to write it down.

100.

Calico

The dark is back, and all around me.

A flutter of white. The envelope opens in Mum's fingers.

The page stutters, a baby bird trying to fly.

Asha's tiny purple writing.

> *dear calico*
>
> *the truth is*
> *you stopped hearing me*
> *a long time ago,*
> *lost sight, and sound,*
> *of who I am*
> *and what I want.*
>
> *truth is,*
> *you made your life*
> *about me,*
> *and lost yourself*
> *along the way.*
>
> *truth is,*
> *even though I know*
> *you'd do anything*
> *for me.*
> *I can't ask you*
> *to do this.*
>
> *for you, it would be giving up,*
> *and that's too big a thing*

for you to carry every day.
truth is
I am dying
anyway.
the when's
the only part
I get to choose.

no more heroic
measures, calico.
I am done.

truth is
it's not your job
to save me,
even though you have
a hundred times before,
and I was glad.
don't do it
any more.

truth is,
I have lived my life,
and now it's time
for you.

truth is
life's
for the living.
and life
is for living.

so live it,
as free
and as true
as you can.

it's your turn now –
you have to
save yourself.

I love you, calico
your sister
asha

The letter disappears, but what it said, what it said remains. Splinters of truth.

Asha took her own life.

How could I not have seen what she wanted? Why did I know best? Why did I think I had the right—

Oh. God. Even then, Mum saved her.

And then I did it again.

And Asha didn't want us to.

I was so scared of losing her, of living without her. But I wasn't thinking about Asha, what she wanted. It was all about me.

I'm sorry, Asha. I'm sorry.

Darkness swims around me.

No more pictures.

Are you there, Asha?

Nothing.

Is this death? Am I dead?

But if we're both dead now, why can't we be together?

Oh.

Maybe Asha's gone to heaven.

And I'm in hell.

101.

asha

some stranger's soul
is stuck inside my sister.
do no harm, do no harm
her never-ending whisper.

she doesn't want to live
inside another body.
do no harm,
do no harm, she weeps,
and like air from a valve,
her soul softly seeps
away
from Calico.

102.

Calico

Dark. Silence.

I float for a moment in peace. It would be so easy to let go, but there's a new space inside me. Not the hollow, that's shrunken and sealed. Healed by Asha. She's given me a gift. Life.

This is a new space. A place to be me.

I curl from the corners into myself.

What will I do now? And how?

There's only one thing I'm sure of. I have to get to the people I care about. The people who care about me. The only people who know me right now. My new family. Jem and Veda and Taylor.

A flash of the execution chamber, sallow walls and burned hair.

I'm half here watching, half there in my body laid out in the chair. Gabe's next to me on a gurney, with Fates leaning over him. Earl is by the door. And on the other side of it are Jem, Taylor, Veda.

The tube, with the needles, is still pressed against my eye. My hands are still strapped down.

'Dammit, they're coming in,' Earl shouts. 'How do they have a key?'

'CALICO!'

Jem.

'Oh no you don't,' Earl says.

There are grunts, thuds, scuffles; the noise echoes off the tiled walls.

I fight against the bindings. Heart thuds, hands sweat.

There are scrabbling fingers at my face. They rip the tape off my left eye. A blur peers down at me. 'Calico? Is it you?' Veda says.

A giant bear roars, drags her off.

I am half here, half there.

'Calico?' Jem whispers.

I can't answer, can't lift my head. I can't see his face, only a haze.

'It's all right,' he says. 'You're all right.' He undoes the straps. I'm free.

'Jem!' Veda screams, and he's gone again.

My own hands fight against what I have to do next. To pull the needles from my eye. To disconnect from where I linger, this halfway place.

My fingers find the pipe. The slightest touch sends sharp scratches through my whole being. But I have to do this.

For me.

I grip the pipe tight, breathe out. And pull.

Searing, screaming, pain. The world swirls red. It's full of howls and shouts and people being hurt. People I care about, being hurt.

I stretch out. My fingers land on a curve of smooth cool glass.

I slowly push up to sitting. The room swims in a sea of red. Vomit spurts from my mouth. I force myself to stay upright, and blink away the blood.

Fates still leans over Gabe. *Do no harm?* He's so twisted he'd kill his own grandson to save himself. Whatever Gabe's said, whatever he's done, he doesn't deserve this.

'DOCTOR FATES!' Earl yells. Jem and Taylor cling, one on each of his arms, trying to hold him still.

'The vessel must be prepared,' Fates rasps. 'That is my priority.'

'DOCTOR FATES!'

Veda drags herself from the ground; blood trickles down her cheek. She swings across to Earl on her crutches. Stops in front of him. 'Shut up.'

But Earl shouts more and writhes so that Jem bashes against the wall and falls, winded. Veda steps forward, rests on one crutch, and brings the other up hard between Earl's legs. He crumples on to the floor. Jem and Taylor hold him down.

'Get his nanocom!' Veda shouts.

Taylor scrabbles at Earl's thick wrist. Earl headbutts him, knocks him back. And now there's only Jem holding on to Earl. But he pivots, slams down hard on Earl's chest, pins his arms with his knees. 'Quick!'

Taylor's back up. He has a scalpel. He slices at Earl's wrist.

Earl bucks Jem off. Veda is there, ready with her

358

crutch. She brings it down hard on Earl's face. Blood gushes from his nose. She raises her crutch again—

'Stop!' Fates says. 'I need him.'

'I don't care what you need,' Veda spits. 'You've lied to us over and over. Hurt our friends—'

'But, don't you see, once Earl transfers me into Gabe's body, I'll be able to put everything right.'

'Not for Gabe,' Taylor says into the sudden quiet.

'You don't know what's right any more, Doctor Fates,' Veda says.

Jem and Taylor and Veda wrestle Earl into the store cupboard. Veda locks it with her key.

Taylor rushes to Gabe. 'Get this thing off him, Fates.' His hands hover over the Soul Holder.

'No!' Fates says. 'His soul is in motion. It would be catastrophic.'

He still has his back to me. He hasn't seen that I'm awake.

I twist my legs round, wipe the blood from my good eye. Swaying a little, I stand. I know what I have to do.

My hand closes around the syringe Gabe was supposed to use on me.

'Lucas?' I say.

He turns slowly. His face a child beneath ancient skin. 'Mother?'

'Yes.' I force a smile.

'But how do you know my name?'

Shit. 'Your p-plan worked. You left a little of the girl behind. I know who you are.'

He steps towards me. 'How do I know it's really you?'

I wrap my arms around his frail body, pull him in. He smells of decay and death. 'You'll just have to trust me,' I whisper, and jab the needle into his neck.

103.

'Calico?' Fates staggers back, falls to his knees. 'What have you done? Where is she? Where's my mother?'

'She's gone. She chose not to stay.'

'No!' He slumps unconscious at my feet.

Jem runs over to me. 'You okay?' He moves my bloody hair gently and presses a wad of fabric on my wounded eye. His hand stays on my cheek. I can feel his breath. He's alive. I'm alive.

'Doctor Fates!' Earl shouts. He hammers at the storeroom door.

'Shut up.' Veda whacks the door with her crutch. 'Doctor Fates is not available.'

'Is he—?' I point at Fates. So small, shrivelled, curled on the floor. Hard to believe he could have done so much harm.

Jem crouches by him, touches his neck. 'He's got a pulse.'

'What about Gabe?' Taylor asks. 'Is he going to be all right?'

'I don't know,' Veda says

'We need to help him.'

'Doctor Perez,' I say. 'Earl locked her in the Cryostore. She'll know what to do.'

Taylor runs off.

My head's full of feathers. The room warps and I sway. Jem catches hold of me. Keeps me from falling.

I lean against him.

Veda stands in front of me. 'Calico. Is it really you in there?'

'Yeah, it's me. Really me. Only me.'

Feet thud down the corridor and Taylor reappears. He goes straight over to Gabe. Doctor Perez comes into the room out of breath, pulling rope from her wrists. There's a moment of shock on her face as she takes in Gabe on the bed with the Soul Holder attached, and me with blood running down my cheeks. But then she sees Fates on the floor and rushes to him.

'Help me!' she calls.

'You're joking,' Jem says. 'Leave that fucker alone. You need to help Calico first.'

'And Gabe,' Taylor says.

'No,' she says. 'I have to prioritise the most urgent case.'

'PEREZ!' Earl rages from the store cupboard. 'LET ME OUTTA HERE!'

Doctor Perez looks over at us. 'Either you help me, or I'll let Earl out.'

'You wouldn't,' Veda says. 'He tied you up, locked *you* in the Cryostore.'

Doctor Perez shakes her head. Fingers flutter to the gold crucifix and then she presses her nanocom and the store cupboard opens. Earl blasts into the room roaring. He shoves Taylor out the way, reaches Fates and picks him up like he's a baby. Puts him on the chair I was lying on before. He turns and heads for Gabe.

'No, no, no!' Taylor screams.

'Earl, stop,' Doctor Perez says, horrified. 'You can't use the boy.'

'Why not? That's the plan – he's already empty.'

'Your plan, Earl, not mine. It's my duty to preserve life.' Perez holds up the other Soul Holder, covered in my blood. 'I'm prepared to transfer Doctor Fates into this,' she says. 'But the boy must not be harmed.'

Fates lets out a rattling gasp. Earl and Doctor Perez both turn to him. She pushes the Soul Holder into Fates's eye.

'You're keeping his consciousness,' I say. 'After everything he's done.'

'Of course she is,' Jem mutters.

'It's not my place to judge him, Calico. And anyway, regardless of his recent behaviour, he has a wealth of knowledge. It will be so helpful for the project Cynthia's setting up.'

'Oh, right, the Library of Lost Souls,' Jem snarks.

'A collation of human knowledge – good and bad.' She touches the gold cross at her neck. 'In science, and in life, the way we learn is from our mistakes.'

Maybe she's right. But it seems like a really hard way to learn.

The feathers are back in my head. I slump on to a stool.

'What about Gabe?' Taylor asks.

'I'll see to him now.' Doctor Perez moves over to Gabe. Earl stands guard over Fates, his craggy face pale behind the blood.

'We need to get out of here.' Jem's twitching.

'Calico needs medical attention first,' Veda says. 'And Gabe.'

'*He's* not coming with us,' Jem sneers. 'Not after what he did.'

'That was our deal,' Veda says. 'He made a bad decision, a mistake, but as soon as he realised what was going to happen to Calico, he did the right thing. He told us what was going on. We can't leave him here.'

'He's as much Fates's victim as the rest of us,' I say. 'More, in a way. His own grandfather did this to him.'

Gabe splutters like an engine coming back to life.

'Right, we need to get him to the treatment room,' Doctor Perez says. 'He needs nanomite serum to save his eye. You too, Calico.'

'Perez!' Earl's voice shakes. 'Doctor Fates – I think – he's gone.'

Everything goes quiet and still.

Lucas Fates is dead?

'Leave the Soul Holder in place,' Doctor Perez says. 'It will absorb the last of his consciousness.'

Lucas Fates is dead.

'Stay with him, Earl. I'll be back soon.'

Jem helps me along the hallway. I feel feather-light, like all my blood has gone.

Lucas Fates is dead.

104.

asha

seed

the air blows
through
me
and I am falli_n
            _g
        fall
            i

                n

            g
                fallen
on to soft earth.
nothing left
of me
but a seed.

it's time to sleep
to rest
in the warmth
of the earth,
let her nurture me
until it's my time
to grow again.

105.

Calico

I lie awake in my hospital bed. Doctor Perez insists I stay still for a week, to give my eye the best chance. She's dosed me with nanomites and bandaged me up. I've only been lying here half a day and I'm fed up already. I'm not good at being still. I want to get out of here. Feels like I'm holding the others back. Doctor Perez has them helping her with the Agers, Gabe, and me. Earl's locked in one of the rooms so he can't do it. Or anything else. He's in there until Doctor Perez decides what to do for the best. It took four of them to get him in there.

Doctor Perez says I'm the worst patient *ever*. And I am. Not like Asha was.

The wave crashes over me again. Asha's dead. Gone for good.

Doctor Perez says this is grief. It comes in waves. She says crying is good. The salt water will help my eye to heal, help my heart to mend. But I am not a girl who cries. Or maybe I'm not a girl who cries easily.

'Hey.' Jem sits on my bed. 'There's a truck we can use, when you're up to it.'

'I'm ready to go now.'

He does the grimace-smile. 'Yeah. Me too. But the chance of saving your eye's got to be worth waiting another few days, right? I'm getting some supplies together. Veda's in Fates's office trying to find "documentary evidence" to back up what's in her journal.'

I nod.

'Keep your head still.' He smiles.

God. I hate to be still.

106.

An alarm screams in my dreams. I wake up, heart thudding. Standing over me, his face half-covered in bloody bandages, is Gabe.

I scramble to sitting. Too fast. The world spins.

'We got to get out of here,' he says. 'That's the fire alarm.'

'Wh—'

He pulls back the covers, grabs my arm.

'Get off me.' I can't see clearly.

'Calico, I know you don't trust me, but there's a fire. Can't you smell it?'

Shit. 'Yeah.' I stand up, bare feet on the floor, wait for the walls to stop warping.

Gabe's moved to another bed with an Ager in it. 'Are you up to pushing one of these?'

'I'll give it a go.'

He pushes the bed towards the lobby.

I go to the next one. This Ager has fine silver hair, like moonlight. Like Shimmy at the end. These people are going to die soon. But *do no harm*. We can't leave them. We have to give them every chance.

I follow Gabe out of the ward with the Ager. The alarm blares even louder out here. Smoke seeps through the lobby. There's not enough room for any more beds. The door to the hallway won't open.

First room on my right is administration. It's not locked. Grey haze swirls around me. Veda is in here fiddling with a panel of switches. 'The sprinklers aren't working,' she says.

'Can we get out through here?' I ask.

'No.'

'Shit. I'll try the staff quarters.'

I pass Fates's office. No point going in there. I know there's no way out.

The alarm batters at my head. Smoke sticks in my throat.

Jem and Taylor come from the staff quarters, coughing. 'The external door's locked. We tried breaking through, but the smoke got too much,' Jem says.

We're trapped.

'Where's the doc?' Gabe shouts through the blaring alarm. 'We need to get the Agers out.'

Yeah. Where is Doctor Perez? And why is the door to the hallway locked? She said she'd leave it open.

We make our way through the smoke towards Gabe.

'I'll go get some wet towels,' Taylor says. 'For our faces.'

Gabe hammers on the door to the hallway, shouting for Perez.

'Wait, where's Veda?' Jem asks.

'Trying to fix the sprinklers in admin.'

'I'll help her. It's our only chance,' Jem says, and turns back. I start to follow but I'm caught in a coughing attack. My injured eye feels like it's about to burst out of the socket.

Taylor gives me a damp towel and I wrap it round my nose and mouth. It helps ease the coughing. I take some towels for Jem and Veda. I get to the admin doorway. Only Veda is in there.

The walls creak. There's a loud groan. And then, sudden ominous silence like the world's taking a breath.

'Get out of there,' I yell.

Flames burst from Fates's office. The fire surges; black smoke pours into the lobby. And I can't see Veda any more.

107.

'Jem!' I scream. 'Veda!'

Rain thunders down on me. And then Veda's at my side. 'Got the sprinkler working,' she says.

The flames flatten. Steam rises in great clouds.

'Where's Jem?' I ask.

Veda looks away.

'What?' I say. 'What happened?'

'He went into Doctor Fates's office,' she says. 'It's my fault. I told him I'd found a letter for you in there.'

I'm already halfway to the office before she's finished speaking, my heart hammering. Jem stumbles out, soaked, clutching blackened papers to his chest. Thank God.

The alarm stops. In the sudden quiet, I can hear Jem's breathing. Like boulders falling in his chest. Too loud, too laboured.

'Are you—'

He drops on to the floor.

'Stay with him,' Veda says. 'I'll find Doctor Perez.' She swings off on her crutches.

I kneel next to Jem. Whisper over and over that everything will be all right. Even though I don't know if it will be. Why did he go back into the fire for some stupid pieces of paper? Haven't we had enough death? It's time to live.

108.

Back on the ward, I look over at Jem in the bed next to me. I'm not supposed to move my head till my eye's fixed. He's not supposed to talk while the nanomites mend his smoke-damaged lungs. But he's muttering to Stan. Veda's checking on the Agers in their beds.

Doctor Perez and Taylor walk into the ward together, their faces grim.

'What is it?'

'Earl's gone,' Taylor says.

'What? How did he get out?'

'Who cares?' Jem mutters huskily.

Doctor Perez sighs. 'I don't know how he managed it. And—'

'What?'

She touches her gold cross. 'Earl's taken the Soul Holder containing Doctor Fates.'

Jem's laugh is hollow. 'Perfect.'

'How did he get away?'

'In the truck,' Taylor says.

'*The* truck.' Veda frowns. 'As in, there's only one?'

'Fuck,' Jem mutters.

'Can't you contact Cynthia?' I ask Doctor Perez. 'Get her to send us some help?'

She shakes her head. 'No. The radio's in the truck.'

'Let me guess – there's only one radio too?'

'Yes,' Doctor Perez says. 'But the supply truck's scheduled to be here in about two and a half months—'

Jem's head jerks. 'I'm not waiting that long to get out of here.'

109.

The bandages are off. I can see, not as well as before, but enough. There are scars like tiny splinters scattered on the skin around my eye. Same for Gabe. Jem's lungs are clear. Doctor Perez has given up convincing us to stay.

Taylor dishes out our documents. Fates had them in his office after all. Charred papers whisper in my fingers. So fragile. I go into the treatment room where Earl and Perez fixed my broken hand. I need to be on my own while I do this. I open my file carefully. The paperwork I originally signed in City Hospital. And Asha's, with Mum's shaky signature on it. Underneath is an envelope with my name, in Mum's handwriting, bold and large and not shaky at all.

I take a deep breath and slide the letter out. A hint of ancient rose. My body fights against me. I unfold the paper.

Dearest Calico,

I've done many foolish things in my life — as you know. But the worst thing I ever did was to let you believe I blamed you for Asha dying.

That night when I left the two of you, I came home and found Asha barely alive. Then I saw the notes she'd left us. I read them both and

374

for a split second — just a split second — I felt
relief that she was finally gone. And then I was
drenched in guilt and rushed her to the hospital.

When you came into that ITU room, I could
not look you in the face. I knew that you would
see what I'd felt, and what I'd done. Destroying
the letters Asha had written us. Disregarding
her wishes. But instead, you thought I blamed you.
And then the wheels were in motion so fast and I
couldn't find the brake.

I want you to know, I came to find you and
Asha as soon as I could. I saw Lucas. He tried
to hide what he'd done but I uncovered his lies.
He'd exaggerated how far along they were with
the reanimation process — yes, they had 'woken'
people up, but no one survived more than a few
hours. And Asha was in Russia! I went there
to make sure she really was. I did everything
I could to keep you both safe and give you the
best chance to live again. I can only hope it was
enough.

It was terrible watching the world move on
and knowing you should have been there. When
the war started, it was the young who fought
off those who were harming people and the planet.
If you'd been alive, Calico, you would have been
one of them, I know it. One of the people making
a difference. The world deserves to have you
in it. And because of me, my guilt, my shame, you

aren't in the world. I can never forgive myself for that.

I hope with all my being that one day you wake up and find your way to where you're meant to be.

You're always in my heart, my thoughts.
I love you and I'm sorry.
Mum

A tear drops from my eye on to the paper, blurring the ink. I fold the letter and put it back in the envelope. There's another letter in here.

Dear Calico

This is George Grayson. Asha's nurse.

I get a flash of the gentle giant in pale blue scrubs who cared for Asha – for the three of us – all the times she was ill. What's he doing writing to me?

I found this letter among your mother's things after she passed—

I put the note down.
Mum's dead.
I think a part of me already knew. Deep down.
I won't get a chance to speak to her ever again.
I go back to George's letter.

After you and Asha died, your mother and I became closer. She missed you girls every day, but went on with her life in her own Ruth Brown way. Bold and messy, full of music. I wanted to tell you that because I hope it will give you some peace.

Peace. There is no peace.

We had a son, Leon. So you have a brother.

I put the note down again.
A brother.
I never thought about Mum carrying on with her life after we'd gone.
Or making a new life.

Your mother's death was unexpected. She went peacefully in her sleep lying next to me. It was a terrible shock for me, but I'm glad she didn't suffer — she'd had enough of that in her life. The world's a much duller, quieter place without her.

Anyway, it feels like I'm talking to myself, but I wanted you to know. I will forward this to that fool Lucas Fates, in case his plan works and one day you wake up.

Yours
George

I close my eyes, see Mum, in the garden at home, brushing her hand through the lavender and rosemary bushes, singing hymns, a voice like silver. I see her in that ITU room, head bowed over Asha, refusing to look me in the eye.

Guilt.

Shame.

Not blame.

I'm heavy with sadness. If only we'd been able to talk to each other, the three of us. Talk and listen. See each other. Hear each other. None of this would've happened.

It did happen though. We made our choices, our mistakes, and now I have to live with the consequences.

110.

Doctor Perez is on the ward but the rest of us gather in the little garden at the front of the facility. The sun beats down on us. This is where Shimmy's ashes were scattered. Gabe has marked it with a cross he made. Jem's portrait of Shimmy leans against it. How she was before the Ageing changed her. He's captured her joy and her sadness, her innocence and her knowing.

'Let's remember her like this.' He takes hold of my hand.

I nod.

Veda clears her throat. 'Shimmy was a person who provoked strong emotions. Honestly, she used to irritate the hell out of me, but there was something about her that meant I could never be fed up with her for long. She had a hard, sad life. And I'm sorry that she's gone. I hope she's found some peace now.'

Jem sniffs.

I stare at Shimmy's portrait until my eyes blur.

Taylor starts to sing.

Goosebumps, ghost bumps.

'It's one of Shimmy's big hits,' Veda whispers.

It's a cover version of an old, old song. Mum used to sing it too.

We build a fire, more smoke than flames, and sit around it to share our memories of Shimmy.

Taylor tells us he had her posters on his bedroom wall at home. 'Her songs always spoke to me, somehow. Meeting her here was weird. She was never, like, totally real to me.'

'When I was really young, I went to see her play live once with my old man,' Gabe says. 'She was so tiny up there on the stage, but her voice was so big.'

And now it's my turn. The words rush out. 'Fates offered me a chance to save Shimmy when she had the Ageing. There was a spare cryopod. He said I – I had to choose between Shimmy and Asha.'

'Oh no,' Veda says.

'I chose Asha.' I stare at the ground. There's silence, apart from the crack of dry wood in the fire.

Jem's arm slips round my shoulders. 'I'd've done the same. I would've chosen Stan.'

'There was no certainty,' Veda says, 'in either choice. You did the best you could with the knowledge you had at the time. That's all anyone can do.'

'Shimmy's death is down to Lucas Fates. No one else.'

'She wouldn't want you blaming yourself,' Taylor says. 'Let it go, sugar.'

111.

Back in my old bedroom – cell – I add the paperwork and letters to my makeshift backpack, one of the old prison laundry bags we've adapted. It's heavy, with the glass bottles of water for the daytime heat and jumpers for the freezing nights.

'Ready?' Jem says.

I glance around the empty space.

'Yeah.'

We go into his room to get his backpack. The file he got from Fates's office is on his bed.

'Aren't you bringing this?' I ask.

'Nah.'

'Why not?'

'Not sure I want to read it. *Shut it, Stan.*'

'He's definitely back then?'

'Yeah.'

'And he thinks you should read it?'

'Yeah. Which probably means it's bad news.'

I pick up the file, open it. There's the consent form his mum signed, and an envelope with *Jeremy* written on it.

'At least bring them with you.'

'Already carrying a lot of stuff.' He turns to go.

I put the file in my bag. I'm not going to read the letter. I'm really not. But it'll be there if he changes his mind.

I catch him up and slip my hand into his. Veda waits with Taylor and Gabe in the reception area. If we manage to stay on course, it'll be a five-day walk to Phoenix. Then Taylor will contact his family and we'll go to the ranch while we work out our next steps. We'll be free. This is our choice.

We walk through the glass doors. Outside. We pass the tree. The single tree. Not as big as the old oak on the common back home, but broad enough that a bird girl could be leaning against it, writing poems, humming. She could be there. But I don't check to see if she is. I know she's not.

I look forward, in the direction I'm going, the direction we're going – me and Jem, Veda, Taylor and Gabe. To life, wherever that will be. Life. Whatever that is.

One Year Later

Calico

So, I'm back to writing. The therapist's idea. She says it's definitely private, but we'll see. I have trust issues apparently. Big surprise. So …

We got to the station in Phoenix and from there went to Taylor's ranch. His family were so overjoyed to see him, which was nice but also hard. Veda wrote to her parents and six weeks later there was a reply. She will see them when they are next in the States for work — probably another two years. The world is so different now. There are no planes, only boats and trains; everything takes so long.

Anyway, in the meantime we contacted Cynthia at EarthKnit. She had said to me at that very first meeting she would help if I needed anything. So here we are — me, Jem and Veda. At EarthKnit. I was wary of living in another facility, but it's different here. There are locks but everyone has their own key. We can come and go as we please. It's a community, not a prison.

I spoke to Gabe and Taylor on the radio yesterday. They're doing good but want to stay at the ranch. Get the feeling there's something going on between them. Cynthia says they're welcome to visit any time.

Doctor Perez arrived a few months ago.

She stayed at the Fates Facility with the Agers until they were gone – as always, putting her patients first. And then she had to transport the Soul Holders here. She's setting up the new Transference of Consciousness lab. They're building up the Library of Human Knowledge. Project C. It doesn't involve forcing a person's consciousness into another person's body, so I feel more positive about that whole thing now. I still have flashbacks to the needles in my eye though.

I'm getting to know Sophia Perez better. She ties herself in knots over the rights and wrongs of everything. But better to be like that than like Lucas Fates, driven by obsession.

No sightings of Earl yet. All the Protection Services are on standby in case he shows up. It's creepy knowing Lucas Fates is out there somewhere. Not his physical body, his soul. If he actually even had one.

Anyway, I try not to think about that too much. I'm working on letting go of things I have no control over. Which is basically everything.

I've written to my half-brother, Leon, and he's written back. It's good having a connection with someone outside of all this stuff. He has a part of Mum in him and so do I. Don't know if we'll ever get to meet. Travel overseas is so expensive and there has to be a good enough reason to go. Like the Amplify man said in our meeting: one person's wants are not worth more than the planet's needs.

Cynthia's teaching me and Jem about how the world changed while we were dead. Things spiralled into a dire mess, but there were always some people who had hope. It was the Green War that turned things around. People came together to save the planet. They had to stop hating others based on what they believed in, what they looked like, who they fell in love with. They had to get over their prejudices. Not everyone managed it obviously, because there are always those who will take advantage – people who value material wealth over humans, like with the breeding programmes. But enough united to hold on to our planet. If the earth dies, it doesn't matter what god you believe in, the colour of your skin or anyone else's, whether the person you fall in love with is the opposite sex or the same. It doesn't matter if you're male, female, something other, or in between. If there's no planet, there's no people – there's no you.

Right now, Veda is still at work with Cynthia – she's doing a kind of internship, preparing to follow her dream of working for the Global Eco Government. Jem and I have finished for the day. He's sitting on the grass in front of me, reading the letter from his mum. Taken him a year of therapy to get up the nerve.

Cynthia asked if I wanted to get involved with the TOC research, but I'm happy working in the gardens with Jem. Up early before the heat sets in. Planting seeds, weeding, watering, growing food and flowers for the few remaining bees. It makes me feel close to Mum. The smell of lavender and roses. I like being useful. Having purpose. Hands in the earth. The green scent of life all around me. Taking care of this planet. Without it we're nothing. And we so nearly lost it.

The therapist asked me what I learned when I was at the Fates Facility. But I couldn't explain — it's too jumbled up, even now, after a year.

She said maybe I'll never disentangle it, but to write it down anyway. We're all works in progress.

So here goes:

Things I learned while I was dead

I learned death is not as scary as I thought it would be. Finding out Asha was ready to die helped me with that. Like dying was just her next step. But I should have known that about her a long time before I did. Should've listened to her, heard her. I made decisions for her. I took away her right to choose.

And I learned what it's like to have no choice myself. To be an object instead of a person. I hate that I did that to Asha too. I don't know if I'll ever make peace with it.

Jem and I talk all the time about the right to choose, to give consent. It's part of what makes us human. It's kind of confusing though. Jem's mum made a decision on his behalf, without his consent, but with the best of intentions. And if she hadn't, he wouldn't be here now, with me. I get why she did it. I couldn't bear the thought of being without Asha either, but …

I've learned family is a fluid thing. The people who make you, the ones who raise you, and the family you find along the way. My first life is full of memories of Asha and Mum. My second life is filling with memories they can't share. And that's okay. It doesn't dilute them. It doesn't erase them. It's all right for me to laugh, and to love other people. My heart is big enough to hold them all.

I learned that Doctor Perez was right. Getting things wrong is how humans learn. Guilt and shame are such a waste of energy, but I still beat myself up about the mistakes I've made. I'm working on it though: trying to make things right where I can, and if I can't, to learn from it and do better next time. It's still a work in progress. I'm a work in progress. I guess that's part of being human too.

I've learned that life without Asha is not as scary as I thought it would be. Sometimes the

weight of her being gone is heavy, but some days
it's not.

And, as she once told me —

Life's _for_ the living.

And life _is_ for living.

So live it, as free and as true as you can.

Acknowledgements

Thank you to the Faber Children's team for the care you take of your readers and authors.

The biggest thanks to my amazing editor Ama Badu, wise and kind in equal measure.

To Natasha Brown, Bethany Carter, Lizzie Bishop, Jack Bartram, Carmella Lowkis, Sarah Connell, Emma Golay, Jessica White, Sarah Barlow, M Rules, the sales team, and everyone who has worked on *Things I Learned While I Was Dead*. Thank you for your creativity and enthusiasm. It's been a real joy to work with you all.

Thanks also to Art Director Emma Eldridge and designer Thy Bui for the stunning cover.

Many thanks to the Imagined Futures Prize judges; to Leah Thaxton for the most exciting phone call. And to my Imagined Futures Prize sisters, Kenechi Udogu and Sally Gales, for the friendship and support.

I wouldn't be where I am without The Bath Spa MA Writing for Young People family:

My tutors, Julia Green and Steve Voake, who nurtured my creativity, and the inimitable CJ Skuse who taught me to be bold.

My fellow alumni and friends – especially Kirsty Applebaum, Sarah House, Helen Lipscombe, Sera Birdie Milano, Kita Mitchell, Julie Pike, Christina Wheeler, and Maddy Woosnam.

Shout out to the WriteMentor crew, especially early

readers Lydia Massiah and Marie Day; to the 2025 debut group; and the writers and readers who have supported me along the way.

To all the friends and family who have been there for me on this (very) long and winding journey, especially:

Dr Diana John for two decades of friendship and philosophical debate, and for explaining the science bits.

Sarah House, dearest friend and weird twin, thank you for being there through all the things.

The Boormans, Clarks, Clarkes, and Howards.

Mum and Dad for taking me to the library when I was small, for reading to me, for letting me be a quiet child with my head in a book.

My sister for everything (apart from the baked beans).

My nephews Sam and Theo for all the chats.

Mike, Grace, Amy, and Jakub. Thank you for being here and for being you.

Resources

Support for various **mental health** issues:
- ❤ CAMHS – https://www.camhs-resources.co.uk/websites

Support for **bereavement and grief**:
- ❤ AtaLoss – https://www.ataloss.org/
- ❤ Cruse – https://www.cruse.org.uk/

Support for **eco-anxiety:**
- ❤ Friends of the Earth – https://friendsoftheearth.uk/